JOY AFTER NOON
A SUGAR SANDS NOVEL BOOK 1

PRAISE FOR DEBRA COLEMAN JETER
AND
THE TICKET–A SELAH AWARD FINALIST

The Ticket is a story that aches to be read … Debra Coleman Jeter has created a character who feels as real as you or me, with doubts, joys, problems, and dreams that seem unreachable. Watch as she reaches out, latches on, and starts becoming the beautiful woman she will be.
—**Ronald Kidd**, author, *The Year of the Bomb*

Wow! … a wonderful book. Debra Jeter's ability to portray the thoughts and feelings … is truly amazing … Maybe this book isn't the kind of page turner a suspense novel is, but this novel is more character-driven than plot-driven, and it's definitely a page turner … that's the finest tribute this older man can pay.
—**Roger Bruner**, author, *The Devil and Pastor Gus*

Complex characters … Jeter's coming-of-age novel considers the problems that might follow a sudden windfall.
—***Publishers Weekly***

Loved it the first time I read it … loved it the last time I read it! … I grew up in the same era, the 1970s. But this book is for anyone who has grown up socially awkward. Or with big dreams … bigger than some say you have a right to … This book is also about what can happen when we allow ourselves to just be who we are and to grow graciously in that role.
—**Eva Marie Everson**, author, *Chasing Sunsets*

The story offers up riveting drama. One would be hard-pressed not to root for the likable protagonist and hope that her story eventually ends with a happy ending. There are some authentic life lessons and talking points to be had here. All in all, this is an enjoyable debut by Jeter.
—***RT Book Reviews***

After [reading *The Ticket*], I was buzzing like I'd just viewed an action-adventure movie and realized that there wasn't all that much physical action in the story. This is excellent story telling. It leaves loose ends that have the reader thinking, not just about the characters or heavy questions generated by what they deal with, but about one's own choices, those already made and those awaiting a decision.
—**Timothy Fountain**, author, *Raising a Child with Autism*

I LOVED this novel. Jeter has caught beautifully and poignantly the angst of the kind of teenager I was and infused the character's life with powerful plot twists and turns that kept me on the edge of my seat. I literally tried to not sob at places. Did this author know my life? And of course, it's the life of most teenagers, even if they come across as having it all together ... I hope Ms. Jeter is writing more books. I can't wait to enjoy them.
—**Kathryn E. Miller**, reader

What happens toward the end of the book took me by surprise and the ending was a touch of genius ... The work of fiction highlights the misbelief that having money is what fixes everything, and readers will come to understand the fact that maybe it highlights more of what is broken in the family unit.
—**Reader**

Loved the style of writing, the subtle humor and the life truths that were shared
—**RVThereYet**, reader

The characters in this book are unique, interesting, and possess strong potential to be memorable. A grandmother who longs to fix mistakes from her youth and find independence, a mentally unbalanced mother, and a daughter who lacks the confidence to pursue her dreams . . . quite a mix with amazing dynamics. The story abounds with tensions and conflict.
—**Kim Peterson**, author

Made me look back at my own [life]... relationship of me and my father ... and my mother ... absolutely loved this story.
—**Reader**

Thoughtful and introspective, honest and sometimes raw, I found myself pulled in to her life. Worth your time—On This Journey of Life,
—**Reader**

It ended quicker than I would have liked simply because I couldn't put it down ... I'm not even sure how to "label" this book genre-wise because it just has the best parts of so many genres.
—**Paige Boggs,** writer and book blogger

The real story is how a girl with self-esteem issues deals with family relationships Most of us can relate to those feelings of being invisible and at the same time -having everyone's critical eyes on you all the time.

—**Judith Little**, reader

Jeter does an amazing job of capturing the essence of a young woman growing up in the South with very limited financial resources. Anyone who grew up during that time outside the "popular crowd" will instantly have memories rekindled. A great story and a great debut novel!

—**P. Thomas**, reader

Cover and Interior Design: Derinda Babcock

Editor(s): Linda Rondeau, Deb Haggerty

Author Represented by the Steve Laube Agency

PUBLISHED BY: Elk Lake Publishing, Inc., 35 Dogwood Dr., Plymouth, MA 02360, 2019

Library Cataloging Data

Names: Jeter, Debra Coleman (Debra Coleman Jeter

Joy After Noon / Debra Coleman Jeter

230 p. 23cm × 15cm (9in × 6 in.)

Description: A newlywed struggles to deal with her stepdaughters, somewhat evasive husband, and troubles on her job.

Identifiers: ISBN-13: 978-1-948888-97-4 (trade) | 978-1-948888-98-1 (POD) | 978-1-948888-99-8(e-book.)

Key Words: marriage, second wife, stepchildren, self-esteem, expectations, family relationships, drugs

LCCN: 2018968300 Fiction

JOY AFTER NOON
A SUGAR SANDS NOVEL BOOK 1

Debra Coleman Jeter

PUBLISHING THE POSITIVE

ELK LAKE PUBLISHING INC.
Plymouth, Massachusetts

DEDICATION

To my beloved husband, Norm, who has read countless drafts, typed numerous corrections, and always finds something positive to say about my writing at every stage.

ACKNOWLEDGMENTS

For their talent, experience, and tireless efforts to make *Joy After Noon* as strong as possible, I thank the team at Elk Lake Publishing, Inc.—especially Deb Haggerty, Linda Rondeau, and Derinda Babcock.

I appreciate the members of my group at Mount Hermon Christian Writers Conference for their comments, criticism, and encouragement in getting this novel off the ground. I also express my gratitude to my Facebook friends and church friends for their enthusiasm in anticipation of my next novel and their help in selecting a cover for Joy After Noon.

Finally, I want to express my appreciation to my family—my parents and sister, my son. Clay, my husband. Norm, and especially my daughter, Nikki—without whose love and support I would never have had the courage, the time, or the confidence to publish my writing.

Be strong and courageous.
Do not be frightened, and do not be dismayed,
for the LORD your God is with you wherever you go.
—Joshua 1:9 (ESV)

CHAPTER ONE

August 6, 1983

Joy opened a cabinet door to gaze at the rows of hand-painted spices—little bottles labeled in delicate, loopy cursive and decorated with yellow daffodils, each flower unique. What kind of woman would take the time to transfer store-bought spices into handcrafted containers? The same woman who painted the daffodils? As a teacher of finance, Joy would question whether she could sell the hand-painted jars for enough cash to compensate for the materials and labor.

In this new marital universe, the question was altogether different. What *was* the question? Joy felt lost.

The jars appeared to be aligned in alphabetical order, and she checked to be sure. Coriander seed, cumin ... tarragon, turmeric. They probably hadn't been used since Carolyn died. Either that or Carolyn had trained Ray and the girls to keep them in their proper sequence.

The ring of the phone startled her, unaccustomed as she still was to her new setting. She recognized the voice at once. Her colleague and coauthor Natalie. Yes, the honeymoon was wonderful, Joy told her. She elaborated on the brilliant turquoise of the water, the amazing world she and Ray explored together beneath the sea. She couldn't tell Natalie the real wonder—to be held, to be nurtured, to feel cherished for the first time in so many years. She flushed at the thought of confessing as much at her age.

"I haven't forgotten our paper," she said instead. "I know I've been negligent lately. I'll get on it. Right away."

Natalie assured her that wasn't why she called, but Joy wasn't certain she believed her. Joy had no close female friends, and she often wished a different personality for herself. If she could choose, she'd be someone who could chat easily and draw people to her with the effortless warmth that had exuded from her mother. She imagined confiding to Natalie how overwhelmed she felt in Carolyn's house, looking at Carolyn's cookbooks, trying to fit into Carolyn's life.

Hanging up the phone, she returned to surveying the meticulous organization of another woman's kitchen. Joy pictured the haphazard contents of the cupboards in her own apartment—or what used to be hers. Tins of pepper and cinnamon sat side-by-side with cans of beans and peaches, crammed in wherever she could find space. Sometimes a box of salt would topple out if she opened a door too abruptly.

She pulled a drawer out, looking for a spoon to stir her coffee. Instead of silverware, the drawer was filled with linen placemats and matching napkins, crystal napkin rings, and silver place card holders. She opened cabinet after cabinet, absorbing the foreign contents. Joy could not bring herself to touch a single item, reminding her of the freeze that sometimes occurred as she struggled to write a research paper. She'd find herself unable to write the first sentence even though she had completed the analyses and assembled all the necessary tools and references. Still, she'd always managed to move past the freeze. She could do so now.

She lifted a Betty Crocker cookbook from a drawer filled with an assortment of cookbooks—desserts, hors d'oeuvres, soups, starters, main courses, crock-pot meals, low-fat meals, and on and on. She flipped through the well-worn pages, some faintly wrinkled as if someone had tried to wash them. Her gaze fell on a yummy-looking recipe for an ultimate chocolate cake. Could that be a cocoa smudge on this page? She tried to envision the woman whose fingers once moved through these pages—beautiful, clever, adept, the perfect homemaker, the perfect wife.

Though today was Saturday, Ray had gone in to work anyway, saying he had a lot of catching up to do. Joy resisted the urge to flee to her own office, where stacks of papers and unread journals piled high, not to mention the project with Natalie that needed to be finalized. How much easier to tackle the tasks she knew rather than the unfamiliar. She plopped into a chair. Her thoughts drifted to the sequence of events that had brought her here.

Their whirlwind courtship was so romantic, so fairytale-like that Joy had not questioned her feelings. Swept into Ray's arms, literally and figuratively, she dared imagine a lifetime with him and his daughters. She'd tried to warn him she was an incompetent cook. Perhaps he hadn't taken her light-hearted confession seriously. When he suggested they elope, she was ecstatic. Of course she'd met the girls but never really interacted with them. Facing hard facts now, she knew she had been afraid of losing Ray because of her lack of finesse with kids and zero domestic skills. She'd been glad—so glad—to be romanced and cherished. Had she made a huge, irreversible mistake by not being more candid?

The lurking fear pushed into the forefront. Did Ray want a wife—or a homemaker and a mother for his girls? Although he'd been raising them alone for nearly four years now, the girls had reached those troublesome teen years where a good mother would be invaluable. Was Joy, inexperienced as she was, capable of providing that sort of guidance? By avoiding the questions, she might have done a huge disservice, not only to herself but to Ray and his daughters. She had tried to discuss her fears more than once, but Ray had dodged her indirect queries about his first marriage as well as his expectations for a second one. Both topics always seemed to turn his good humor into a sour one. So Joy had caved—much too easily.

Ray was gorgeous, with his long, rangy body, his face tanned and creased from years of Sugar Sands' sun. His eyebrows and eyelashes were inky black, a startling contrast to the bright caramel hair on his head and faint stubble on his chin. Joy couldn't help feeling—both then and now—that he was out of her league. Dating him, much less marrying him, had seemed too much to hope for. Yet, here she was in these beautiful, sun-filled rooms that were about to be jarred from their history of perfection.

With the vast expanse of glass that overlooked the Gulf of Mexico and the vaulted ceilings, the rooms seemed designed for entertaining. The pastel chintz couch and chairs, however, barely appeared to have seated guests, much less two growing girls. She'd been a rambunctious child and imagined she'd have certainly knocked over and broken the huge matching urns. Most likely Ray's kids didn't do somersaults inside the house.

The dining room was done almost entirely in white, the least practical color Joy could imagine for a room where food was served or eaten. The very thought of making this display of elegance and wealth her own both thrilled and terrified her. Even the girls' portraits intimidated Joy. Original art in outdoor beach or park settings—paintings, not photographs.

Joy knew she was blessed. Why, then, was she acting like she'd been struck by misfortune? Misfortune had struck Joy once, struck her hard, and this was its exact opposite. Overcoming the lethargy that threatened to paralyze her, she pushed herself from her chair, almost toppling it.

She scanned the country-themed kitchen, the only room furnished in line with Joy's taste, with its glazed tile flooring and colorful throw rugs. She returned her attention to the assortment of cookbooks and selected a recipe for pecan pie, something she knew Ray loved. She perused the complicated instructions. How easy to slip off to the grocery and purchase a preformed crust. But no, the taste and texture would be different and would never do.

She checked the cupboards for the listed ingredients and found everything she needed. This would never have happened in her apartment. Always there would have been something lacking, forcing a substitution or a run to the store.

Within minutes, clumps of damp flour dotted the granite counters and tile floors. A powdery fog blanketed the air, and Joy's hands were a clammy mess. What she had failed to do, however, was produce a pie crust. Staring at the disaster before her … a crumbly, perforated mess with holes like Swiss cheese … Joy threw up her hands in despair.

"Mother always says you should clean up as you go." Marianne spoke from the doorway. Something about her face struck Joy as ethereal. She was so beautiful, nearly luminous, with her heart-shaped lips and red-gold hair falling to her shoulders. Fourteen months older than her sister, Marianne seemed more mature than her fifteen years. Despite her small stature and flat chest, she possessed an ageless quality—a miniature adult.

Mother? Not Mom or Mama?

Joy forced a smile. "Cleaning up as you go sounds like good advice. I'll have to try it next time." The gunk clung to her fingers, refusing to wash off. A sign, perhaps, she couldn't, or shouldn't, give up. Not this time.

With chunks of dough clinging to her damp hands, Joy redoubled her resolve to salvage the mess in front of her, whether Marianne was watching or not. The girl remained in the doorway, making no move to help except for an occasional remark. Finally, the crust was nearly intact, and Joy turned with some relief to preparing the filling.

"Mother always scoops out the last of the egg whites with her thumb," Marianne said.

Noticing her use of the present tense, Joy squelched a gasp at the feeling—as if Carolyn stood next to her daughter, smirking at Joy's incompetence. Then, getting a grip, she forgave Marianne for the comparison. Joy had known loss and the refusal to accept that loss as final. She almost said as much, but didn't.

"Mother always sprays the pan first." This time, Marianne's gaze met Joy's. Was there hostility in those gold-flecked eyes? Resentment at the intrusion? *Fear?*

Joy took some of her suggestions and ignored others, determined to survive the process without breaking down in front of this woman-child. Marianne left after a time, a certain smugness marring the lovely features. Now, the younger daughter, Jenny, was the one who watched when Joy removed the pie from the oven.

Joy's heart thudded in anticipation, the way her body behaved when she opened a letter from a journal, hoping for a positive review but fearing a rejection.

The crust was black around the edges.

"I never eat pecan pie anymore," Jenny said, "not since Mother died."

Her shoulders slumped and her face sullen, Jenny wore a white tee shirt with Michael Jackson's face above the scrawled album title, "Thriller." Her feet were bare beneath a pair of lace-edged black leggings ending just above the ankle. Her toenails, so short they might have been bitten off, were painted a fluorescent fuchsia. Joy's heart went out to the younger, less beautiful daughter.

When Joy was Jenny's age, she had rescued a skinny, bedraggled kitten from a dumpster. Mom, allergic to cat dander, had allowed Joy to keep the kitten only after exhausting every effort to find Buttons another home.

"Please, please, please!" Joy had cried. "Look at her. She needs me! We can't abandon her, can we?"

Joy had lavished all the pent-up love she possessed on dear little Buttons, who had soon grown into a not-so-little but still dear and loving cat. Did she identify Jenny with Buttons or with herself? Maybe a little of both.

She would take Jenny out for ice cream and encourage her to talk. Somehow, Joy knew she'd find a way to connect with this somber-faced girl.

"If you change your mind, you can have the first piece." Joy kept her tone as bright as if the pie being offered were perfect.

Jenny shrugged, something wistful in her face distracting Joy from the fear that her pie might be inedible. The girl's eyes were lovely, the color of burnt sienna.

"You want the first piece?" Joy tried again.

"I guess."

When Joy removed a slice, the center oozed, running to fill up the empty space, the filling in Jenny's piece spreading rapidly to the corners of her dish as well.

"Maybe we should have waited," Jenny said. "Mother never cut the pie right away."

Joy stared at Jenny, fighting a sudden impulse to burst into tears. Instead, she sank into a chair beside her stepdaughter. With spoons instead of forks, they ate pie together in silence.

By the time Ray came home from the bank, Joy had only the burnt but runny pie to show for her afternoon in the kitchen. She'd hoped her creation might settle into something firmer after cooling, but no such luck.

Hearing his footsteps, she jiggled the pan one last time, grabbed the miserable concoction and headed toward the trash can. "Whoa!" he said, and she whirled to find him leaning against the doorframe. "What have you got there?"

Sheepishly, she showed him the pie. He frowned for an instant. The caramel-colored stubble on his cheeks and chin glinted gold in the fading sunlight slanting through the windows. Then he laughed, grabbed her around the waist and twirled her. "How about pizza?"

Over his shoulder, she caught a glimpse of Jenny's expression, a curious blend of sadness and surprise. Joy wondered how many times Jenny had seen her dad swing the first Mrs. Jenkins like this, and wondered if the girl was thinking that never again would she see her parents together.

CHAPTER TWO

Jenny removed the reed from her clarinet, sucked on it for a bit, and repositioned it on the instrument. She took care to cover each hole completely with the pads of her fingertips before trying again. She blew tentatively at first, then louder. The clarinet emitted an ear-piercing screech, and Jenny tossed it onto her bed in frustration. Why couldn't she do anything right?

A couple of off-color circles stained her pale yellow comforter. Must be where her clarinet leaked spit the last time she swabbed the instrument. Gross! Mother would have had a fit. Jenny wondered if Joy might be willing to let her redecorate the room. Shabby chic, Mother called it, but Jenny would have preferred something modern. Geometrical patterns or abstract art, maybe. And definitely not *yellow*.

From the next room, the rhythmic vibration of Marianne's familiar dance exercise routine grated on her nerves. Without looking, Jenny could picture Marianne's perfect moves.

Jenny picked up the clarinet and blew gently. Her insides quivered at the prospect of the upcoming band tryouts. She didn't need to be first chair, like Marianne would probably be if she were in band. Which she wasn't, thank goodness. Still she really, really wanted to move up from third clarinet this year. Why did she always panic during tryouts no matter how much she practiced?

The clarinet vibrated with a long, delicious note. Finally! The sweet sound almost compensated for all the irritating, nerve-grinding squeals. A tap on her door interrupted the thought, and Marianne's head popped into view. The reddish blonde hair swung forward in thick, smooth drapes, like a shampoo commercial. "We need to talk."

"Okay." Jenny laid down her clarinet and waited.

Marianne dropped gracefully onto the edge of Jenny's bed, and Jenny resisted the urge to smooth out the wrinkled bedcovers. Not for her own sake, but for Marianne's, who, like Mother, wanted everything to be perfect. Hopefully, the wrinkles camouflaged the stain circles a bit. Marianne had never commented on them, so maybe she hadn't noticed. Mother always said you had to keep bed covers clean, because they never looked the same once they were laundered.

"How do you feel about Joy?" Marianne grasped her tiny foot in one hand, drawing a pink-leotarded leg toward her face, then stretched the limb out in a perfectly straight line at an impossible angle.

Jenny hesitated. She almost felt sorry for Joy yesterday during the pie-baking episode, but mostly she resented the woman for taking so much of Dad's focus away. After Mother died, Jenny felt as if she was the most important person in Dad's life. He said as much to her once.

Well, not exactly. What he said was, "You're my special girl. You know that, don't you?" Of course, there was Marianne too, but somehow the bond between Jenny and Dad was a little stronger—like the one between Marianne and Mother. A bond the new wife would ruin.

"I hate her," she said.

"Good. So do I." Marianne released the foot, tucked both legs under her and smiled.

Jenny smiled back in spite of herself. Marianne was only nice when she wanted something. Still, whenever Marianne turned that brilliant smile in Jenny's direction, she lapped up the attention the way she was doing now. She was that pathetic. Jenny crossed her own legs like Marianne's … a doable pose … and waited for Marianne to continue.

"What I'm thinking is this—" Marianne paused, and Jenny's heart raced in anticipation. "Whenever we get the chance, we bring up Mother. We say, 'Mother always did it this way,' or 'Mother never did that.' You get the idea?"

"Why?"

"I've been watching her. When I say something like that, she swallows so hard you can see her throat move, and she gets this funny look on her face. I think it gets to her big time."

This strategy seemed a little mean, but Jenny smiled as if the idea was the cleverest ever.

"Are you with me?" Marianne asked, an uncharacteristic urgency in her voice, though her face was creamy smooth and expressionless as usual.

Jenny nodded.

"We don't want to overdo it though," Marianne continued. "We can't say this stuff in front of Dad either. And if we do it too often, the strategy won't work as well. Often but not too often. You know?"

Jenny was not sure she did, but she nodded anyway just as Dad's familiar knock—three quick raps, brisk and sharp—sounded on the door. Jenny froze, and Marianne nudged her to answer.

"Come in!" Jenny called out, feeling her face flush.

"How are my favorite little women?"

She couldn't speak, certain her guilty role in the new strategy was written plainly in her eyes.

Marianne replied for them both. "Just fine."

Jenny snuck a sideways glance at her sister's expression—as cool as a dilly bar.

Throughout the next couple of weeks, Marianne was tireless in her efforts to dethrone Joy, and she was seemingly successful. And yet she was not. When Jenny joined her in uttering the fatal words, "Mother always …" Joy paled. The trouble was their father. No matter how out of place Joy proved herself to be in their home, he didn't appear to mind or even notice. How could anyone love someone so obviously flawed, so—so different from Mother?

When Dad had brought Joy home to meet his daughters for the first time, Marianne had almost laughed. She was really old. Nearly forty, most likely, and nothing like Mother, who, as Marianne recalled, was so very beautiful. She had trouble picturing Mother some days. Too often she had to rely on her dresser photo to remember how perfect Mother was. But sometimes Mother was right there with her, clear as day, so real she could almost reach out and touch her. She couldn't summon her up when she needed her, though. Oh, no. Mother only came to Marianne when a visit suited her, not when it would suit Marianne.

In contrast, Joy was pale and boring, with a shy, self-conscious smile as though she already knew Marianne would never like her. Freckled like a girl, though Joy had lines in her forehead. Everything about her was pale—skin very white and flushing to pink at times, dishwater blonde hair, and eyes, a translucent blue. Even her eyebrows and eyelashes were pale. No makeup. You'd think she was a Quaker or something. Marianne had to admit, though, that Joy seemed different—softer and glowing—since she and Dad came home from their honeymoon. Marianne could almost understand what Dad saw in the woman. Disgusting, though. When they were together—Joy and Dad—sometimes he'd put a hand on her back. Then she'd look up at him with those pale blue eyes. Such puppy-like adoration made Marianne want to puke.

A sudden thought—how would she have felt if Dad had brought home some drop-dead gorgeous young thing in her twenties? Better or worse? He was handsome enough. Dad always acted like he was completely oblivious to flirtations by the women of all ages at church, who had made an obvious play for him. Especially in the early months following Mother's death—four years ago today—a day Marianne would never forget. Had Dad forgotten so soon?

What made him change? This thing with Joy would never last. Marianne would make sure of that.

Really? A fire drill on the first day of the new school year? Bored and miserable, Marianne hated standing outside for so long on such a hot day. Sweat stained her armpits and her calves felt sticky. For weeks, Marianne had planned to wear her new blouse, khaki capris, and sparkly sandals for a splash of color. This morning, she had almost changed her mind at the last minute before deciding to stick with the original plan. Now, she wished she had worn a short skirt and sleeveless top instead.

Nearby, students chattered and giggled with friends they hadn't seen since school had let out for the summer. The cheerleaders huddled together. From time to time, they raised their heads, and their laughter rang out.

"Just join them," Mother would have said. "don't stand there like a dummy."

Marianne wished she had a friend, or even better, a few friends. A circle of friends. She imagined herself surrounded, everyone wanting to know how she spent her precious free time, everyone sympathizing at her admission of the evil stepmother's intrusion into her perfect life. If Mother were still alive, she would have understood and helped her through the transition. Of course, if Mother were alive, none of this would be happening. Marianne would still be homeschooled, and there would be no Joy in their home.

She caught a glimpse of Jenny standing apart from her sixth-grade class, though she was not alone. The girl next to Jenny looked older and was dressed in a tiny, hot-pink skirt and a long-sleeved, low-cut top that revealed the edges of a purple-laced bra. As if this weren't enough to make the girl stand out, she'd pushed up her sleeves to reveal what appeared to be the tail of a mermaid tattooed on her right arm. Just then, the girl bent forward to adjust one of her sharp-toed, high-heeled boots showing off yet another tattoo—an octopus on her left breast.

If this girl was in the sixth grade, she must have flunked a grade or two. She and Jenny were engrossed in animated conversation. What on earth could they be talking about? Marianne edged closer to send her sister a warning glance. As she approached, a hand fell on her arm. Marsha Blanning grinned at her. "Hi, Marianne."

"Hello." Marianne had no time for Marsha, an unattractive girl with thick glasses and braces. Since Mother died, and Marianne entered this school, the only kids who gravitated toward her were the oddballs. The popular kids acted as if being homeschooled had marred her for life.

Marsha apparently didn't pick up on Marianne's indifference or didn't care. "How was your summer?" she asked. Did she have to sound so cheerful?

"Fine. Yours?"

"It was good. We went to Disney World."

What are you—five? Before Marianne could zip a sarcastic remark, she was transported back to the time when her family made the trek to "The Happiest Place on Earth."

Marianne had been a small child and shy around the costumed characters from her favorite stories. Jenny had been even smaller, of course, still in a stroller, and she'd dozed off in the middle of the afternoon. "Come on, Marianne!" Mother urged, taking her hand and standing in line with her. When they got to the front, Mickey Mouse draped one arm around Marianne and one around her mother, and Dad snapped a photo. The framed photograph still sat on Marianne's dresser. In it, Mother was laughing, her eyes sparkling, her teeth white and perfect. Marianne was looking not at the camera but at Mickey Mouse's huge hand resting on her shoulder, and the corners of her mouth curved slightly upward in delight.

In the photo, a strand of hair escaped from her ponytail and swept across her cheek. Painfully, she remembered how Mother tried to correct the problem before the picture was taken. Now Marianne could not look at the photo without wishing she hadn't shrugged off her mother's hand the way she did. Sometimes, when she looked at that photo, she pinched herself—hard. At other times, she put the picture into a drawer for a while but always took it back out, usually within a few minutes. She loved the photo, and she hated it.

Marianne rushed over to the spot where Jenny had stood only moments earlier. Though her class was still nearby, Jenny and the girl with the mermaid tattoo were nowhere in sight.

Marianne scanned the school grounds, finally catching a glimpse of hot pink behind the oak tree in the center of the parking lot. She stared until, sure enough, Jenny emerged from behind the tree, then stepped behind again.

What were they doing over there?

A spiral of smoke drifted from where Jenny stood, and Marianne gasped. At least one of them was smoking. She took a step toward the tree, then hesitated, wondering whether she should risk getting caught with them.

Before she could decide, the principal announced the drill was over. "Return to your classes as quickly as possible," she said. "For those of you interested in trying out for cheerleading, assemble in the gymnasium for important instructions."

Cheerleading? Marianne considered the activity to be pretty much pointless, but it might be a way in, a means of making some friends who weren't weirdoes. Although she didn't like the cheerleaders especially—she couldn't forget how they had snubbed her last year. But, she'd give anything to be popular.

Her ballet lessons might give her a competitive edge. She headed toward the gym, dreaming of the possibilities.

CHAPTER THREE

"We're having the next Bible study meeting here," Ray announced. His matter-of-fact tone indicated Joy had no say in the decision.

"What?" Joy's head reeled. For an instant, she was back in Fiji, where she and Ray spent their honeymoon. Most of the time she remembered only the good—the intimacy, the pure pleasure—of being with Ray all day and all night. But there was a moment or two when Ray's behavior had struck her, for an instant, as dictatorial.

They'd arrived in Nadi too late to transfer to their island the first day. So they spent the night in a small hotel high on a hill. The distance from hotel to beach required a long hike or a shuttle. Joy wanted to go, loving the beach as she did—anxious to feel the water at her ankles, the sand beneath her feet.

"No," Ray had said, as if addressing one of his daughters instead of his bride. "We'll have plenty of beach time when we get to the island." Then, just as she was about to protest, he leaned toward her and brushed her lips with a kiss. She had marveled afresh at the way his touch thrilled and reverberated right through her, as if there had been a faint ember, almost dead, languishing inside her for years. Ray could bring the ember to full blazing glory with a few deft strokes. Surely this was enough.

At Taveuni Island, the turquoise waters dazzled Joy. A welcoming band of singers greeted them, and cool drinks and friendly smiles followed at the reception desk. After that, the honeymoon was exquisite, and Joy had almost forgotten the rocky start.

Until now, when Ray's announcement about the Bible study meeting brought the memory surging back. Suddenly, all the little slights she'd dismissed since their return surfaced—magnified. The times when he pulled away from her touch. The way he sometimes withdrew into his own thoughts when she was trying to engage him in conversation. His reticence about anything remotely related to Carolyn. Was she merely insecure? Why insist Ray talk about Carolyn if remembering made him sad?

Still she longed to know. Did he kiss Carolyn the same way he kissed Joy? Did he call for Carolyn in his sleep the way he sometimes did for Joy? Had he rubbed his thumb over Carolyn's knuckles when they held hands and walked on the beach? Had he talked to Carolyn more, loved her more?

Although Joy and Ray had first connected at a small Bible study group meeting, she wasn't totally comfortable with the concept. She longed to be the kind of wife and hostess Carolyn had been. She so wanted Ray to be proud of her. Still she couldn't help the dread seeping into her bones at his announcement. With an effort, she kept her face neutral to hide her dismay—dismay that he would volunteer without asking her, dismay at the blunders she would undoubtedly commit, dismay at her uncharitable reaction.

When the day of the meeting arrived, Ray confided, "You know, since Carolyn died, I hadn't felt up to having the meeting here."

He so rarely mentioned Carolyn at all that relief washed through Joy alongside her misgivings. Despite all her mishaps in the kitchen, he wasn't fearful of her failure at least. If he believed in her, she would rise to the occasion. The others would be bringing plenty of food, Ray had promised, so she was only baking brownies. Out of a box. This was something she'd been doing for years, and she had perfected the technique of removing them from the oven early enough, so the texture was moist, almost but not quite gooey, and altogether mouth-watering.

She barely had time to check the brownies with a toothpick, decide they would do, and turn the oven off when the guests started to arrive. The first was Eileen Reynolds, who had been Carolyn's best friend. Eileen offered a kiss on the cheek—an awkward near miss, but a gesture nonetheless. Joy tried not to envision Eileen and Carolyn sitting cozily in the kitchen nook overlooking the Gulf, sharing a pot of tea.

Joy sighed. Was she wrong to wish she and Ray could start fresh in a different house? She'd brought up the notion to Ray a few times, but his response had not been encouraging. "Maybe," he'd said, but argued the housing market wasn't strong enough to sell this one except at a huge loss.

The evening began promisingly enough. The house was so lovely Joy couldn't help feeling a little proud of her new home, with its beachy charm and elegant furnishings. The group assembled on the large balcony off the living room, where Ray had dragged enough chairs to accommodate everyone. Even more beautiful was the view—the expanse of gulf and sky, God's handiwork.

As on the evening when Joy and Ray first came together, the tall, bespectacled Alfred led the discussion. "This passage is from 2 Corinthians, chapter 7, beginning in verse 4," he said without preamble and began to read. "And in all of our troubles I have great joy."

Not despite our troubles … in our troubles. Was she capable, like Paul, of finding joy in trouble? With Ray, she'd found happiness, intense pleasure, for what felt like the first time in her life. That was the easy part. How would she react when troubles mounted? Joy tried to read her Bible every night, but lately she'd been remiss too often. She vowed to do better.

"And we were even happier to see that Titus was so happy," Alfred read on. "All of you made him feel much better. I bragged to Titus about you. And you showed that I was right."

As the group discussed the Scripture, Joy's attention wandered to the speakers' faces, wondering which of them might prove to be a good friend. She kept returning to Eileen Reynolds, perhaps because of her connection to Carolyn. Eileen wasn't nearly as lovely as Joy remembered Carolyn being. Yet, there was something similar in the way they styled their hair, wore their clothes, carried themselves, as through they'd been to a finishing school where girls were taught how to give off the vibe of privilege. Eileen's lips were a little too thin, her nose a trifle too sharp to be truly beautiful. But she was certainly striking, with her bouffant black hairdo and her lavender eye shadow. Suddenly, Joy heard Alfred mention her name and focused her attention with the startled guilt of a student woolgathering in class.

"We need to welcome Joy as a full-fledged member of our group," Alfred was saying. He put his Bible aside and turned his gaze squarely on Joy. Embarrassed at being singled out in this way, she felt heat rise to her cheeks.

As they adjourned to the dining room, she found herself surrounded by friendly, welcoming faces. "How are you doing?" asked a young woman named Sybil.

Joy recognized her as someone she knew from church, though not from the earlier group meeting. Sybil had lovely skin and large wide-spaced eyes, and Joy could picture her balancing a toddler on her hip at church. But no husband present. Joy had no idea whether Sybil was a single mother, or simply one whose husband didn't accompany her to services.

"I'm fine."

"Honest?" The eyes that met hers were so guileless Joy fought back the sting of tears.

Sybil touched Joy's arm gently and led her to one side of the group. "Do you want to talk about it?"

Joy shook her head, unable to speak, overcome by everything that rushed to mind, everything that was fine … and everything that was not.

"Maybe later," she managed, touched by this caring girl, so much younger than herself and undoubtedly with problems of her own. Yet she seemed in command of hers as Joy was not.

Eileen approached, her plate dotted with an assortment of miniscule portions. "Aren't you two going to eat?"

"We were just about to fill our plates," Sybil said, and Joy followed her to the serving line, which had dwindled to one last couple. There was plenty of food left, all of which looked delicious. Jalapeno cornbread, fried corn, sweet potato casserole, homemade pimento cheese, sweet pickles, and pickled okra.

As she and Sybil heaped casseroles and sandwiches onto their plates, Eileen stared at Joy's pan of brownies. "I wonder who made those," she said. Only one square had been removed so far.

Something in Eileen's tone made Joy cringe. Bravely, she admitted, "I did. Why?"

Eileen stabbed a brownie and showed the fork to Joy. Moist crumbs clung to the prongs and a hint of something gooey. "Do you want me to put them back in the oven for a little while, honey?" Her tone was hushed, as if the topic was almost too painful to discuss out loud.

"I like them that way," Joy said, and Eileen shrugged expressively.

"So do I," Sybil said, and once more Joy blinked away the threat of tears at this young mother's kindness.

As they settled into chairs to eat, Eileen sighed. "I can't help thinking of Carolyn," she said. "Sorry, honey."

Joy could not abide people who called you honey but hardly knew you, though she told herself they meant well … usually. Of Eileen's address … Joy was not so sure.

"Seems wrong not to talk about her from time to time," Eileen continued. "She was such an important contributor to our group, to the women of the church in general. I mean, you name one worthwhile activity that goes on at the church, and I can show you how instrumental Carolyn was in developing the program—or at the least, improving it. When we started the coat closet ministry, for example, who do you think …"

As her voice droned on and on about Carolyn's achievements, Joy gnawed at a rough edge on her fingernail. True, she'd been wanting to learn more about Carolyn, but she had wanted to hear about her from Ray, not from Eileen. Perhaps, though, that would have been even worse.

A masculine voice interrupted Eileen's soliloquy.

"That's quite enough, Eileen," Ray said, icicles dripping from his usually gentle baritone. Joy had not heard him approach, but now he stood beside her. She wondered how long he had been listening.

Nervous, Joy ran her tongue over her teeth, where a fingernail sliver had lodged. There was no graceful way to remove the fragment. Should she excuse herself, or would the timing be too awkward? Everyone would surely think she was upset by the comparison between herself and Carolyn, which of course she was.

To change the subject, Joy turned to Sybil. "Who's keeping your"— she hesitated, trying to remember whether Sybil's toddler was a girl or a boy and hoping that the fingernail sliver, which felt enormous, wasn't visible—"your little one tonight?"

"Oh, he's with Mrs. Davis. Their Bible study group is meeting on Saturday this week, and she offered to keep him so I could come. Wasn't that sweet?"

"Yes. Very sweet," Joy agreed, mulling over Eileen's words and Ray's reaction to them. Obviously, he still suffered agonies when reminded of the many virtues of his first wife. How long before he recovered, if ever?

She pressed her tongue against the fingernail sliver, but the nuisance would not budge. In a few minutes, she would discreetly excuse herself and take care of the problem in the privacy of her bathroom. Carolyn's bathroom, actually, as undoubtedly Carolyn had selected everything from the marble countertop to the fluffy guest towels. This house was as much Carolyn's canvas as the sky and the sea were God's.

Marianne appeared in the doorway. Her face as anguished as though she were in the throes of appendicitis, she waved a paper in their direction.

"Today was the last day to turn in the permission slips," she wailed, "and now I can't go!"

Ray took the paper from her hand, read it at a glance, then passed it over for Joy to see:

_____ has my permission to attend the field trip on September 1 to the opera, "The Marriage of Figaro," at Sugar Sands State University.
SIGNED _____ DATED _____.

"You'll learn," Eileen said, only slightly smug. Her lavender cowl-necked sweater slipped off one rounded shoulder. "You have to go through their backpacks every single night or—"

"Or something like this," Joy finished the thought.

"I'll give the principal a call," Ray said. "Maybe it's not too late."

He shot a look at Joy, one she couldn't quite read. Disappointment? Perhaps she should have offered first. She was so far afield here. Carolyn must have been the one to attend to matters like this—if they ever arose during her reign, since she'd homeschooled the girls.

Joy gazed toward the horizon—the blue sky melted into shades of petal pink, lavender, and orange-gold, luminous in an unexpected harmony. She thought of the apostle Paul, of his ability to find great joy in his troubles. Still, she needed time to adjust before the troubles mounted sky-high. Was that too much to ask?

CHAPTER FOUR

"There's no easy way to say this, Joy."

Gary Morgenstern's brow crinkled, and Joy could not tell from his expression whether he was in fact her worst critic or her strongest supporter. The rumor mill said he was tough on junior faculty in these decisions. When he was appointed as the chairperson of her tenure committee some months back, she'd been uneasy at first but told herself she had no reason to worry. Her record was fine, after all. Wasn't it?

Her stomach lurched. She feigned interest in the notes she had been reviewing for class while she collected her thoughts. She looked up to where Gary lounged in her doorway. "Sit down, please."

"The thing is," he said, perching stiffly on the hard chair most often occupied by one or another of Joy's students, "we're worried about your record."

Joy stared at Gary's orange patterned tie, a characteristically odd choice against his raspberry oxford shirt. "I thought my record was good," she managed to say. Then she raised her eyes from his tie to his face, daring him to dispute her statement.

He bent his head while he fingered his tie tack, refusing to meet her gaze. "It is good. It's very good. We're just not sure that it's good enough." He cleared his throat.

"But ... but if you compare me to the others, the ones who've gotten tenured in the past few years ..."

"Unfortunately, that's part of the problem," he said. "We're getting tenured up."

"Tenured up?" she echoed, as if she had no idea what he meant, though, of course, she did. She knew universities preferred to keep a balance of tenured and untenured professors in their ranks. Otherwise they ran the risk of complacency. They needed people to be a little hungry.

"Times are tough, and there are no guarantees about student enrollments." He adjusted his glasses, which perched crookedly on his rather large nose, or perhaps the nose was lopsided. "The administration is looking to cut costs everywhere possible. If they don't get better in the next year or so, they may have to reduce the number of faculty."

Once more Joy's stomach flip-flopped. She hadn't expected her tenure to be a serious problem, though she knew there were no guarantees. Her record was much stronger than either John Kincaid's or Kevin Herrington's, both of whom seemed to glide through without a hitch.

"Surely that isn't relevant to my case."

"I'm afraid it is." He uncrossed and re-crossed his legs. "Then too, there is the matter of trend."

"Trend?" She could do little more than echo his words.

"Since your marriage—" He cleared his throat again. "In the months since your change of circumstances, it has been noticed that you are working shorter hours and that you haven't gotten any new papers under review. The committee looks at what's in the pipeline, you know, as well as what you've published."

After Gary left her office, all efforts to prepare for today's class fell on numbed senses. Staring at her notes, she saw instead Gary's face, Gary's tie, and the face of another colleague, Natalie Winters. She'd always thought of Natalie as one of her allies at SSSU. Now she wasn't so sure.

Joy replayed a recent conversation with Natalie. "I hate to complain," Natalie had said, "but it feels like you're somewhere else lately, even when you're here. You know what I mean?"

Though she hadn't wanted to admit it, Joy had known exactly what Natalie meant. "I'm not sure."

"It seems like I'm always having to nag you just to read the latest version of the paper—when I'm the one who did most of the work."

Heat rose to Joy's cheeks as often happened when she was hurt or offended. "Be fair," she said. "I was totally involved in the early stages."

"I know that." Natalie twisted a strand of dark hair around her index finger. "And this project never would have gotten off the ground without you." She sighed, her delicate facial features knotted into a small tight configuration like a fist. "I knew I shouldn't say anything. I mean, I know you're still getting used to being married and all."

"Of course you were right to say something. And my marriage shouldn't be affecting my work. I'm not being fair to you if I let that happen," Joy said. "I'll see that it doesn't happen again." Natalie had slunk out of her office unhappily, and Joy knew she must have sounded dismissive.

Coming back to the present, Joy glanced at her watch—already past time for her class to begin. She scrambled to collect her notes, if not her thoughts, and make her way to the classroom.

As she stammered her way through the day's material, a messenger arrived.

"Dr. Jenkins, I am sorry to interrupt," the young man said.

He didn't look sorry. Her hand trembled as she reached for the slip of paper he held out to her. *Please, God, don't let it be Ray.*

She glanced at the paper:

YOU ARE WANTED AT YOUR DAUGHTER'S SCHOOL ASAP.

She should protest. She had no daughter. They must have the wrong person. But of course she had a daughter—she had two daughters. Joy's insides quivered at the prospect that one of them might be seriously injured or ill.

She hesitated, her hand still shaking while she shifted her weight from one leg to the other, trying to sort out her spinning thoughts.

The young man stood as if waiting for a reply.

"Thank you," she said, and he sauntered off. He glanced back over his shoulder, as though expecting Joy to reveal the contents in her facial expression. You know as much as I do, she did not say.

Joy stared out at the sea of faces in the classroom, which had become uncommonly quiet. They too were waiting. Above their faces the clock on the opposite wall gazed blandly back at her. Twenty-five minutes remained in the period, if she was thinking straight. Could she muddle her way through somehow? Should she try?

Yesterday, she would have canceled class in a heartbeat. But now, with the recent complaints about her trend toward shirking—would Natalie have actually complained to someone?

Joy wavered. The last thing she needed was for word to get around that she'd started canceling classes because of her new stepdaughters. Of course none of this would matter if one of the girls was in danger of some sort. How serious would a problem need to be to interrupt a college class?

Joy had no idea. She chewed on a raw cuticle while her thoughts darted about her brain like fruit flies around an overripe banana.

She should at least come up with a smooth exit line, or an in-class assignment, or perhaps a reminder of the assignment for the next class. Her mind went blank. "That's all for today," she said simply, and the students' faces erupted into thinly disguised delight.

Among the jubilant faces, one expression was more hesitant. A girl in the front row with a fish-shaped birthmark on her forearm opened her mouth as though to speak. Maybe she wanted to ask Joy if something was wrong, or perhaps she needed clarification about the assignment Joy had forgotten to give.

She did not wait to find out. Already she was on her way, her heels clicking in the hallway, her heart in her throat.

"Where did you get it?" the principal asked Jenny for the third time. He was a small man with a disproportionately large head and a pitted complexion.

Jenny said nothing. She stared at his shoulders. They sort of bulged in the direction of his big head. Probably over-sized pads in his suit jacket, like the ones in Claudia's bra that made her look as well-developed as any of the girls in Marianne's class. Jenny would not tell. She would never, never squeal on her friend.

When Jenny got caught with the weed, Claudia was barely out of sight. "Run!" she'd told Jenny, and Jenny had tried. She'd wanted to run. But, as in a dream, her legs froze.

She'd been too terrified to inhale, too scared of being discovered to enjoy the experience that led to exactly what she feared. "You'll love it," Claudia had promised. "There's nothing like it."

"But ... but it's a drug, isn't it?"

Claudia laughed. "It's less of a drug than the cocktails our parents swig in restaurants. And it's way better."

Not mine, Jenny thought. Her father didn't drink, and neither did Joy. At least not so far as Jenny knew. "So how do you know?"

"Just try it. You'll see."

Jenny wrapped her lips around the cigarette and pretended to suck in the essence. But she didn't really.

At that moment, a teacher's aide had popped into view, and Claudia had disappeared, only her voice lingering. "Ru-u-u-n-n-n!" the voice called. If Jenny could have reacted as fast as Claudia, she wouldn't have been caught. She had no one to blame but herself.

Now Joy was here, listening to the principal's explanation. He presented the incriminating evidence—the sad, stiff evidence that promised so much and delivered so little. Joy looked at Jenny, and Jenny simply couldn't meet her stepmother's eyes. Joy would surely hate Jenny after this and think she was worthless.

Maybe she was worthless. Still … always before, she'd tried so hard to be good. And where had being good ever gotten her?

"I hope you understand the seriousness of the offense," the principal said, his pale lips puckering into a tight bow. Jenny was a little afraid of him before this happened, even when he didn't know who she was. Now she would never be able to look at him again without quaking inside.

She nodded.

"Where did you get it?" he asked.

She said nothing, forcing her lips into a steady line. Joy had been kind, and Jenny hated the position she was in—the position they both were in.

The night before band tryouts, Joy had come to Jenny's bedroom and listened while she tried to play the notes. "Let me see that," Joy said when Jenny screeched a long, ugly note that hurt her own ears.

Joy took Jenny's clarinet and examined it closely. She removed the reed, checked it for cracks or splits, and replaced it carefully. "Try again."

Jenny had licked the reed, placed her fingers carefully over the keys and holes to cover them completely—to avoid letting even a little air into the wrong place—and blew. The harsh, ugly sound pierced the air.

"I think there's something wrong with your clarinet," Joy said, and the next day she accompanied Jenny to school to talk quietly with the band director before the tryouts began.

Joy had been right. There was a loose pad causing Jenny's problems. The band director tightened the pad by holding a lit cigarette lighter to her clarinet. "This is a temporary fix," he said. "Bring the horn back to me after class."

Oh, the thrill of satisfaction when the note resounded properly—a long and deep pleasing note. Because she had tried so long and so hard, she did much better than she expected in the tryouts. Not well enough to be one of the first clarinets, of course, nor even the best of the second clarinets, but good enough to be several places from the bottom.

Now Joy would probably never help her again. The principal droned on about consequences, whether Jenny should be suspended, and why he must take a tough stance. "You know we have a zero tolerance policy. We have to set an example for the other students," he said, "and since she won't tell me where she got the weed ..."

He shrugged, as if to say Jenny sealed her own doom. Her stepmother had said almost nothing so far. Joy spoke suddenly. "Don't you believe in second chances?" she said to the principal. "Experience has taught me we all need them on occasion."

Jenny met Joy's surprisingly gentle gaze, and Jenny's heart gave a happy little leap. Maybe, just maybe, Joy did not hate her after all.

"I'm sorry," she whispered. Yet, even as she spoke, the image of Claudia's smiling red lips came to her. She still wanted to be Claudia's friend, even though she didn't know what that might entail. Would Joy keep on understanding?

Joy was in over her head. *Let's face it. You know virtually nothing about parenting.* No, not virtually nothing—exactly nothing. Should she scold? Should she explode? Yes, she was disappointed in Jenny, but also Joy was curious.

The girl was silent as she sat in the passenger seat of Joy's car. Cassette tapes lay scattered at Jenny's feet. Joy glanced at the assortment of music she sometimes listened to during her drive, a habit she formed in her solitary days before meeting Ray. She wondered what Jenny thought of her taste in music. Not much, she imagined.

John Cougar and Lionel Richie and Chicago. Radio stations always seemed to have too much talking and not enough music. Lately, though, Joy had so much swirling in her head. She would arrive at her destination most days before she even thought to pop in a cassette. Funny, how at times her life before Ray felt like a bad dream, but at others—like today— the old life beckoned like a tantalizing dessert. Then her new life was the one that felt like the dream. Or nightmare.

Jenny's punishment was a three-day suspension. "I'm letting her off easy," the principal had pointed out with pursed lips. "I could have expelled her for this—probably should have." Joy didn't like the man.

What would Ray say? Surely he would know how to handle the situation. Yet, as Joy sank into the comfort of this solution, Jenny spoke. "You aren't going to tell Dad, are you?"

What? "I'll have to tell him. We'll have to tell him."

"No!"

"He'll find out anyway—when you don't go to school."

"Not if we're careful." Jenny's expression had been alternating between anger and shame. Now, though, she looked thoughtful.

"What do you mean?"

"He's so out of things lately, he might not notice. Not if we *act* like I'm going in the mornings. Okay?"

"That would be deceitful. Besides, what about your sister?"

Jenny's face darkened. "Yeah, there's that."

"Trying to hide your suspension will only make matters worse. The truth will eventually come out … always does in the end." Joy forced a firm tone, trying to sound more experienced than she was.

Jenny turned sullen. "I should have known you wouldn't help me."

"I didn't say that. I do want to help you." This was true. She wanted to do what was best for Jenny. If only she knew what that was.

"Then don't tell Dad. You don't know how hard he's always preached to us against drugs. He really, really hates them, and I—I don't want him to hate *me*. Okay?" Her voice broke … her words barely audible.

Joy's heart ached for Jenny more than ever. "Oh, honey, he could never hate you."

Jenny sobbed quietly, the tears coursing down her cheeks.

Even the girls had noticed how distracted Ray was lately. A slow-moving station wagon pulled out directly in front of them, and Joy slammed her brakes. Jenny lurched sharply against her seatbelt, and Joy muttered an apology. What was Ray's problem anyway? Perhaps he'd really rather not know, would prefer to have Joy find a way to help Jenny without involving him. What would Carolyn have done?

Jenny probably knew exactly what her mother would have done. But would she be honest if asked? Besides, Joy hated to sound so desperate. She hated to reveal—even to this child, or perhaps especially to this child—her insecurity, her lacking. Of competence, of confidence, of control.

"Please ... please don't tell him!" Jenny pressed.

Joy came to a sudden decision. "How about this? If you'll tell me where you got the stuff, I won't tell your dad. Not right away, at least."

Jenny hesitated, and Joy wondered whom she was protecting so fiercely. "All right," she said, "but you promise not to tell?"

Joy nodded, and Jenny began to talk. Her eyes lit up when she spoke of her new friend, the longing so sharp in the young face, Joy longed to be hopeful for Jenny—hopeful for this fledgling friendship. Instead, apprehension flooded every pore.

Jenny was so clearly infatuated, so enamored, with the girl's differentness, her boldness, her sophistication, all qualities that frightened Joy. Lightning shot across the sky in front of them, illuminating a large section of a sky that had suddenly darkened. Then, in the next moment, rain poured down. Joy switched on her windshield wipers, and a shiver ran down her spine.

Keep your enemies close, she thought. "Let's have her over for dinner sometime soon, shall we?"

CHAPTER FIVE

Science class never ceased to be boring, except when a telltale buzz rippled through the room, like now—a sure sign of some gossip-worthy event. What baffled Marianne were the furtive glances in her direction. What could she possibly have to do with whatever juvenile thing had created this tumult?

"What?" she whispered to Marsha Blanning. "What's going on?"

Marsha flushed. She obviously knew something.

"What?" she whispered again, more insistently this time.

"It's your sister." A fleck of something green was trapped in Marsha's braces, and she lisped slightly on the word, "sister."

"Jenny?" Marianne said stupidly, as if she had several.

Marsha nodded. "I guess she's gotten into some kind of trouble."

Marianne's heart raced. Mrs. Subhawong rapped on her desk for attention, but Marianne didn't care. She had to know.

"What kind of trouble?"

Marsha glanced at Mrs. Subhawong, then back at Marianne. Several other students were staring in their direction now. "I'm not sure exactly," Marsha whispered. "Everyone's saying it has something to do with drugs."

She whispered the last word in an even more hushed voice, and suddenly Marianne knew. That new friend of Jenny's!

"That's ridiculous," she said, loud enough for not only Marsha but all the other curious onlookers to hear. Then she turned her face squarely in the direction of the teacher, wondering if the tingling in her body showed in her face.

She pretended to be raptly absorbed in the subject at hand, something to do with molecules. Meanwhile her brain processed this new development. How could she turn Jenny's problem to her advantage?

When she got home, Joy and Jenny were seated at the kitchen table, listlessly playing a game of gin rummy. They turned guilty eyes on Marianne.

"There's something we have to talk to you about," Joy said before Marianne had a chance to slip off to her own room.

"What is it?" Should she admit she already knew—that it was all over the school?

"There was an incident at school today involving your sister, and—"

"So you won't tell Dad, will you?" Jenny interrupted. "Please!"

Joy held up a hand to Jenny. "Wait until I've told her."

A bubble of something like laughter welled up inside Marianne as she listened. She could not believe Joy had agreed to this madcap scheme. She was too stunned to do more than gape at the pair of them.

When Joy finished, Jenny blurted, "So please promise me you won't say anything to Dad! You know how he is about ... about ..."

"Why do you start every sentence with 'so' when there's no reason to?" Marianne glared at Jenny. "You either start with 'so' or end with 'okay,' which drives me nuts!"

Jenny bit her lip. "So ... I mean ... are you going to tell him or not?"

"I've got to think about it." Marianne turned on her heel and left the room, her head spinning with the possibilities. She didn't know what she was going to do yet, but clearly a great opportunity was being handed to her on a platter. What series of events would most surely turn Dad against his new wife once and for all?

She changed into her practice leotard and began her stretching exercises. She was less than halfway through when Jenny tapped on the door. Marianne's mind was about a million miles away from her routine—something that normally demanded her full focus—but after all, she'd been through the steps a million times.

"So, have you decided?" Jenny asked, eyes and cheeks bright with excitement or embarrassment, or both. She looked prettier than usual. She was changing, dropping some of her babyish roundness, developing angles, cheekbones. She reminded Marianne of someone in that moment, but she couldn't think who. Then she did. She was starting to look like Mother. "Why are you staring at me like that?" Jenny asked.

Marianne hummed a few bars of "Puff, the Magic Dragon."

"I love that song! Mother used to sing it sometimes. Do you remember?" Jenny asked.

"You've got to be kidding."

"What?"

"Don't you know what that song is about?"

"A dragon that lived by the sea, and a little boy who loved the dragon." Jenny hesitated a beat before adding, "Isn't it?"

Marianne rolled her eyes. "No, the song is about smoking weed."

"No, it's not!"

"Yes, it is." Marianne paused to let this sink in. "What were you thinking?"

"I guess I wasn't thinking, okay? Don't you ever do anything without thinking?" Something lurked beneath the surface in Jenny's usually guileless expression. She started to drop to the floor, then seemed to change her mind. Turning away, she paced like an anxious father-to-be.

"It was her, wasn't it? She talked you into it."

"No!" Jenny whirled back to face Marianne, suddenly defiant. "She didn't talk me into anything. I wanted to, okay?"

"Why?"

Jenny's expression changed abruptly, the guilelessness back, a pleading note in her voice when she spoke. "She's so totally cool, Marianne. Nobody like her has ever paid attention to me before. I just want her to stay my friend. She's been everywhere and done everything … and she actually likes me."

Marianne dropped onto her mat and stretched her hamstrings while she half listened. Obviously her sister was enamored, which was pathetic, but that wasn't Marianne's concern at the moment.

"Don't you see?" Marianne wasn't in the mood to hear Jenny rattle on about Claudia's virtues.

"What?" Jenny sank to the floor beside Marianne's mat, her shoulders slumped, cross-legged.

"How did you convince Joy to hide this from Dad?"

"I guess she just doesn't want me to get in too much trouble."

"Hmm."

"So, she doesn't know if we should dump more on Dad just now," Jenny added.

True, Dad had been acting a little odd. Probably, he already regretted his marriage to Joy, and this would simply prove to be the last straw. "Don't you think this is a great chance for us to turn Dad against Joy?"

"What do you mean?" Jenny's brow puckered in puzzlement.

"When he finds out she's been hiding stuff like this from him." Marianne spoke with deliberate patience. Jenny was so slow sometimes.

"No! He can't find out."

Marianne felt like the only sane female in this household. How could both Jenny and Joy possibly believe they could hide something like this indefinitely?

She stretched her leg so far back over her head it touched the floor. "Sweet!" she said.

Over the next couple of days, Marianne watched in fascination as Jenny and Joy performed an odd sort of dance in Ray's presence. "Hi, Dad," Jenny would call out gaily when he came home from work. "How was your day?"

Without waiting for him to answer, she'd add, "Mine was great" or "Mine was boring." Jenny was a lousy actress. However, no matter how exaggerated her tone of voice, Dad never quizzed her about what exactly made her day so great or so boring.

In the mornings, she went through an elaborate charade of getting ready for school. Jenny and Joy would carry on the strangest fake conversation, causing Marianne to roll her eyes skyward in disbelief. "Guess what happened at school yesterday," Jenny might say.

"What?" Joy would glance at Ray to see if he was paying attention.

"I made the highest grade on my science test," Jenny would conjure, or "I made an A plus on my essay." Really? When had Jenny ever made an A, much less an A plus, on an essay? But if you were going to lie, you might as well make the lie a good one. On the other hand, if you were going to lie, wouldn't you want the fiction to be remotely believable? Unless you wanted to get caught.

At least once he shot Jenny a curious look while Marianne held her breath, waiting for him to recognize the truth staring him in the face.

All he said was, "That's great, honey."

CHAPTER SIX

Something in the house smelled sour. Joy was sure the house never smelled this way when Carolyn the Perfect was alive. Joy was a lousy housekeeper, always had been. She'd tried so hard to do better. For Ray, for the girls, for herself too. Two days had passed since Jenny's suspension, and maybe they were going to get away with the subterfuge. She didn't know whether to be relieved or disappointed. Was Ray really so out of touch with her feelings and the household in general as to be totally oblivious?

He would surely notice this odor. Wouldn't he?

She lifted the lid to the trashcan in the kitchen, almost afraid of what she might find. She sniffed tentatively. Nothing noticeable. She inhaled more deeply. Still nothing specific. She went to the sink, sniffed around the garbage disposal. Nothing.

Barefooted, she padded outside onto the deck, and inhaled. Ah, nice. The saltiness of the sea. She could not console herself that something outside had crept in. No, the problem lay inside. She sucked in mouthfuls of the clean, sweet air again and again. Then, sighing, she returned to the search.

Where was the smell the strongest? She tiptoed cautiously into the hallway, the bathroom, and the bedroom she shared with Ray, as if expecting the odor to attack her. By now the stench had dulled, or perhaps she was simply becoming used to it. Could it be inside her head, the stink of the lie?

She wished she had someone to confide in. Before Ray, she knew who she was, at least. She knew her goals, her strengths, her weaknesses. At least she thought she did. She'd accepted her lot in life. Now she was in a muddle. At work, her desk overflowed with reminders of things left unattended, plus all the things she'd addressed only half-heartedly. Today, when she should be taking advantage of a day free from teaching to catch up, what was she doing? Playing hooky with Jenny.

A rap at the front door startled her. Who could that possibly be?

"Eileen. Hello." Joy gawked at Carolyn's best friend. A woman who, Joy suddenly suspected, had wanted to marry Ray herself. She stared at Eileen's tailored yellow linen pantsuit—not a single wrinkle—then down at her own stained T-shirt and bare feet. No doubt Eileen's house was immaculate and odor-free as well.

"Aren't you going to invite me in?" Eileen smiled broadly, revealing teeth so perfect Joy wondered if they were capped.

For a long moment, Joy said nothing, thinking frantically. What excuse could she offer for refusing? "I'm afraid I'm coming down with a cold or something. You probably don't want to come any closer," she said at last.

"Oh, don't worry about me. I never catch cold." With these words, Eileen literally brushed Joy aside and entered. "I wasn't sure you'd be home, but I thought I'd stop by on the chance."

Was Joy imagining things, or was Eileen lifting her nose, dog-like, to sniff? "Let's go out on the deck, why don't we? It's so much nicer out there," Joy said, thinking suddenly of Jenny. Please let her stay in her room. She escorted Eileen onto the deck. "Can I get you something to drink? Tea, water?"

"Sweet tea would be great."

Joy left Eileen on the deck to fill two glasses with ice cubes. She was wondering whether she should warn Jenny to stay in her room when Eileen spoke. "What's that odor?"

Startled, Joy turned to find she'd been followed into the kitchen.

As Eileen's words registered, Joy's eyes blurred with tears of frustration and defeat. "I don't know."

The good news was that Eileen could smell it too. Surely a smell in your house was better than a smell inside your head. She stifled a nervous giggle.

"What's funny?"

"Nothing." Joy poured tea into the glasses. "Do you want sugar or artificial sweetener?"

"You didn't sweeten the tea when you brewed it?" Eileen raised one thin, carefully plucked eyebrow.

"No, I drink mine unsweetened."

"I forget that you're practically a Yankee," Eileen said.

Before Joy could protest that she wasn't even remotely a Yankee—both her parents were born in the South, and so was she—Eileen was prattling on. "You know, Carolyn and I both descended from Civil War colonels. One of the many things we have—*had*—in common. Sugar won't dissolve in cold tea. Carolyn always kept the artificial sweetener right up here."

Eileen opened a cabinet door and located a box of pink packets.

"Let's take them back out on the deck," Joy said. "I'm always happier outside on a nice day. Aren't you?"

Eileen shrugged but followed her outside. They settled into deck chairs, and sipped their tea in silence. Joy had opened her mouth to attempt hostess chitchat when she caught sight of Jenny through the glass doors. Her mind blanked, and she fell silent. She tipped her glass again, sloshing an excess of tea down the front of her T-shirt.

"How's Ray?" Eileen asked.

"Oh, he's fine." Another lie. Just last night Joy lay awake, feigning sleep while she listened to him toss and turn. When he did sleep, his sleep was fitful, interrupted by occasional groans as though haunted by night terrors.

Lately, when he noticed her and the girls at all, he was uncharacteristically short-tempered. When Jenny had knocked over a glass of milk that morning, he'd barked, "What's wrong with you?"

Jenny had scrambled to clean up the mess, and Ray apologized. "I'm sorry. I shouldn't have yelled. I've just got a lot on my mind—but that's no excuse."

Joy remembered how she had just been wishing for someone to confide in, and here was Eileen, ready and eager to listen. What in the world was Jenny doing to make such a racket inside the house? She cleared her throat loudly, ready to blurt out something sufficiently juicy to distract Eileen.

Before she could speak, Eileen said, "What's she doing home at this hour? Why isn't she at school?"

Jenny frowned at them through the glass. Joy sighed. She could not bear to tell another lie. She would tell Eileen the truth. As she opened her mouth once more to speak, Jenny caught her eye, shook her head sharply, sending an unmistakable message. Joy was not the best reader of people, but she caught the drift. Eileen might have been Carolyn's friend, and she might even be a good Christian woman in her way. She was not, however, Joy's friend.

Jenny emerged onto the deck. She coughed into a tissue.

"Oh, are you sick too?" asked Eileen.

"So you know how anxious everyone is these days about flu germs?" Jenny said, shooting Joy a curious glance. "They don't want you at school if there's any chance you've got something catching, okay?"

What a cool liar she is.

"Carolyn always kept the girls on vitamin C," Eileen said, "as a preventative. And they hardly ever got sick when she was alive."

Joy's head reeled at the thought of all the personal things she might have blurted out to this woman. What a narrow escape. She smiled gratefully at Jenny.

By the time Eileen left, Joy's spirits were surprisingly lighter. They were only slightly dampened by Eileen's final barb as she stood by the door. "I hope you sort out that odor before Ray gets home. He's very sensitive to smells, you know."

On the heels of her departure, Joy headed to the laundry room, where she'd suddenly recalled having seen a nearly hidden mouse trap set in a corner. She cringed at the thought of a little Mickey or Minnie dying in agony, but steeled herself to face—and touch—the stinky truth. Even before she set foot inside, she knew what she would find there.

CHAPTER SEVEN

Joy could no longer deny it—the coolness between herself and Ray. Most nights, she lay on her side of the bed and Ray on his, barely touching. She waited for him to reach for her, but he did not. She stared at herself in the mirror after he'd left for work, and she hated what she saw. Joy had never liked the way she looked, not really. For a brief interval Ray had made her feel beautiful, and she'd almost believed herself to be transformed to be sensual, desirable.

"Joy," Ray had murmured the first time he kissed her, her name a caress on his lips. His touch had almost erased those other times.

As a child, as a teenager, Fatima Joy hated her name, which conjured up images of dark, sensual women with slender legs and tiny waists, with sultry eyes and drapes of heavy black hair. The other kids at school mispronounced her name on purpose, scoffing, "Fat Emma! Fat Emma!"

She always blushed furiously, not being quick enough to come back with a good retort, never able to put the rude boys in their place the way some of the girls could. The more she reacted, the more they taunted.

"I'm not either fat!" Her cries had been met with hoots of delight.

"Fat Emma, Fat Emma!" Oh, why had her parents burdened their pale-skinned, sturdy lump of a child with the name of an Arabian princess?

On her sixteenth birthday, they talked her into having a party. "It'll be fun!" Mama promised.

"What if nobody comes?" She secretly feared that even if they did, she would somehow manage to turn the party into a disaster. Surprisingly, all had gone well. The kids came, ate the food, listened to the music. They talked and laughed.

She was giddy with relief … until that awful moment … the one she'd tried so hard to erase. From the bathroom, she overheard two of the boys discussing her. "Sweet sixteen. Never been kissed," one of them said.

"Who'd want to kiss Fat Emma?" said the other. "No thanks!"

True. Fatima had never been kissed, and in that moment she felt certain she never would be. She stared at her face in the bathroom mirror, hating the acne splotches on her cheeks, the way her hair hung limply around her face, the line that was already popping into her forehead from anxiety and worry. No boy would ever want her.

She ran from the bathroom, threw herself on her bed, and sobbed. Before long a rap sounded on her bedroom door. "Are you in there, Fatima?" The voice was Mama's.

She stifled her sobs, lay quiet, and hoped Mama would leave. The rap became a pound. "Fatima Joy!" Daddy called out in a voice not to be ignored.

She dried her eyes and let them in. "I'm not Fatima anymore."

"What?" Mama said, her face mirroring her husband's bewilderment.

"Call me Joy."

"But why?" Daddy had asked.

"Just call me Joy."

"All right," Daddy said. "if I can remember."

"And now," Mama added, "you'd better go downstairs and say goodbye to your guests. Right now, Fatima."

She glared at Mama. "Did you mean Joy?"

She'd made the change happen. Occasionally she forgot, but most of the time, she simply refused to answer to Fatima.

Later, in college, there had been a few awkward, fumbling, teeth-bumping kisses, nothing like the sweetness of Ray's. When Ray took her face in his hands, when he looked into her eyes, she was beautiful. For the first time in her life. And for that, she would learn to be a homemaker. To cook and clean. To manage his daughters. Running Ray's household was going to be a joy—if it killed her.

Now, the old Fatima Joy was back and homely as ever. Some enlarged pores, a few tiny pink streaks in her cheeks where the blood vessels were visible, the beginnings of a slight sag beneath the jawline, bags and circles under the eyes. She manipulated the skin on her face, stretching the flesh to lift the corners of her eyes. Would surgery help? She lifted her breasts and punched her belly while hopelessness crept over her like a fungus.

Yet, within the hopelessness came a certain courage. To look at a direct comparison. Side by side. Joy and Carolyn. One photograph of her mother stood always on Marianne's dresser, and there were others in a drawer Joy had stumbled upon one day. Quickly she'd slammed the drawer, as if the pictures could peer back at her. No matter how she avoided seeing them, they never went away. She might as well look and look hard.

She slid open the drawer to the desk where this truth resided and stared in dazed admiration at the lovely, smiling face. In a flash, her first meeting with Carolyn flooded back, a memory she'd managed to keep buried until now.

Joy had been new at church then, and the former preacher, Barry Davis, introduced them. "Joy, this is Carolyn Jennings, one of our most active members. She has a hand in just about everything that goes on around here."

"I'm pleased to—glad to meet you," Joy stammered, feeling instantly inadequate in the presence of this poised and beautiful woman. Why did some women, by their very togetherness, have this effect on her?

"Joy is a career woman," Barry Davis said. "She teaches at the university."

"Oh, I'm sure I don't know how you do it all," Carolyn said. "I can barely manage to run a household myself without even thinking of adding another job on top of that." She went on to say something self-demeaning on the surface, yet with obvious pride beneath—about the juggling acts necessary with two daughters and committees and cooking and so on.

"I don't do any of that," Joy admitted. "It's just me so there's really not much of a household to run, and my cooking consists mainly of microwavable dinners and peanut butter sandwiches."

"Oh." The single syllable somehow conveyed the way Joy shrank before her eyes—into a pitiable spinster who was nearly invisible to someone like Carolyn. Carolyn drifted away, and the extent of their relationship quickly settled into a nodding acquaintance.

Joy dug out every photo she could find. Except for the one on Marianne's dresser, all the photographs of Carolyn seemed to be here, in this one drawer. Joy stared at the shining eyes, the vibrant hair caressing her cheek so sweetly the viewer wanted to reach out and touch the photo to see if the hair was as soft as it looked. How horrible for Ray to be constantly reminded of his loss—so hard he'd swept these tangible reminders from his sight.

Suddenly frantic now, Joy pulled open every drawer and flung out the contents, searching. *For what?* She did not know. Drawer after drawer, closet after closet, shelf after shelf, she kept searching.

And then she found it. In the very back of a little used closet in the pantry, on a shelf so deep Joy had to stand on a kitchen chair to reach it. An old cigar box. Odd, she thought, wondering if Ray once smoked cigars. She'd never seen him with one, had in fact gotten the impression he hated smoking in all its forms.

She lifted out a delicate scarlet fabric. When she held the cloth up to the light, its shape took life before her eyes and she blushed. The teddy was cut so sharply it would scarcely cover any part of the wearer's curves, made of a fabric so transparent that the bits covered would be just as visible as those not, tantalizingly visible. She brought the article to her nose and sniffed. Was it her imagination, or could she smell sex lingering in the garment? The image of Ray and Carolyn making love was one she'd avoided with an art akin to obsession. She surrendered now, yielding to the vision of Carolyn in red and Ray drinking in that vision, body and soul.

There was something else in the box. Gingerly, she lifted two folded sheets of paper and smoothed out the creases. The pages were thin, too flimsy to be used in a printer, and yet the words on them were typed. By an old-fashioned typewriter perhaps. Some of the letters had faded to a dim grey, though she could still make out the words. *My dearest, my darling, my only love for all eternity …*

The tears would not be contained, and still she could not put the letter down. As painful as the words were, she had to know. The rest was so private, so intimate, so graphic, she could not bear it. Flushing furiously, she put the letter and the teddy back in the box, and the box back in the closet.

Ray must never know she'd seen it.

Fearful of discovery at any moment, she retraced her steps through the house to hide all signs of her rummaging. Though neither the girls nor Ray were due, schedules could turn unpredictable at the worst possible time. What had she been hoping to gain? She'd gotten exactly what she deserved, and now she would never be able to forget what she'd seen. Why did the very things which hurt you the worst seem to stick with you the longest? Ray needed a mother for his girls—as simple as that. Yet, even at this, she was failing—and failing abysmally.

Joy found herself back in the pantry, inside the closet, with the cigar box once more in hand. She yielded to the impulse to read the letter one more time, to pretend just for a moment that the words were intended for her and not for her rival. Clutching the flimsy red fabric in trembling fingers, she weighed her options. She could destroy the contents and burn the box, but the image burned into her brain couldn't be eliminated so easily. Squaring her shoulders, she took a last look and put the box back where she found it. Carolyn may have been hot once, but she wasn't anymore. Joy was alive and here, and she loved her husband. She would not be defeated by a ghost.

CHAPTER EIGHT

Joy stared into the expectant faces of her students, trying not to see the red teddy or the typed words emblazoned on her brain, trying to get a grip. She never wanted to think about the items that lay inside the cigar box ever again. How quickly her resolve failed. Her students could not know her world was crumbling. She looked down, surprised to find a stack of overhead slides in her hands. She was more organized than she thought; after all, the material was not new to her.

She flipped the switch on the projector, which obediently shot a square of yellowish light onto the chalkboard. The screen. She needed to lower the screen. For a few seconds, she was able to concentrate on the logistics of positioning the slide, of turning the knob to focus properly, before her thoughts slid back to the box, to the light that illuminated the marriage that came before hers. The faces of the students blurred, and all she could see was that blood-red teddy. What a ridiculous word. The image in her head reshaped itself into a small red bear. The students stared, wide-eyed. As if they could see inside her head, a couple of them began to snicker, and the laughter rippled through the classroom.

She turned her back to the students, forced her brain to scuttle away from the box and toward the topic of today's lesson but could not grasp it. Beginning to sweat—a cold sticky sweat—she remembered reading once that fear had a distinctive odor. Would her students be able to smell fear on her—the fear of failure, or *failures* plural? Failing to be a desirable partner in marriage, failing to cook or entertain or decorate like Carolyn, failing to sign parental consent notes for the girls, failing to hold up her end in her research with Natalie.

Her legs began to tremble, and she put out a hand to steady herself against the table on which the projector perched. Recalling belatedly that the table was on wheels, she lurched awkwardly. She stumbled forward but managed to stop her fall by stretching out one arm toward the tray that held the chalk and erasers. This too wobbled but did not break. Instead of the titter she expected, the classroom was eerily quiet … almost sympathetic. Somehow this unexpected support enabled her to focus just long enough. Long enough for today's topic to swim to the surface of the muddled waters of her brain. She wrote the words on the board to the right of the screen: Substance versus Form. She faced the students as she asked, "What does this mean?"

Students averted their eyes, looked down at their notes or their books, a sure sign they did not want to be singled out. "Anyone?"

Silence.

"Did anyone read today's assignment?"

More silence.

"Substance versus Form," she said. A welcomed host of examples sprang to mind. Few of them had anything to do with financial matters, but today she did not care. She simply had to get through the lecture.

"Think about it," she said. "Feel free to glance at your books if you wish." Remaining silent when the students didn't answer right away had never been Joy's strong suit, though she'd heard often enough that silence was a valuable ploy in negotiations, in classrooms, probably in marriage. Why was it so hard for her to resist the urge to fill unwanted silence with prattle? She would learn to do better.

She located a chair and seated herself, prepared to kill a few minutes while the students read. Immediately the images were back. The box, the letter, the words of passion she longed to hear from Ray. Words he must have uttered to Carolyn, words he had obviously written to her. Would he ever write a love letter to Joy? What if she asked him to? She flushed at the thought, at the vision of his startled expression, his refusal.

The students stirred, waited for her to resume the lecture. Already she'd forgotten the exercise she'd given them only moments before. She glanced through the slides, seeking something to trigger her memory. Again she turned her back, stared at the words on the board. *Substance versus Form.* Of course, that was her topic. She slapped a slide onto the lighted projector and as she did, the entire stack of slides toppled to the floor. She stooped to retrieve them, where they lay scattered haphazardly about the floor. She grabbed a handful.

She shuffled the slides frantically, wondering why she hadn't thought to number them. This one went before that one, surely, but where was the lead slide? Tears of frustration pricked her eyes. Who really cared if today's lecture was lost? Not the students. She thought of all the times when she'd pushed herself to keep on topic, to complete every last detail when all they wanted was to escape. To meet their lunch date, or talk to their friends, or slip outside for a smoke.

"Can someone tell me what this means?"

"Like capital leases?" ventured a girl in the front row.

"Yes, exactly like that." Capital versus operating leases were, of course, the subject of the lecture notes that lay in disarray, some on the floor, others on the table, a few in her hands.

"I'll give you another example," Joy said. "Take marriage, for instance." *What was she doing?* "You've heard about these couples that get married just so one of them can get a green card? They are married in form—not in substance. Do you understand?"

A few heads nodded, while most of the students still looked perplexed. Perplexed but also curious.

Joy plunged on. "Technically they are married. But in their hearts they are not. I suspect a lot of marriages are like that, and not just for green cards—the couple has the marriage certificate, and they've dotted all their *i*'s and crossed all their *t*'s. They may file a joint tax return and be covered on the same insurance plan. They may go places as a couple and sign their names as Mr. and Mrs. Yet, in their hearts, they are as separate and as far apart as two people can be."

She looked out at her students, who listened now with rapt attention. They never seemed this interested when she was on topic. Even the boys in the back row, who always slouched in their chairs and took off the second class ended, acted vaguely curious. Of course, they might simply be wondering what manner of foolishness Joy would fall into next. One girl raised a tentative hand, and Joy called on her.

"Then why do they get married in the first place?"

"I don't know," Joy said. "I just don't know."

Another girl spoke up without raising her hand. "I know! You don't have to be a genius to figure that one out. What happens is that one, or both, of them changes. Why do you think so many of us have divorced parents?"

Several students nodded their agreement. And then they were clamoring. Someone asked, "Can substance change?"

Another, more serious-minded student added, "Can a capital lease turn into an operating lease?"

Joy let the students talk amongst themselves, while her own mind wandered far afield. She was thinking of Ray, of how he'd been on their honeymoon. He must have loved her then, at least a little. Could his lovemaking have been all form with no substance? She couldn't believe that. She wouldn't.

Another example came to her. Before she could weigh the reasons for keeping her mouth shut, she blurted out loud, "Think of the story of the Good Samaritan in the Bible."

Startled, the students quieted their discussion of hearts and love affairs. They waited for her to go on. Was she violating some kind of school policy about religion? Probably. She continued anyway.

"There was this man on the side of the road, and he was hurt and bleeding. And there were all these religious types of the day who prided themselves on following every rule and eating the right stuff and avoiding working on certain days and so on. They just walked right on by. But one man, a Samaritan, stopped and helped the injured man. And he was the kind of guy who didn't live by any of their religious traditions. Jesus told this story, and he asked the question, 'Who was the real neighbor to the hurt man?' In other words, who had the substance of being a Christian?"

The thought occurred to her that no one was called a Christian at that point in time, most likely—while Christ was still alive. Not able to think of another term that worked as well, she let the word stand.

One of the guys in her class spoke up. "Is that going to be on the test?"

The class exploded with nervous laughter, and Joy realized with relief that the time was almost up for today. Thank goodness. Another half hour, and who knew what she'd have said? She might have spilled her guts about her tenure case or, worse yet, about her marriage.

CHAPTER NINE

One of the benefits of teaching college was sometimes your schedule allowed you to go home early if you needed to. A benefit Joy didn't often use. Today, she saw no point in sticking around. Instead of heading home, she drove to a point of public access to the beach.

She parked her Volkswagen and sat for a moment staring into space. In her suit and pumps, she was hardly dressed for the beach. She roused herself from the stupor, slipped her jacket and shoes off and locked them in the trunk. An old ratty blanket caught her eye, something she used to carry to the beach occasionally in the days before Ray. She grabbed the blanket and draped it over her arm.

The wind whipped her hair, and she tilted her head and opened her mouth wide to see if the sea spray was strong enough to taste. She once held her head out of the car window of her parents' Chevrolet, trying to catch the wind. "What if you catch a bug?" Daddy had teased, and Joy made a big pretense of spitting out an invisible insect. Then she and both parents all sang at the top of their lungs about the old lady who swallowed a fly. "I guess she'll die!" they chorused.

To the west, the water turned silver. The sun poked through gray clouds, as though the sun were gliding to the right, passing behind the clouds, creating a pattern. Like a dancer behind a screen, silhouetted and provocative. Carolyn sprang to mind, as she so often did. Joy's eyes stung, and she brushed at them with her knuckles. Must be the wind.

A few families with small children dotted the beach, but the day was too windy for the row of striped umbrellas, which stood in a line, unfurled, as limp and lifeless as an inept teacher. The sun emerged, a yellow so brilliant she could no longer look at it. A finite ball a moment before, now the sky was a blazing mass of color—and though there was still a ball at the core, the intensity nearly blinded her. Like her love for Ray, the sun blazed so suddenly, so vividly, as to sear her vision. She could no longer see clearly, couldn't see her way, couldn't see herself for what she was—or wasn't.

She tried to spread the blanket, but the wind whipped the fabric so that it billowed and bucked like a ship sail in a storm. Finally, she managed to drop onto the blanket quickly, before the wind could whisk it from her. She lay flat on her back, throwing an arm over her eyes. A sudden chill told her the sun had slipped behind a cloud once more, and she looked up. At the horizon, the sky was a rosy sheet of peach and gold, though the time was only four o'clock. A blue patch of sky toward the east caught her attention, below a bank of gray-white clouds and just above a mass of white fluffy ones. Just a streak here and there of the brightest blue.

How marvelous it all was, and how insignificant her problems seemed in the grand scheme of things. Still, not to her. *Not to her.*

"What's wrong with you?" Ray said over spaghetti. He wound a forkful expertly, and for some reason this too made Joy want to cry. She sliced sharply through her noodles with the edge of her fork so she wouldn't have to embarrass herself by trying to wind them and failing.

"Me?" She was surprised he'd noticed.

"I don't see anyone else at the table."

Both girls were away for the evening, sleeping over at friends'—more of an acquaintance than a friend, Marianne had corrected. At least she went. Joy was glad not to have to deal with their angst on top of her own. "What about you?" She put down her fork and watched him eat for a moment. "You haven't exactly been the picture of cheer lately."

"No, I suppose not. But you usually are."

Ha! Was that what he thought? Joy stared at him in stupefaction for a long moment, and then she burst into tears.

He pushed his plate aside and reached for her hands. "Tell me. Please."

She could not tell him about the box or the letter. She could instead talk about her disaster in the classroom, and she could tell him some of her worries about the girls. So she did.

When she paused for breath, he rose from his chair and pulled her to her feet and into his arms. "I'm so sorry," he murmured against her hair.

"It's not your fault." Her body trembled under the tenderness of his touch.

"I hope not." He stroked her hair and her arms and her throat, and then he led her to the bedroom. "We should take advantage of this opportunity. Don't you think?"

"Opportunity?"

"Having the house to ourselves for once."

She nodded, and all of a sudden she felt as though the honeymoon never ended. How had she forgotten the way he could make her feel?

Surely what she saw in his eyes was not pity, not when they burned so deeply, so brightly she felt blinded for the second time today. Together, they climbed to a height of passion surpassing even that reached on their honeymoon. How little Joy knew of these matters. She was astonished to find her body capable of such pleasure in the wake of stress and trauma.

Later, as they lay curled into each other, Joy reached up to stroke his chin, the delicious stubble that presented itself at this time of day. With her forefinger, she caressed the faint cleft in the very center.

"Tell me," she whispered before she could stop herself. She so needed to hear him voice the words of love he must surely be feeling.

"Tell you what?"

"Nothing." Her sureness evaporated the way a rainbow dissolves in the sky when you try to capture the image with a camera lens.

He lifted her face to look into her eyes, and his were still burning—not with passion—rather with an emotion just as raw. He opened his mouth as if to speak, and then closed it without saying a word. A shadow passed through the deep hazel eyes, so like Marianne's. What was he thinking?

The phone rang. "Don't answer that," Joy said, longing for this day to last forever, hoping against hope that he was on the verge of allaying her worries.

He turned his back on Joy, grabbed the receiver, and listened. When he hung up, he reached for his trousers and without a word, prepared to leave.

She grabbed her clothes and dressed quickly. "I need to clear the table."

CHAPTER TEN

"I don't know," Marianne said. "I think I'm too old for this anyway." She frowned, her arms draped with elaborate Halloween costumes, ranging from princess gowns to astronaut and space alien suits.

"Of course you're not too old," Ray said. "You know as well as I do there will be people older than me who'll be dressed up tonight." Although Joy didn't normally attend, she knew about the church's Halloween festival from prior years' photos. The event was mainly for the kids but really for people of all ages. A time when even the most staid elder had been known to clown around and act silly, just to get a chuckle or two from the youngsters.

"Do any of those still fit?" Joy indicated the stack in her arms, enough to stock a small costume shop.

Marianne, Jenny, and Ray all turned to stare at her. Jenny answered. "We never wear the same costume twice."

"No." Joy was abashed. "Of course not." *So why did you drag all of those out of the closet?*

"There wouldn't be anything wrong with that, of course," Ray said. "No one would remember most of them."

"We would, Dad." This from Marianne.

"We can come up with something new, I'm sure," Ray said. "We shouldn't have waited until the last day to start, though."

"I could be run over!" Jenny said.

"And go as a zombie," Marianne chimed in, a slight smile lifting the corners of her mouth.

"So all I need is an old shirt, okay? Then you … " Jenny looked at Ray.

"I can run over it with mud on my tires," he said.

"Yes!" Joy felt a surge of appreciation for this awkward but loving daughter, gratitude too for Ray's willingness to pitch in and dirty his usually immaculate car. If only she didn't feel so useless herself.

Ray turned to Marianne. "Maybe you could go as Groucho Marx. You've always liked him."

She shook her head. "Not scary enough."

"How about Don Corleone?"

"Who?" asked Jenny.

Marianne shot her a withering look. "You know, the Godfather. What would I wear?"

"I've got a pantsuit that might work as a start," Joy offered. "It will be too big, of course, but we should be able to pin up the pants and cuffs."

"Let's see it," Ray said.

A while later, when the girls' costumes had begun to come together, Ray directed Joy to a disorderly drawer to search for old Halloween makeup. "She—we—kept the stuff in there."

"Here, let me look," Jenny said. "So what about you two? You have to have costumes too, okay?"

"I don't know. What do you think—hero or villain?" Ray asked, twisting his eyebrows and mouth into a ludicrous evil scowl.

The girls and Joy laughed.

"Ooh, I'm so scared!" Jenny said.

Marianne rolled her eyes. "You look ridiculous, Dad. I repeat … hero or villain?"

"Hero," Jenny said at the exact same moment Marianne said, "Villain definitely."

"I guess you'll have to decide." He turned to Joy.

Half and half, she thought unworthily, true to recent behavior. Jekyll and Hyde. "Do they frown on scary stuff at the church?" she said instead. "I really don't know much about this sort of thing."

"They're all pretty cool." Marianne stared critically in the mirror at her eighth attempt at the perfect Godfather mustache.

"So … a really scary costume would be okay?"

"Sure," Ray said.

"How about Jack Torrance from *The Shining*? Or were the kids even allowed to see that?"

"Nope. But they've all heard about the film."

"All work and no play makes Jack a dull boy," Marianne quoted with a wicked laugh.

Ray chuckled. "Everyone always has fun guessing the ones that are less obvious. We tell no one, and see who can figure ours out first."

"So what about you?" Jenny asked Joy. Her head emerged from the makeup drawer where she'd been rummaging for some time, not content with the odds and ends they'd produced so far. She triumphantly waved an elaborate kit of markers and tubes. "I just hope these haven't dried out."

Joy laughed self-consciously. "Oh, I don't have to have a costume, do I? Can't I just go as myself? That's scary enough."

"You have to have a costume." Jenny's voice left no room for debate. She drew a tentative pattern of lines across her forehead. "Still works! Maybe you could redo one of Dad's old costumes. That's not the same as him wearing it again, okay?"

"I've got it!" Joy said. "I'll be the Joker from Batman."

The entire group, even Marianne, entered into the spirit of designing costumes with a camaraderie that lifted Joy's spirits. When at last they were dressed and made up more or less to everyone's satisfaction, Ray fetched the camera while Jenny and Marianne debated the best spot for photos.

"Here!" Jenny lurched zombie-like to the front of the fireplace.

"Or here?" Marianne struck a pose in front of a bookshelf.

The phone rang, and all three females watched Ray as he listened to the voice on the other end. "I see." His tone was grim.

Marianne groaned. "No, Dad!"

"You can't go to work tonight." Jenny's eyes were sad, her tone pleading.

Ray's tight voice left no room for argument. "Don't give me any more grief. I've had about all I can handle just now."

Joy stared at him for a second, biting back a retort and forcing a smile for the girls' benefit. But the pain inside, bright and sharp, matched that implied in her Joker grin. She allowed herself a protracted sigh. "Are you going to wear that to the bank?"

"We were wondering if you were going to make it," Eileen said, hugging each girl in turn. Joy observed, with ungenerous satisfaction, that the girls endured her embrace but did not reciprocate. Eileen pulled back to look over their costumes without comment. She was wearing a fairy godmother costume herself, and Joy half expected her to wave her wand in an effort to transform their costumes into something she would deem more appropriate. "Where's Ray?"

"He had to go to the bank." Joy and Jenny spoke in unison.

Eileen lifted one waxed eyebrow. "On Halloween night? That's certainly not like him."

Isn't it? Joy wondered if perhaps this woman did actually know Ray better than she did—the last thing she wanted to admit. "He wasn't happy about it, but—work is work."

"He's always here on Halloween. I can't think of one he's missed—can you?" Eileen looked expectantly at Joy before adding. "Oh, that's right. You don't usually participate in the festival, do you?"

The girls were already dashing off to check out the booths. Joy hurried after Jenny, not sure what to do on her own and not wanting to lose sight of the girl. "If you'll excuse me," she said over her shoulder to Eileen. Inside the huge painted grin of the Joker, she felt her lips cracking in fake friendliness.

She followed Jenny from one booth to the next, pretty sure Jenny wasn't enjoying herself much more than Joy. She finally managed to talk the girl into trying the bean bag toss. "Go ahead," Joy urged. "It'll be fun!"

Jenny overshot the hole with her bean bag by such a margin she hit a toddler at another booth smack in the chest. Several girls about Jenny's age snickered, and Jenny's face flushed scarlet.

Joy rushed to check on the child, who was howling more from surprise than pain. The little boy's mother scooped him up and shot Jenny an apologetic look, as if he were the one out of line.

"He's not really hurt," she reassured Joy, who returned to Jenny's side. The other girls were still giggling, making no effort to absorb Jenny into their circle.

"What's that on your shirt?" one of them asked, and Jenny explained about the tire tracks.

"Oh," the girl said, clearly not impressed. Jenny shot a wordless appeal in Joy's direction, and together they located Marianne.

"How are you doing?" Joy's Joker mouth smiled at her older stepdaughter.

Marianne shrugged. "To tell the truth, it sort of stinks. I don't know why everything is so much more fun when Dad is here."

What could she possibly say to that? Joy stared at the girl. Then an idea struck her, and she glanced from one sister to the other. "I've been seeing the ad all week for a haunted house in the old mansion behind the park. We could do that instead. What do you think?"

Jenny said nothing, looking to Marianne for guidance.

"I don't think so," Marianne said. "It wouldn't be any fun either without Dad."

Eileen sidled up to them and smiled cheerily. "Having fun?"

Joy turned her Joker face to Eileen. "You bet."

"There's something about your costume," she said to Joy. "Of course the girls' aren't up to their usual standards. But yours. Something about it …"

She hesitated, and Joy wondered if she was actually going to pay her a compliment.

"Yours is downright creepy. Don't you think it's a little too scary for an event with small children?"

Joy's already tremulous smile faltered further. A wave of nausea washed through her. How Halloween-appropriate if she hurled a stream of vomit in Eileen's direction just now. The two girls looked back and forth from Joy to Eileen, as if trying to assess whether she had just opened fire, and warfare was now the order of the day.

Marianne spoke abruptly. "I like her costume. Don't you, Jenny?"

Jenny nodded. "It's supposed to be creepy, okay? It's Halloween."

Marianne turned to Joy, her back to Eileen. "I think that haunted house sounds like a great idea after all." She leaned against Joy for the briefest moment, but it was enough. A thrill ran through Joy, warming her right down to her toes, and she realized she had been chilly ever since they arrived at the church building.

Funny, she thought, how this gesture meant more to her than a published research paper. Not that she'd had any of those lately. Perhaps this was what motherhood was all about, the big fuss she could never quite fathom.

Until now.

CHAPTER ELEVEN

Marianne looked away from the ballet barre—where she was taking her frustrations out on her body—to the doorway where her father stood. She made no move to turn down the stereo, which was blasting, "Do You Really Want to Hurt Me?"

"I don't know what's wrong with you, Dad."

"What do you mean?" Dad stared at her, his face so clueless she knew he had no idea that he'd broken a promise. Joy, she knew too, had told him he'd better see Marianne in her room. Anger bubbled up inside her like the vinegar they added to bicarbonate of soda in science lab.

Marianne strove to control her voice and her emotions before replying. She stretched one leg into a position so extreme as to be painful. "You don't even know what I'm talking about, do you?"

She watched his face, knew the exact moment when he remembered his promise to be there this afternoon. "How did your—your event go?" he asked, his sheepish expression belying the casualness of the question.

"Like you care."

"I do care."

"I don't believe you. Did you forget, or did you just blow me off?" She knew this phrase would displease him, but was nonetheless mild compared to the words she wanted to hurl at her father. She longed to scream, to rant and rave, but she knew that if she gave in to the impulse, she'd feel sick afterward. Sicker than she felt already.

Dad's face paled. He too looked sick—did his face actually have a greenish hue? "I forgot. I'm so sorry."

"You forgot! How could you?"

"It's been rough at work lately. I realize that's no excuse."

Marianne abandoned her workout routine. She glared at him, her legs spread, nothing dainty or lady-like in her stance now. "You were never like this before," she said. "It's all her fault."

"You're wrong. My behavior has nothing to do with Joy," Dad said, making no pretense of misunderstanding Marianne's reference. His voice was hushed. Here she was—the injured party—and he was worried about *Joy's* feelings!

"Of course not," she said. Then, because she really wanted to know, she dropped the sarcasm ... for the moment. "Then what?"

He hesitated, and Marianne turned her back to him. She resumed her routine with renewed vigor, as if she could teach him a lesson by inflicting pain on her limbs and joints. He spoke to her image in the mirror.

"One interesting thing came up at work today," he said.

"Oh, well, that explains it then," Marianne said. "One interesting thing would obviously knock your daughter clean off your radar."

"Of course not. I said I was sorry."

"All right, you might as well tell me. What came up?"

"Could you turn that down please?"

She obliged, then shot him a look to say she hoped he'd gotten the message from the lyrics. He spoke so rarely of what went on at work, she was genuinely curious. Flattered too, in spite of herself, that he was talking to her like an adult. She was reluctant to let him see, though, because she suspected this confidence was his way of distracting, or pacifying, her. She resumed her workout to let him know she had more important things on her mind.

"I had a phone call from Peter O'Neil. He wants me to lead a small Bible study group the rest of this quarter and maybe the next one too. The majority of the meetings would be held here. What do you think of that?"

"What did you tell him?" Marianne asked, her voice carefully noncommittal. She executed a perfect attitude leap, wishing she could feel more pleasure in her success.

"I told him no, that I couldn't possibly. He said for me to sleep on my decision."

"Well, that's just peachy."

"So you agree it's a bad idea?"

Deliberately ignoring her father, Marianne attempted the most difficult move in her repertoire. Multiple *fouettés en pointe*. She almost succeeded. On the last one, she lost her balance, grimaced, and turned back to her dad. "I mean, you are totally clueless about what's going on here, and now everyone in the small group will be around to witness it."

"What do you mean? Witness what?"

"You didn't even notice when Jenny was suspended from school for almost a week!" As Marianne waited for her words to register, she saw Joy standing, stunned, in the hallway just outside the door.

Joy's face was white, and Marianne should have felt thrilled. For some reason, she didn't.

Marianne met her stepmother's glance, then watched as Joy's gaze turned to Dad. "I see" … Joy's eyes seemed to be saying … "I'm an outsider here."

Dad looked back at Marianne. She shrugged and turned away from her stricken father.

Torn between sorrow and triumph, she whirled back to face him. "Do you think Jenny and I don't see what's going on around here? Do you think we're as blind as you are?" In the most mature voice she could muster, she added, "I suggest you talk to your wife before you make any more decisions."

When she looked back toward the doorway, Joy was gone.

CHAPTER TWELVE

"For this next exercise, I want you to choose a partner," Christine Bookman said. Christine was a very tall, very thin brunette of indeterminate age. With her hair pulled back in a ponytail and flawless skin, her features were so perfect Joy suspected plastic surgery. She wore a tailored navy pantsuit, a white silk blouse, and strappy red sandals with very high heels. She was the kind of woman whose very existence made Joy acutely aware of her own flaws.

At her words, a shiver ran through Joy, coupled with the nausea she'd been experiencing off and on of late. It had always been like this, since she was in first or second grade. The fear of being rejected, of no one wanting to be her partner. Ironic, since that fear was the exact reason she was here today. When the brochure came in the mail, with the letters shakily written out as if by hand—F-E-A-R—Joy had tossed the mailer into the trash, retrieved it, trashed it again, and finally convinced herself that the seminar was meant for her.

Now she was not so sure.

In front of her, the pastor's wife, Acadia O'Neil, turned around in her seat. Catching sight of Joy, she smiled broadly, seeming genuinely pleased to see her. She mouthed something, and though Joy could not make out the words, she nodded. Not that Joy was anything more than incidental to Peter O'Neil's request to host Bible study group meetings. Ray was the one he wanted, and Ray just happened to be married to Joy.

A few minutes later, Acadia was seated beside Joy on the back row, and they were listening as Christine Bookman completed her instructions. One of them was to play the role of an irate parent who believed her son was being discriminated against at school, though completely innocent of false accusations brought against him by the real troublemaker. The other was to assume the part of a well-meaning guidance counselor who knew the boy in question to be guilty of far more wrongdoing than had yet been revealed to the parent.

"Which part do you want?" Acadia offered.

"I don't care. You pick."

"I guess you should be the mom—since I don't have any children."

A ripple of pleasure traveled through Joy to think she was the one with children—pleasure mingled with trepidation at her ineptness in the role. "Okay."

The two women stared at each other in silence and then burst out laughing. "I don't see the point," Acadia said.

"Me either. What does this have to do with fear—other than the fear that I'm no good at role playing?"

"You got me." Acadia smiled her appreciation at Joy's wit. "The sad thing is I feel even more frustrated now than I did before I came."

"Me too! The brochure made it sound like this seminar was going to solve all my problems. All it's done so far is to convince me that Christine Bookman is infinitely better at everything than I'll ever be."

"You and me both." Acadia sighed, and Joy thought how lovely she was, with her dark hair and clear skin and gray eyes, even now when she looked so sad.

When Joy had arrived at the session and noticed Acadia a few rows in front of her, she'd almost slinked away right then. She'd been hoping for invisibility. Now she felt surprisingly light-hearted for the first time in days, maybe in weeks.

Still, she wondered what Acadia had to feel sad about. As if reading her mind, Acadia said, "I know that as Christians we're supposed to find joy in everything, even in disappointment. And I don't even have anything concrete to feel disappointed about—but some days, the more I tell myself that, the worse I feel."

"I'm glad I'm not the only one," Joy admitted. A couple of women across the aisle from Joy and Acadia were enrapt in a heated dialogue about a boy named Herod.

"Who would name a child Herod?" Acadia whispered, and they both laughed.

Acadia rummaged through a large vinyl handbag and finally produced a tube of mints. "I can never locate anything in here. Sometimes I think

I'm the least organized teacher on the planet. Want one?" She held out the crumpled, half-empty paper tube.

"Sure. Thanks." Joy took one and popped the mint into her mouth.

"I tell you what," Acadia offered. "We'll pretend like we're role playing, and instead we'll have a fast pity party. I'll tell you what bothers me if you'll do the same."

Joy sucked in a quick breath and nodded, not certain how much she could reveal to the minister's wife. Still, there was something about Acadia that made her believe she could share some of her troubles at least. She shifted the mint from her jaw to her front teeth and bit into it.

"One condition," Acadia said. "Whatever we learn about each other stays between the two of us. You know how careful a preacher's wife has to be!"

Joy had never really given the matter much thought. But now that she did, she saw that Acadia could be on even more tenuous ground than she was, and the thought reassured her. The two women stared at each other once more in silence, and then Joy became aware of the observant eyes of Christine Bookman on them.

"Maybe we should act like we're yelling at each other or something," Joy said.

Acadia grinned, and then the grin faded abruptly. "It's my husband," she said, and she raised her voice and pointed her finger in Joy's face. "He's making me crazy!"

Joy was taken aback for a second before she realized that Acadia had taken her suggestion to heart. "How so?"

"He's so good and kind all the time, it's exhausting," Acadia said.

Joy resisted the impulse to chuckle. "If that's the worst of your problems," she said instead, and immediately felt guilty. Exactly what Acadia did not need to hear. "I'm sorry. I didn't mean that."

"You know how he manages to be that way?" Acadia continued.

Joy shook her head.

"I don't know if I can tell you, but I feel like I have to tell someone or—or I'll explode." She was convincingly irate, and Joy couldn't tell how much of Acadia's delivery was role-playing and how much was genuine.

"Go on."

"He keeps everything inside," Acadia said, and now her voice wasn't so loud. Joy sensed real anxiety. "He never tells me how he really feels about anything. I think he's scared that if he ever started complaining, he would never be able to stop."

"Or maybe it's just because he's a man, and men don't know how to communicate. Ray certainly doesn't." Thinking of the letter he wrote to Carolyn, she wondered if what she was saying was true. Or if the truth was simply that he couldn't communicate with her because, if he did, he'd have to admit that he didn't really love her. Not the way he loved Carolyn. An admission too painful to share.

"I worry that there's something else going on with Peter," Acadia said suddenly. "Something he's not telling me."

The admission struck so close to home, Joy was startled. "I wonder the same thing. How can we ever know if they won't tell us?"

She and Acadia stared at each other once more, and Acadia's gray eyes widened a fraction. Her long dark lashes reminded Joy she'd rushed out this morning without bothering to apply mascara. Her own lashes were pretty long but practically invisible without mascara. Acadia opened her mouth to speak just as Christine Bookman rapped on her podium for attention.

"All right," Christine said. "Who wants to share what they learned from the exercise?"

A giggle escaped Acadia, and Joy found herself biting back laughter. As others in the room shared their experiences, she and Acadia shook with silent mirth until the tears were streaming down Joy's cheeks. "I feel so much better," Acadia whispered.

Acadia rummaged in the large black bag again, and pulled out a dilapidated package of tissues. She offered the wad to Joy, who took one and dabbed at her eyes, glad now she wasn't wearing mascara after all.

When the seminar was over, Joy had not learned much from Christine Bookman, but she and Acadia O'Neil had agreed to meet for lunch the following day. When she filled out the evaluation questionnaire, she decided to give Christine Bookman a break.

I didn't know how much I needed this, she wrote.

CHAPTER THIRTEEN

How much do you love me? Joy wanted to ask, wanted and feared at the same time. *Do you love me at all?* She reached out a tentative hand to Ray's back.

How cool he had been toward her in the days following Marianne's revelation about Jenny's suspension. They had been as distant as nodding acquaintances who happened to be living in the same house, and could she really blame him? She had waited for him to ask why she didn't tell him, had even practiced her reply. He did not ask. Several times she started to bring the matter up herself. Something always stopped her. Something in his face, or something inside Joy. A familiar but despised reticence she longed to overcome—a reticence that had driven her to retrieve the F-E-A-R brochure from the trash.

Still they did not communicate. Instead, they moved past the revelation as though it never happened. A novel on the nightstand beside the bed drew Joy's attention. The cover showed a man gazing down at a woman with an expression of such adoration, so much tenderness. Even as she told herself they were paid actors or models, Joy's heart ached with longing. She'd always loved romantic novels and movies—stories where the hero eventually tells the protagonist exactly how much he loves her. Was it possible, even remotely, that Ray loved her and just couldn't find the words she needed to hear? Men could learn so much about what women want if they would just occasionally, read a book written by and for women. Most men, she suspected, would scorn these types of books, and Ray was no exception.

Ray sighed in his sleep, shrugged as if to throw off Joy's hand, then rolled over toward her. In the new position, curled on one side facing Joy, his face was as handsome as an Adonis. Albeit, a Greek god who was now snoring loudly.

Joy too sighed and rose quietly. She headed to the bathroom, brushed her teeth, and turned on the shower to adjust the temperature before stepping inside. Very hot, the way she liked it. As the water beat into her body, she imagined herself with another body, a different face. Her hair thick and dark, her features perfectly symmetrical yet mysterious, her expression animated. She threw back her head, the mane of dark hair streaming behind her, and laughed aloud.

"What's so funny?"

The masculine voice, spoken in near proximity, startled Joy so that she leapt into the air, slipping and almost falling on the wet floor of the shower. "Ray! I was just—just daydreaming." She raised her voice to be heard over the noise of the shower.

"Share the joke," he said, and Joy blushed furiously, glad he could not see her inside the shower.

Though she couldn't see herself either, she knew the flush suffused her entire pale, freckled body. "I couldn't," she mumbled and, rinsing quickly, turned off the water. She reached for the towel she had draped over the shower door and wrapped herself like a mummy before stepping out.

"Suit yourself." Ray was shaving now, making the curious faces he always did in this process, his face lathered in white creamy foam.

"Did you sleep well?"

"Well enough." He grimaced. "Darn it, I nicked myself."

"I went to a seminar yesterday," Joy offered, something she had not planned to share. Then again, why keep the venture a secret?

Ray said nothing, probably assuming the meeting to be one of her usual financial seminars at work.

"Acadia O'Neil was there."

"Oh?"

Joy had his attention now. "We're going to lunch today."

"What kind of seminar was it?"

Joy hesitated. "The idea was for us to gain inspiration into time management. The seminar was kind of a disappointment." She congratulated herself on a reply that was honest but not too honest.

"I see." A pucker appeared in the handsome brow. What was he thinking?

"How are things at work?" she asked.

The pucker deepened. "Not great. How about you?"

Joy hardly knew where to begin. The string of rejection letters that arrived in the past few weeks told her what she already knew. In her desperation to get some papers published before the upcoming review, she'd sent them out prematurely. Now they were bouncing back. Rejection on top of rejection.

Almost she blurted out her self-pity, yearning for sympathy—yet hating to be this way. She thought of her talk with Acadia and knew she should be forthright with Ray if she expected him to be so in return. Instead she simply shrugged. He lifted a quizzical eyebrow.

"It was good, I guess, to see that other women have a lot of the same problems I do."

Ray put down his razor and turned to face her, the pucker turning to a deep-seated frown. Belatedly, she realized her error. He was assuming she referred to her situation with the household as a problem. Because this was partially true, she could not think how to make amends.

He bent to rinse his face in the copper sink, leaving a pattern of tiny dark bristles around its rim. Always meticulous, he toweled his face dry before proceeding to clean and dry the copper vessel bowl. Carolyn had trained him well. She studied him for a moment, then reached for the blow dryer. Soon the noise of the dryer drowned out the silence between them.

"I feel like such a failure sometimes," Acadia said.

Although Acadia seemed like anything but a failure to Joy, she was realizing people were often not what they seemed. "Me too." Joy wouldn't have volunteered this information if Acadia hadn't done so first. How did a person learn to be so honest?

They had chosen Poseidon's Fork for their lunch, a restaurant Joy drove past often but had entered only once or twice before. She liked the cozy feel of the place.

"Do you come here a lot?" Joy asked, not quite ready to elaborate on her string of failures. After all, there were failures and there were failures. Like those who occasionally messed up a pecan pie, and like those who could not maintain a relationship of any depth. She suspected Acadia's were of the first, more benign variety.

"I used to," Acadia said, and a shadow passed behind the lovely gray eyes. Acadia wore a red jogging suit but somehow managed to look elegant even in that. Red was a good color for her. She changed the subject abruptly. "That seminar was such a disappointment."

"Wasn't it?" Joy said. "Except for bumping into you," she added and flushed. For Joy, the remark was unusually presumptive.

"I agree totally."

The aroma of fried seafood permeated the air, and Joy's stomach rumbled. The sensation in her gut was more queasy than appreciative, though. She studied the menu, willing herself to overcome the nausea. "What's good here?"

"Pretty much everything. I'll probably just have one of the lunch specials. There was a time when I resented having to pinch pennies so much. A preacher's salary and all. I really don't mind anymore. There is a certain satisfaction in getting the most, or the best, for the money. For me, at least."

Joy thought to offer to buy, but she dismissed the notion, afraid Acadia would be offended. Acadia was looking at the back side of the menu, so Joy flipped hers over too. Their table boasted a roll of brown paper towels and an assortment of hot sauces. Nothing fancy, but the customers around them ate, laughed and chatted, relaxed and at ease. Local artists' works crowded the walls, side-by-side with fishing paraphernalia and magazine clippings where critics heaped praise about the food and hospitality here.

"The lunch specials look good to me too," she said.

"They include iced tea or coffee and dessert, and the desserts here are out of this world."

"Why don't you come as often as you used to?" Joy asked. Seeing Acadia hesitate and the shadow return to darken her face, Joy sensed she had touched something very delicate and very private. "You don't have to tell me," she added quickly.

Acadia drew a sharp, audible breath. "No, it's all right," she said. "I lost someone—do you remember Beatrice Wood?"

"I do, but I didn't know her well." Joy laid her menu down and met Acadia's open and honest gaze, the gray eyes swimming with unshed tears.

"Beatrice died during our first year here. She and I used to come here all the time."

"You were very close." Joy remembered a petite, sweet-faced woman, much older than Acadia. A surprising friendship, perhaps. Then again,

Joy didn't really know that much about friendships between women. Or relationships in general, for that matter, as she was rapidly learning.

"Yes. Without Beatrice, I don't know if I'd have survived that first year. I was such a mess, and she was so wise and so gentle." A tear slid down Acadia's smooth cheek. "This is actually my first time here since she died."

"I'm sorry. I didn't know," Joy said, though in fact Acadia had been the one who suggested the place.

"Don't be. I think I needed to tell someone, and I needed to come back here. I had the feeling you and I could be close. That's why I suggested it."

"I'm glad," Joy said, astonished and pleased.

"The thing is ... I feel like it's sinful for me to keep mourning Beatrice. She was ready to go, and she was in a lot of pain at the end. I still miss her."

Joy nodded. She waited for Acadia to go on, but Acadia seemed to have said all she was going to on the subject. "You know what I dread?" Acadia asked.

"What?"

"Thanksgiving. Isn't that awful?"

"Me too." Joy laughed aloud. Acadia was certainly full of surprises, both in the things she thought and the things she said. All of Joy's preconceived ideas of what a preacher's wife would be like were way off base. "I'm just so inadequate in the kitchen, and I know Ray's expecting a real turkey dinner with all the trimmings."

She wanted to ask Acadia if she had known Carolyn, if she liked her, but she was obscurely afraid of the answer. *Oh, I adored her,* Joy did not need to hear. Besides, Acadia was unlikely to have known Carolyn since she would have died before Peter and Acadia's arrival in Sugar Sands. Wouldn't she? Funny, how this notion flooded Joy with relief. How silly she was.

"You know what we should do? We should combine forces. That way we'd only be responsible for half as many dishes," Acadia said.

Joy was thrilled. An hour earlier, she would have just dreaded having two more people at her house to serve, but Acadia's honesty knocked down a bunch of Joy's instinctive barriers to friendship. *Still* ... "It's not really fair to you unless I cook more than half. After all, there are only two of you, and we have the girls. Besides which ... in a moment of weakness, I told them they could each invite someone if they wanted to."

"I don't think that really makes much difference." Acadia tucked a strand of dark hair behind one ear. "Most recipes make plenty. My worry is more about getting them to come out right. In fact, when you cut a recipe down to a two-person serving, I think you just multiply the probability of disaster."

Joy chuckled, remembering Acadia was a math teacher, not all that far removed from her own training in finance. The more she got to know this woman, the more they seemed to have in common. "Okay, but you've got to let me have the meal at our place."

"Done," Acadia said.

The waiter, a not-so-young man with a ponytail and goatee, approached their table, smiling and ready to take their drink orders. "Sorry for the wait," he said. Then, recognizing Acadia, he added, "I haven't seen you in here in the longest time."

Joy watched to see if Acadia would be jarred afresh by the remark, but she seemed pleased to be recognized. "It has been a while… but I won't wait so long next time."

They both ordered iced tea, and Acadia told the waiter, "I think we're ready to order our food too." She glanced at Joy, who nodded her agreement.

Joy ordered the Greek-style fish, Acadia the grilled liver with onions. "I love liver," she said, "but Peter can't bear the smell, so I almost never have it."

While they waited for their food, they settled into discussing the menu for Thanksgiving. "What I don't understand about cooking," Acadia said, "is how something that takes so little time to consume can take so much to prepare."

"Not to mention the anxiety," Joy added. "I think there are people who actually enjoy it."

"Yeah, I wish I was one of those."

Their food arrived, and they ate in silence for a few minutes. Joy's nausea passed, and she found herself savoring the flavors. From time to time, Acadia excused herself to address someone at another table or someone who had just entered. More than once the newcomer came over to their table to be introduced to Joy. "Don't you know Edna Haygood?" or "Have you met John Tillman?"

And then Joy did know someone—Eileen Reynolds. Joy had caught sight of Eileen the moment she entered and was debating whether to greet her when Eileen spotted her and came over. Eileen wore a two-piece cream-colored suit and was more carefully put together—with every hair in place, heavy makeup, and several strands of gold around her neck—than any of the other customers. Of course, she knew Acadia too, and she addressed them both.

Joy could not help herself. She bristled at Eileen's presence and her annoying tone. As Eileen left their table, Joy found herself tempted to mention Carolyn, how threatened Joy felt by the constant comparisons everyone made between her and Ray's first wife.

Before she could broach the subject, Acadia was talking again. "Where were we? Oh, yes. The hellishness of Thanksgiving." They both laughed, a little sheepishly, and the moment passed. "Beatrice always told me to let go of the reins. Some things are just bound to go wrong no matter what we do. You know?"

"Yes, but letting go is really hard for me," Joy said.

"Me too. Let's make each other a promise."

"What?"

"When we find we're at that point where we're lying awake trying to figure out how to make things work—no matter what time it is—we pick up the phone and call. Any time, day or night. Are you in?"

Joy thought of the popular girls in school with their clubs and cliques that never wanted or needed her. What if Acadia was looking for someone to replace her friend Beatrice, and Joy was just going to disappoint her, the way she was disappointing Ray? She hesitated, and then she saw Acadia's expression. So earnest and so beautiful. Wanting her, Fatima Joy Hancock, to promise.

And so she did.

After her lunch with Acadia, Joy went home and walked on the beach. It was a non-teaching day for her, and she felt no compulsion to go to her office. The weather was unseasonably warm, but breezy. She gazed toward the horizon. The waves rolled in like a bulldozer, bound on destroying everything in their path. She thought of the passages in the Old Testament—Isaiah or Jeremiah—where God finally lost patience with the children of Israel after repeated warnings. Looking at the waves on a day like today, you couldn't question the majesty of his power. If he chose, he could destroy any nation or tribe, surely.

Against the pale blue sky, the water sparkled silver and turquoise. Several boats practiced their runs in preparation for the boat race this coming weekend. They skimmed the surface, rearing up on the choppy water the way the boys used to rear up on their bikes, showing off for the girls, when Joy was a kid. A yellowish green, lemon-lime boat appeared to be the fastest, although you couldn't always tell by the practice runs. Some of the other racers might be holding back.

A few brave souls ventured into the water. Near Joy, a stiff-legged man about fifty or sixty with a sunburned chest and navy blue swim trunks resembling boxer shorts made his way cautiously into the water. A courting couple strolled past Joy, headed in the opposite direction. Though Joy wasn't a great judge of age, especially teenagers, the two looked barely old enough to be in middle school. She glanced at her watch. School shouldn't be out yet, but perhaps they were homeschooled.

Gulls squawked as they plunged into the violent waves in search of a meal. The sun beamed down with hot insistence. A trio of pelicans, also searching for fish, began a graceful descent, then lunged into the water as if startled by its abrupt onslaught. All three came up empty, and Joy found her spirits soaring with the pelicans. What a beautiful world, and how thankful she was to have a new friend.

CHAPTER FOURTEEN

Helping Joy fold napkins and set the table for Thanksgiving dinner, Marianne was so nervous she almost regretted inviting Chrissy. But after Chrissy arrived, things seemed to be going fine for at least thirty seconds.

When Joy had initially told Jenny and her they could each invite someone for Thanksgiving dinner, Marianne had said, "Probably not. No matter how much we entertained the rest of the year, Thanksgiving was always just a family affair when Mother was alive."

The truth had been that she could think of no one to invite. Then she just happened to overhear Chrissy Mahoney, who was head cheerleader, telling Renee Taylor how her life was so screwed up after her parents' divorce, she had nowhere to go for Thanksgiving. "Mom *has* to spend the holidays on a cruise ship with her new husband," Chrissy said, her voice thick with sarcasm. "And Dad is dating a woman so young I get sick to my stomach. How can you be expected to eat with that in your face?" she said to Renee.

"I'd have you over but we always go to my Grandma's in Maine. Everyone's so boring there, I wouldn't wish that on my worst enemy," Renee said.

Before she could chicken out, Marianne blurted, "You can come to my house, Chrissy—if you like. My new stepmother said I could invite someone if I wanted to."

"For real?" Chrissy looked pleased, grateful even.

"Sure." Marianne's heart had soared. Maybe everything was going to be okay now. Maybe she and Chrissy were going to be friends. She just hoped Joy wouldn't mess up the meal too badly. For the next several days, she'd offered a steady stream of suggestions to Joy, all based on her memory of how Mother did things. She divided her time between trying to dissuade Jenny from having Claudia over and trying to prevent another kitchen catastrophe from Joy.

"I simply adore your house," Chrissy had said to Joy when she arrived.

Marianne's heart swelled with pride. "Actually my mother did all the decorating here."

"Didn't she use an interior design artist?"

What was an interior design artist, Marianne wondered. "I don't think so."

"Hm." Chrissy's nose tilted slightly higher into the air, and Marianne cringed. Why hadn't she pretended they had an artist? But then Dad might have overheard, and he had such a thing about honesty. Whenever he caught her or Jenny telling a lie, you'd think they had murdered someone.

Now, to Marianne's horror, Chrissy was talking to Claudia. "How long have you been living in Sugar Sands?"

"Oh, I don't know," Claudia said. Her black eyeliner slanted up at the corners, giving her a cat-like vibe. She wore faded jeans and a black tank top, cut low enough to reveal the top of a tattooed breast. "I don't keep track of time. But it feels like forever."

"I hear you," Chrissy said. "There's absolutely nothing to do around here."

Marianne, who loved Sugar Sands but had never lived anywhere else—felt compelled to defend the place, as if their criticism of the town was somehow an attack on her and Dad and everything they stood for. "Don't you like the beach?" she said. Everyone liked the beach, didn't they?

"Not especially," Chrissy said. "I always end up with sand and stickiness all over—and what do you suppose all that salt does to your complexion?"

"Not to mention the sun," Claudia said. Claudia actually shuddered, as if she cared a flip about her complexion. How could someone who took no notice of time think far enough ahead to worry about sun and salt damaging her skin? She had to get Chrissy away from this hypocritical freak.

"Want to see my room?" she asked Chrissy, who tilted her head faintly in what might or might not be construed as a nod.

Marianne chose to think positively and headed in that direction, hoping Chrissy would follow. Marianne had tried really hard to be good at cheerleading. She'd been so excited when she was selected, believing this would be her ticket "in." Not so! Granted, she could do the cheers almost perfectly by now—she honestly thought she made the fewest mistakes of anyone. Still she never seemed able to satisfy Chrissy's critical eye.

Chrissy would roll her eyes in Renee's direction whenever she corrected Marianne. Chrissy never said a harsh word about Renee, though Renee could not pull off a forward flip properly, much less a backward one, whereas Marianne could do a string of either easily. No, getting on Chrissy's good side wasn't about how perfect you were. But what *was* it about?

"I guess your mother decorated your room too," Chrissy said. Looking at the room through Chrissy's eyes, Marianne saw how childish and, well, *lame*, the décor must seem, with the crisp ruffled curtains and polka-dotted bedspread.

Until now, Marianne hadn't wanted to change a single thing that had Mother's touch. "I guess it's about time to remodel," she said with a guilty twinge. What would Mother think—if she was up there listening from heaven?

Chrissy plopped onto the bed. "Who else is coming for Thanksgiving dinner?"

"How did you know anyone was?" Marianne hadn't told her yet about the preacher and his wife, afraid this piece of information might cause Chrissy to back out altogether.

"Didn't exactly take a rocket scientist. I counted the place settings. Tell me it's not your grandparents."

"No, our preacher and his wife."

"You've got to be kidding me!"

"Nope."

"Isn't that a hoot? *Them* together at the table with your sister's little friend and all."

Little was definitely not the word that Marianne would use to describe Claudia, but she got the point.

Marianne looked out the window as Acadia O'Neil hauled dish after dish from a beat-up Volkswagen. How beautiful she was. Marianne had seen Acadia plenty of times at church, of course, but now that she was in their house, Marianne was suddenly acutely conscious of her own looks. Marianne wore her new brown leather boots, which she loved to death—the leather was so soft—with black tights and a short black and tan striped dress. But now she wondered if she'd overdressed, making everyone think she was trying too hard, which she definitely was.

Acadia was in a pair of slim black pants and a long, loose sweater that somehow managed to accentuate rather than obscure the figure beneath.

Chrissy and Claudia sat together on the sofa, their long jean-clad legs stretched out side by side. Chrissy wore a snug turtle-necked sweater in a shade of blue that just matched her eyes. Joy darted here and there, looking harried in a white oxford-cloth shirt that had been clean earlier in the day but now sported an assortment of splatters representing just about every dish she'd prepared.

"I'll watch the food if you want to go change," Marianne offered, and Joy agreed, seeming grateful.

Joy was also trying too hard, and Marianne couldn't help feeling a little anxious for her stepmother as well as for herself. Except for her bad case of nerves, everything seemed to be coming out perfectly.

"Can I help?" Chrissy escaped from Claudia long enough to ask Acadia, and Marianne chastised herself for not having offered first.

"No, thanks. I think we've got it," Acadia said, setting down a casserole dish and slipping off her oven mitts.

Returning in khaki pants and a spotless white shirt, Joy brought out the turkey, golden brown in all its glory, complete with a moist portion of cornbread stuffing just visible. Everyone *oohed* and *aahed*, and Marianne had to admit she'd never seen a more perfect turkey.

Dad carved away while the others chatted. Only Marianne was absorbed by the process—absorbed to the point of speechlessness. The more he sliced, the more apparent it became something was wrong.

The meat was still bright pink. "How long did you bake the turkey?" he asked quietly.

Joy's lips went white. "Four and a half hours," she said. "I wanted to err on the side of safety. But—but—oh no." She glanced from Ray to Peter O'Neil, and her face flushed scarlet. "I'm sorry," she said, and she ran from the room.

The table had gone completely quiet now. Marianne glanced at Chrissy, who grinned—actually smirked, as if amused by the whole debacle. Suddenly, Marianne knew what had happened. The oven had a built-in timer, which they'd set for the pecan pie at some point. The heat automatically shut off when the pie was done, leaving the turkey "baking" in a cold oven.

"I never really wanted to be a cheerleader in the first place," Marianne blurted out, breaking the silence. The unbidden image of Marsha Blanning, with her thick glasses and braces, popped to mind. She should have invited Marsha instead. They would have laughed together about this.

"Then why did you try out? You know you knocked one of my *friends* out of the running."

"Well, she can have *my* spot. I quit!" Tears welled as Marianne pushed back her chair and ran after her stepmother.

CHAPTER FIFTEEN

Before long, Chrissy called for a ride. Jumping at the chance to escape the confusion, all the adults spoke up at once, offering to drive her. They reminded Jenny of the way birds on the beach lurch toward a single crumb of bread.

Chrissy coolly declined all offers.

Jenny and Claudia exchanged glances. One part of Jenny wanted to be glad for her sister's defeat, but mostly she wasn't. This was what always happened. No matter how hateful Marianne sometimes acted, as soon as things went wrong for her, Jenny couldn't help softening. She knew the reason too. Deep inside her, there was this place where she secretly longed to be her sister's best friend. These kind of friendships happened in books, like *Little Women*, where Jo and Beth adored each other, so why not in real life?

Every once in a while, Marianne would say something sweet too, just enough to make Jenny think the idea wasn't all that lamebrained. Only yesterday Marianne had questioned Jenny about Claudia. "You're sure she's the one you want to invite?"

Jenny was sure.

"But why? What do you like about her?"

With a pleasant jolt, Jenny realized that Marianne was a little bit jealous of Claudia. Maybe Marianne secretly wanted to be Jenny's best friend, just as Jenny wanted to be hers. Marianne was always complaining that being homeschooled for so long had ruined her chances to make normal friends in public school. Well, the situation was the same for both of them—something they had in common. If she hadn't invited Claudia, maybe Marianne wouldn't have invited Chrissy, and the whole turkey catastrophe wouldn't have seemed so awful. The preacher and his wife appeared to be the sort who would have just laughed it off.

To her credit, Claudia made no comment on Marianne's outburst at the table. Instead, she complimented both Marianne and Acadia lavishly on each and every non-turkey dish. Jenny appreciated Claudia all the more because of Chrissy's smug stuck-up attitude.

Did Claudia really like those gooey casseroles? Broccoli with all kinds of stuff in it—cream and cheese and nuts and who knew what all. Squash casserole with chunks of onions and sour cream and crumbs on top. Sweet potatoes mashed up and loaded with butter and marshmallow cream and brown sugar. Jenny liked her foods simple, one straightforward thing at a time.

Just looking at the polite portions of casserole on her plate left her slightly nauseated.

School was the same way. When the teacher switched gears from math to spelling, just as something was about to click for Jenny, she'd get that nauseated feeling, like everything was all mixed up together in her head. Why was she always a pace behind? Her brain wasn't quick like Marianne's or a lot of the kids in Jenny's class.

"This corn is delicious," Claudia smacked her lips. "What's in it?"

"Cream cheese," Acadia said, and Jenny wondered why there should be anything besides corn in the corn, except maybe a little salt.

Marianne and Joy slid back into their chairs in time for dessert. Marianne's eyes were only slightly puffy, and her lips actually curved up in a semblance of a smile. Jenny was so relieved she wanted to laugh out loud. There were three choices for dessert—pumpkin pie, chocolate cake, and pecan pie. The decision was easy for Jenny.

The pecan pie turned out, though not exactly firm, much better than the last time. "Yum!" Jenny said, and Dad smiled his agreement.

Claudia practically swooned over the chocolate cake topped with ice cream, though she only ate half her piece. "Whew! I'm stuffed," Claudia said.

As soon as they were back in Jenny's room, Claudia dove into her handbag and pulled out a joint.

Jenny gasped. "Not here," she said. "We can't."

"Why not?"

"They'll smell it. And I'll be grounded forever, okay?"

"They won't know what they're smelling," Claudia said slyly. "Not unless they've smoked weed themselves. Besides—"

She delved into her handbag and to Jenny's amazement, produced a handful of odd-looking sticks and a book of matches.

"What's that?" For a second Jenny thought she was about to be introduced to a heavier-duty drug than weed, and an accompanying heavier fear clutched at her chest.

"Incense. To hide the smell. Also, incense makes a terrific distraction. If your parents come, they'll get so caught up warning you about fires and matches and all—"

"I don't know." Joy would never be fooled that easily, not after last time.

But Claudia was already busy, lighting the incense and the weed almost simultaneously. She handed the cigarette to Jenny, who took a very tenuous draw and began to cough.

Afraid the coughing was echoing throughout the house, she tried to stifle the sound. Unfortunately, the more she resisted, the stronger the urge to cough. "What else have you got in that bag?" she asked, as much to distract herself from the tickling in her throat as from curiosity.

Claudia took a long draw before producing a large bar of dark chocolate and a bag of peanuts. "For the munchies," she explained. "We're bound to be hungry after that pitiful excuse for a Thanksgiving dinner."

Jenny bristled. "So ... but you said ..."

Claudia grinned. "Did you buy that? Maybe they did too." Before long, Claudia was giggling like crazy, and the urge to cough had left Jenny. She tried to join in with Claudia's laughter, but she kept worrying about whether the sounds could be heard down the hall.

"Come on," Claudia urged. "This is good stuff. Don't waste it—you've got to inhale to get the effect."

Jenny puffed and sucked, all the while fighting the impulse to cough. After a few more draws, though, she began to feel better. Less worried anyhow. In fact, her worries suddenly struck her as silly, and she too began to giggle.

Just then a sharp rap sounded at her door, and Dad's voice boomed out. "What's going on in there?"

Jenny's heart thumped so hard she thought it might explode in her chest. He cracked the door, and Claudia smiled sweetly, her giggle vanishing as quickly as all evidence of the marijuana.

"Just a little incense. I hope that's all right. I know we should have asked first," Claudia said.

Jenny held her breath as Dad sniffed the air. "Hm," he said distractedly. "I guess it's okay. Just be careful with those matches. We don't want you setting the house on fire."

As soon as he was out of earshot, Claudia exploded into laughter once more.

Jenny could no longer share her appreciation. "So—when do you have to go home?"

CHAPTER SIXTEEN

"We know what a tricky time this must be for you at work," Alfred said to Ray, having thanked him for the third time for agreeing to lead the small Bible study group.

"What do you mean?" Ray looked disconcerted by the remark. They were seated on the balcony during this conversation, and Ray had spent some time rounding up enough chairs for everyone.

"Just what a difficult time the banking industry is having," Alfred said. "All I know is what's in the press."

"Oh, of course." Joy watched her husband's color return. Why would Alfred's comment elicit such a response? In the glow of the setting sun, the lines in his forehead seemed deeper than she remembered. "I haven't done anything yet. The burden—I'm sorry, that's the wrong word— the responsibility is more Joy's than mine. She's the one you should be thanking," Ray said.

"I really haven't done anything either," Joy said, hating to be the center of Alfred's attention. She stared past him, out to sea. The waves crashed in to shore, as though furious at the undertones in this conversation. Funny, how the gulf could be calm as a lake at this time of evening on some days and as volatile as a teapot about to boil on others. Like her mood swings of late. Had life really been as predictable before Ray as she remembered? Alfred's voice droned on, and she realized he was addressing her.

"We need to decide on our plan for the month," he said. "Do you want to have early meetings with dinner? Or later meetings without food, or just snacks?"

When Joy hesitated, he added, "Of course, everyone will pitch in to bring dishes, regardless of what we decide."

"How about desserts?" Eileen suggested. "We could all get dinner on our own, and then have dessert here. If that's all right with Joy."

"Sure," Joy said. "It's fine with me."

"Good. Then that's decided," Alfred said. "How about a six-thirty start time, for a while?"

Before anyone could answer, a sudden wind blew up, dumping what looked like a bucket full of rain on Ray and the other members sitting nearest the edge.

"Oh!" Mildred Brubaker jumped up, and several others followed suit.

They rushed in to escape the rain, and Ray dragged the chairs back inside. Joy brought a stack of towels to absorb the puddles. A couple of men lingered on the balcony, apparently enjoying the rain, but then they too headed indoors.

Once inside, Joy became aware of an odor she hadn't noticed before, a certain fishiness. Was she always to be haunted by strange odors? She read somewhere that imagining odors could indicate a brain tumor. But, no, the odor was real. She shuddered. Did the wind bring the smell? Normally Joy loved the rain, could sit for hours watching it pepper down on the beach. She longed to do so now, begrudging her new role as hostess, which prevented her from enjoying the downpour properly. She wondered why the smell was stronger inside the house than on the balcony, wondered if the odor was inside her head. She glanced around to see if anyone else was sniffing. Apparently not. They were merely dabbing at their chairs and damp clothes with towels, smoothing their shirts and blouses and hair, and reseating themselves tentatively as if fearful the rain would find its way indoors.

When they were situated, Alfred began to read Scripture, and Joy tried to focus on the words.

"Woe unto you, scribes and Pharisees, hypocrites! For ye make clean the outside of the cup and of the platter, but within they are full of extortion and excess. Thou blind Pharisee, cleanse first that which is within the cup and platter, that the outside of them may be clean also. Woe unto you, scribes and Pharisees, hypocrites! For ye are like unto whited sepulchers, which indeed appear beautiful outside, but are within full of dead men's bones, and of all uncleanness."

"Comments?" Alfred asked.

As the comments swirled about the group, Joy found herself gauging her husband's reaction. Ray had paled once more. Whether from the comments of the group or the Scripture reading, she couldn't tell. But one thing was certain: Ray looked about as guilty as a schoolboy caught in a lie. Was he cheating on her? Nausea flooded through her pores at the mere possibility. And if he was, who was the other woman?

After a time, the discussion of legalistic traditions wound down and turned to more personal matters. Marianne and Jenny had joined the group, along with Jenny's tattooed young friend. Something in Marianne's lovely face was uncharacteristically still. Still and sad as she listened to what Eileen was saying. She looked as if she'd rather be anywhere than here.

"Most girls your age would kill for a chance to be a cheerleader," Eileen said. "And you just up and quit. What's going on?"

Marianne turned her gaze toward her father. "It was Dad," she said. "He made me quit because he didn't like the skimpy uniforms."

A murmur of approval went through the room. Stunned by the lie, Joy looked out through the balcony doors to collect her thoughts before she blurted out words she might regret. The rain was coming down harder than ever, straight down now, as though the wind had given way to some more insistent force. Marianne was lying, but why?

Joy struggled to picture the cheerleading uniform but failed in the attempt. Was it really skimpy? What kind of parent was she to fail to notice—and what else had she missed?

The meetings fell into a rhythm after that, and Joy grew accustomed to her role as hostess. Tonight, thunder crackled in the distance, and a dark mass of clouds covered the moon. With the later timeslot and chillier evenings, they'd given up on balcony seating and clustered inside in the spacious living room.

"If more women stayed home and raised their children the way my mother did," Alfred said, "this country wouldn't be in the shape it's in."

"What do you mean by that?" Surprisingly, Jenny's friend Claudia was who spoke up. Although she'd been to a few of these meetings by now, she had never said a word before.

Joy could not help feeling relieved this was the last study before Christmas. With the holiday just over two weeks away, schedules got hectic this time of year, and everyone agreed to wait until the new year for their next group session. Joy usually just made her brownies for the meetings. However, Eileen had let her know, not so subtly, that a bit more was expected of the hostess, even if they were only having desserts.

"What I mean, young lady," said Alfred, disapproval written all over his face, "is that if women stayed home instead of being out in the work force, there wouldn't be so many—er—illicit affairs, for one thing." He cleared his throat audibly. "And for another …"

A reddish hue had crept up over Ray's throat and into his face, confirming Joy's worst suspicions. Absorbed in Ray's reaction, she lost the thread of Alfred's argument. Then again, she couldn't really believe Ray was cheating on her. She knew infidelities happened. All the time, if you could believe the statistics. But for Ray, who was so noble and true … something else must be the matter. Did he agree the woman's place was in the home? Would he be happier if she quit her job?

Of course he would. Carolyn never worked outside the home. Yet, could Joy survive if she abandoned her career? She, who had devoted virtually everything to her work until she met Ray, might flounder without a job, might fall apart completely. And yet … perhaps her work had been a default of a sort, since she had no real competing interests back then. She, Ray, and the girls might all be unequivocally better off if she quit.

"Many women, especially in younger couples, have to work to help pay the bills," Eileen pointed out. Legs crossed, she swung one high-heeled sling-back so that the shoe dangled precariously from her toes. The possibility of an affair flickered again …was Eileen the one? Or, perhaps, Ray wished he'd married her instead.

"That's different, of course," Alfred agreed. "In a case like that, it's for the benefit of the family. Hopefully, those situations are only temporary."

"The trouble"—put in Sharon Mabry, a working mom herself—"is that once the family becomes dependent on two incomes, it's tough to go back to just one."

"Exactly," Alfred said, "and that's why I believe it's better if they can survive at all, the women stay home from the beginning. Or, at the very least, from the time the first child is born."

Joy watched Ray intently. What was he thinking? The flush appeared to have receded now. Could she have imagined it in the first place? Perhaps there was something weird about the lighting. The rain had stopped—funny how, for a place with so little rain, Bible study nights always managed to bring on the storms. The moon lay low on the horizon, brilliant in its shimmering glory. Silver, though, not red. She was pretty sure it was not the lighting.

"I think one of the chief problems with our society is the Jones phenomenon," Alfred said.

"The what?" Claudia spoke again. Did she actually just roll her eyes?

"Keeping up with the Joneses," Alfred said. "You'd understand if you were a bit older. It's what happens when everyone gets the *wants*. They want a bigger house, a newer car, a more expensive couch, and so on." Joy wondered how large, or small, Alfred's house was, and whether his remarks were directed personally toward her and Ray, or everyone in general. Joy glanced at Alfred's sky-blue sweater, which looked like genuine cashmere.

A chorus of voices agreed with Alfred's last statement.

Claudia frowned. "What does that have to do with whether or not a woman should have a career?"

Joy waited tensely for the reply, at once enthralled and appalled.

"Most people work because they have to," Alfred explained with exaggerated patience. He picked a piece of lint from his sweater and rolled it between thumb and forefinger. "But they only think they have to because they're filling up their lives with stuff they don't really need. And in the process, their teenage daughter comes home pregnant and their son comes home with tattoos all over his body." As he spoke, Alfred's patience morphed into something else, and Joy wondered what had happened with Alfred's children. She knew he was divorced. Though she'd heard he had two grown children, she couldn't remember ever seeing them visit.

There was an uncomfortable silence as everyone stared at Claudia's tattoos. Then she spoke again. "That's a lot of crap if you ask me."

A nervous giggle escaped Joy. She jumped up. "I need to check on something in the kitchen."

Her remark proved prophetic, as almost simultaneously she smelled something scorching. Sure enough, the pot of cinnamon and apple spice she'd been boiling so the house would smell nice had scorched—a nasty stench. She grabbed the handle of the pot, nearly burning herself from the steam, and moved it to another burner.

She looked up to find Marianne in the doorway. "Can I help?"

"Sure. Let's cut up some fruit for a platter," Joy suggested. "I meant to do that before the people started arriving."

"But they came early." Marianne's tone was uncharacteristically amiable. In berry-colored leg warmers over black leggings and an oversized Mickey Mouse shirt, she looked lovely as always. Shining red-gold hair flowed behind a black headband, and the gold-flecked eyes were gentle.

"Yes, they did." In companionable silence, she and Marianne sliced and peeled apples, oranges, and peaches.

"Bananas?" said a voice from the doorway. Joy recognized Eileen's flowery perfume even before she looked up from the cutting board. She sliced into her fingertip as she did.

"Oh!" She sucked on the finger, tasted the metallic flavor of blood. At least the cut wasn't deep.

Eileen held up a bunch of bananas.

Joy nodded. "Definitely. Bananas."

"How do *you* slice them?" Eileen picked up a knife.

Still distracted by her cut, Joy took a banana and began to chop the fruit into small disks.

"Very original," Eileen said with no effort to hide the sarcasm, as she sliced her banana length-wise.

Joy should have expected a trick question from Eileen. A previous meeting came to mind. Eileen had bitten into one of Joy's brownies and asked, innocently enough, what kind of nuts she'd used. "Nuts?" Joy had stammered. "There are no nuts." She recalled having rushed through the stirring of ingredients, much the way she'd rushed her research in recent weeks. A few random clumps of unblended flour created paler, nearly white spots dotted sporadically in the texture of the brownies. Too late to lie, even if she wanted to, Joy had confessed, "I guess it's just flour."

Eileen had raised a carefully waxed eyebrow then as she did now. Tonight, however, Eileen's snide remarks barely fazed Joy. She was too preoccupied with Ray's reaction to Alfred's remarks.

When Eileen left them alone, Joy glanced toward Marianne, a question at the tip of her tongue: *Do you think your dad would be happier if I quit my job?* Better not broach the subject. Suddenly, she wished Acadia were in her small Bible study group tonight. She and Peter rotated from group to group, and tonight wasn't their turn. She thought of her pact with Acadia. With its memory, she felt a slight lightening.

Later, when the last guest had left, she called. No answer. Acadia was probably still at her own group meeting. At the beep, Joy blurted out her name, then wished she hadn't. "It's not important," she said. "You don't need to call me back."

CHAPTER SEVENTEEN

Joy threw herself into work. The semester was winding down, and she had to act soon if she wanted to salvage her students' respect in time for course evaluations. Even more, she truly coveted their respect. She needed their approval. If she couldn't run a household like Carolyn, at least she could run a classroom. She spent the entire morning going over her lecture notes so she would be letter perfect. Still, her mind kept wandering until finally she gave up. There was such a thing as overpreparing, wasn't there?

Perhaps that was the problem. In the middle of her lecture that afternoon, she sensed the students' attention drifting, hardly surprising since she was having some trouble staying focused herself. As if on automatic pilot, the words would flow smoothly to a point with no effort on Joy's part. Then something … the overtly bored expression on an attractive, usually enthusiastic young man in the front row … would throw her off-guard and she was lost. Years before—how many years now?—she'd experienced the same confusion in the middle of a band solo. The sheet music, which she had known so well, suddenly looked foreign to her. She had been humiliated, not knowing where to go. Back to the beginning, or starting from a random point?

Instead of the well-organized presentation that was *supposed* to be in her head, a host of troublesome images swam, each fighting for the surface:

Marianne's smug expression—"Mother always scooped out the egg white."

Ray's frowning face at the breakfast table—*where was he these days?*

Eileen's curious expression, her eyes as round as her mouth—"What kind of nuts are in your brownies?"

A hushed voice penetrated Joy's trance. "What's wrong with Professor Jenkins?" The question came from the girl with the fish-shaped birthmark, her eyes mirrors of concern. Joy tried to think of her name but failed.

With the clicker frozen in her hand, Joy scanned the puzzled faces of her students, tried to think of a single name. She knew their names. Of course she did. Only last week she knew them all.

"Let's talk about sunk costs," she managed. "Can anyone give me a definition?"

Silence.

"How about an example?"

She waited. Nothing. She would wait them out, she would not yield to the urge to babble. At last a hand shot up, then another. The name of one of the students came to her. "Ed," she said, almost faint with relief.

"Like when you sink too much capital into a project and you can't recoup your investment?" he said.

"You're on the right track. Anyone else?"

She pointed to another student, the girl seated beside the boy with the bored handsome face, a little less bored now. Their names still eluded her. "Like when you buy a car and it depreciates as soon as you drive it off the lot?"

"Not exactly," she hedged. "What distinguishes a sunk cost from other costs?"

Someone in the back row spoke up without being called on. "They're under water."

A few kids tittered.

Joy turned to the board and wrote shakily, *decision making*. "How do the costs affect decisions?" she asked.

"They don't," someone said.

"That's right. It's a cost that was already incurred in the past, prior to some decision point, and is irrelevant to current and future decisions. Does that make sense?"

A few heads nodded while most faces remained perplexed. "Think about life choices," Joy said. "Can anyone think of an example from your own life?"

Soon there was a murmur of whispering. To stop the chatter, she answered her own question. "Suppose you have a used car for sale. Someone offers $1000, but you don't think it's enough. The next week the car breaks down and you have to spend $500 to get it going again. Now how much do you need to sell the car for?"

"Fifteen hundred," someone said.

"Depends," another student spoke up.

"On what?" asked Joy.

"On how much you can get." His name was Geoffrey, she remembered suddenly.

"That's right. How does the $500 enter the selling price decision, Geoffrey?"

"It doesn't. It's a sunk cost."

"Exactly right." Joy thought of her investment in a PhD, of all the hours of studying and fretting over exams and papers, the uncertainty about passing or getting her topic approved for the dissertation. Was the entire experience a sunk cost that should be disregarded in future decision making? Students were glancing unabashedly at the clock now, and Joy saw they were right. The class period had ended five minutes ago.

"Don't forget your assignment," she said abruptly, and the students filed out.

Stopping by Joy's lectern on her way out, a girl asked timidly, "What assignment?"

Back in her office, Joy dropped her head onto her desk, banged it once, twice. She should stop before she gave herself a headache. Someone would walk by and see her like this, but at this moment she simply did not have the energy to care—or, more accurately, to care enough to rise and walk the short distance necessary to shut the door.

She had an open door policy with her students. One of them was likely to show up any moment. She willed the door to shut itself. Her phone rang, and not for the first time. There was probably a button somewhere that would silence the ring, if only she knew where or how.

Finally the ringing stopped, then a second later started again. She lifted her head—how heavy it was—and looked from the open door to the ringing phone. A passing student glanced curiously in. Not one of hers, at least not one she recognized.

In frustration, she grabbed the phone. "Yes?" she snapped into the receiver.

"This is Acadia."

"Oh. Hi."

"I got your message," Acadia said.

"Oh." Joy tried to sound lighter than she felt. "I can't even remember what I called about. Nothing major, I'm sure."

Acadia waited, and the silence stretched out until finally Acadia broke it. "Are you ready for Christmas?"

Joy laughed, a mirthless laugh. "Hardly. Is it coming?"

"A couple of weeks, if it sticks to schedule."

"To be honest, I haven't even thought about Christmas. I don't usually do a lot for the holidays. Not since"—Joy hesitated, tempted for the briefest instant to blurt out something about the event that altered Christmases for her—"not since I was a girl."

Silence stretched out again, and Joy thought she was going to ask why.

"You're going to have to do better this year," Acadia said, not harshly but firmly. "You've got Marianne and Jenny to think about."

"I know, I know." Joy groaned. "I can just imagine all the preparations their mother did this time of year."

"You've still got two weeks. I don't suppose Ray's much help." Acadia's tone was sympathetic, and her sympathy was balm to the raw sore that was Joy's psyche … soothing but not healing. "When are your classes over?"

"There's only one more class, but then there's an exam review. And I have to make out the exams." Joy was tired, just thinking about everything that needed doing.

"And grade them."

"Yes. And assign final grades." Joy felt whiney, talking so much about herself. "What about you?"

"I've got another week, and then pretty much the same as you. Exams, grading, etc., etc., etc."

"Your classes meet every day, don't they?" Acadia's high school teaching schedule was way more rigorous than Joy's. Of course, Acadia didn't face the research requirement, but most people outside academia didn't understand that aspect of a college professor's job … the pressure, the stress. Still, teaching every day would offer a different sort of stress—perhaps even more challenging than teaching college students.

"I have classes every day. But that's not what you want to talk about … is it?" Acadia said.

You called me, *Acadia.* Shame edged the thought. Acadia was reaching out in *her* moment of need. Still, Joy was in no mood to be helped. Why were people so often at cross-purposes in their timing? Was this why so many relationships floundered, why so many marriages failed?

"I was in Bible study that night when you called. I imagine you'd been too," Acadia prompted.

Everything came rushing back—the discussion that led, in large part, to Joy's present frame of mind. What harm could there be in confiding in Acadia? Yet, Joy hesitated, waited for Acadia to break the silence once more.

When she did not, Joy at last blurted, "There was this discussion about women working outside the home, which got me to thinking."

"Thinking how?" A note of skepticism crept into Acadia's voice. Although not certain, Joy thought she'd detected the faintest hint of a groan before Acadia spoke.

"Thinking maybe Ray would be happier if I quit my job." Joy dropped her voice, glanced through her doorway to see if anyone was in hearing range.

"You don't think he's happy now?"

"Honestly—no." Joy flushed as she reached for a pen. At once relieved and appalled by her admission, she scribbled furiously on a partially blank pad.

"Are you sure?"

"I'm not *sure* about anything," she said, stilling her pen. "But I'm pretty sure about that."

"If you're right—and I'm not saying you are—I doubt if it has anything to do with your job."

"There were a lot of people at the meeting—almost a consensus, at least of the ones who spoke up—saying women shouldn't work outside the home unless they need to. Financially. Do you and Peter ever have this discussion?"

"Peter's pretty supportive that way," Acadia said. Then, as if compensating for sounding unsympathetic, she continued, "I shouldn't grumble about him so much, even to myself. It's just that he gets so caught up in his work and his congregation, I feel like he forgets me for long stretches at a time. I don't know how I'd survive if I didn't have other outlets."

A student passing by peered curiously into Joy's office. "Could you hold on a minute?" Joy laid down her receiver to close the door. "The thing is," she told Acadia, "I'm not sure I *am* surviving. Here at work, or at home. I'm afraid I'm drowning."

Acadia fell silent for a long moment, perhaps waiting for Joy to elaborate. At last she said, "Everyone feels that way sometimes. You shouldn't decide anything when you're in that frame of mind. Seriously."

"I guess you're right." Joy was not convinced, but she'd told Acadia more than she intended already. She needed to sort things out for herself.

Another rap on her door, or perhaps the next door down the hall. She couldn't be sure which. Joy chose to ignore the disruption.

Seeming to understand Joy's reticence, Acadia changed the subject. "Are you staying in Sugar Sands over the holidays?"

"Yes. Are you?"

"No. We're going to visit family." Joy could hear the sigh of dread in Acadia's voice.

"And that's a bad thing?" Joy asked, trying to think how to draw Acadia out. Joy realized with a twinge of guilt that Acadia's problems made her feel marginally better about her own. Maybe, though, what made her feel better was the sharing.

"No, of course not," Acadia said and then added, "Truthfully, yes and no."

Joy wanted to tell Acadia how lucky she was to have family. Better, though, not to bring on questions Joy wasn't prepared to answer. Besides, she didn't want to sound preachy; she stifled a giggle at the thought of preaching to a preacher's wife. "Carolyn's parents may be coming here," she said instead. "Ray invited them, but he says they probably won't accept."

"What if they do?" Acadia sounded so horrified Joy had to laugh. At least she wasn't alone in regarding this as a potential nightmare. Your own family was one thing; the family of the perfect ex-wife another thing altogether.

The rapping came again, more insistent this time. She was pretty sure someone was looking for her. "I guess I should go see who's banging on my door," she told Acadia. "I have office hours scheduled."

"Sure, we'll talk later. Call me when you're free."

"Professor Jenkins, are you all right?" came a muffled female voice through the door.

Joy rose, noticing the pad on her desk. She'd scribbled all the while she was talking to Acadia. The page was covered in crudely drawn fish and the words SUNK COSTS. What had she been thinking? She ripped out the page and crumpled it. Holding the wadded paper, she opened the door to the girl with the fish-shaped birthmark, so like the fish she had just drawn.

After answering the girl's questions, Joy went home. Despite her remark to Acadia, she felt no compunction about ducking out during her office hours. Not today. She sat on the balcony, gazing out toward the gulf. The wind blew hard, and huge waves pounded the shoreline. Even the gulls had to pump hard to make any headway against this wind. In one direction, they could coast, while in the other they appeared to be almost staying still. Was that what Joy was doing with her life until she met Ray—just marking time by pretending to want a career, while really waiting for someone like Ray to appear and magically transform her into wife and mother?

That other women had as little insight into their motives as Joy did hardly seemed possible. Yet surely she wasn't entirely alone in this confusion and uncertainty. Perhaps all this was just more evidence of a man's world, where women had to fight to find their place. Joy honestly didn't know what to think or believe anymore. One thing she knew—she wasn't ready to give up on her marriage. She longed to believe Ray wanted their union to work as badly as she did. She remembered reading somewhere that relationships were never really equal—that one of the two always loved more than the other. Was she strong enough to be the one who loved more?

If making her marriage work meant giving up her career, she was willing to do so. Besides, in some ways she might be relieved to escape the cloud hanging over her at work. There was no joy in having a tenure clock ticking away. So why did the thought of giving notice leave her with such a hollow ache inside?

CHAPTER EIGHTEEN

"Let's go out for a coffee—or a soda," Joy suggested to Jenny. The girl had been moping around. Recalling her intention to bring Jenny out of her shell, Joy felt negligent. She resolved to do better. At home. At work. She would not give up, or give in.

"I don't know." Jenny looked up from crumpled bed covers, where she lay flat on her back staring at the ceiling. A book lay open beside her, its pages too pristine to have been studied.

"Come on—it'll be fun. Maybe a piece of pie too."

Jenny's brown eyes brightened, just perceptibly. She wore the black, lace-edged tights she'd worn on the day Joy talked her into trying the first piece of that awful runny pecan pie. There was a hole in one knee and, when she stood, Joy noticed how much shorter they were now … well above her ankles. She wore a very short orange dress, and Joy suspected its length had more to do with a growth spurt than with fashion. After their coffee and pie, she would take Jenny shopping. Every girl loved new clothes, and not needing to worry about how much things cost would be a novel experience for Joy.

Half an hour later, seated in a cozy corner booth, Joy dumped the contents of a half-and-half creamer into a steaming coffee and then, for good measure, a second one. Jenny sipped coke through a straw while they waited for her pecan pie to be served. "Did you want ice cream with that?" the waitress asked, and Jenny looked at Joy.

"Sure."

The pie arrived, the vanilla ice cream already beginning to melt around the edges onto the warm pie. "Good?" Joy said.

"Mmm." Jenny didn't sound overly excited, but she wasted no time before digging into the dessert.

At least it wasn't runny. "You know what we should make for Christmas?" Joy forced an enthusiasm she didn't quite feel.

"What?"

"Sugar cookies in shapes like trees and bells and stuff. When I was little, my mother used to bake those every year."

"So why don't you ever talk about her?" Jenny pulled a strand of hair into her mouth and chewed on it while she peered into Joy's eyes.

"I just don't." Joy gulped her coffee so quickly she scalded her tongue.

"So how old were you when she died?"

"Sixteen." Joy's tongue felt like sandpaper. What happened to her mother—to both her parents—had been so horrific, she could never bring herself to tell a living soul. Of course, there were people who knew. The police, school counselors … but they were part of the past now. Someday she would find the words. Someday, not now. She changed the subject. "Would you like to invite Claudia over for Christmas Eve?"

Jenny hesitated. "I don't think so."

"Aren't you friends anymore?"

Jenny shook her head, as noncommittal on this subject as Joy was on that of her parents. She ate her pie in silence, and Joy sipped her coffee, more cautiously this time. Her tongue still felt furry.

"I had a phone call from your Grandmother Whitworth this morning," Joy said at last.

Jenny looked up and abruptly stopped chewing.

"She's coming to visit for a few days."

"Oh, no!"

Joy was surprised by this reaction, which matched her own exactly. "Why? Won't you be glad to see her?"

"You'll find out." Jenny sighed, and with renewed vigor, went back to her pie. She retrieved the last few crumbs with her fork and pushed the empty dish away.

Three topics broached, all duds. "How about your Grandfather Whitworth?"

"He's okay."

"So there's that." The coffee was delicious now that it had cooled, and smelled even better than it tasted. Was that a hint of cinnamon?

"I suppose. Mostly he just talks to Dad about banking stuff."

"Was he a banker too?"

Jenny nodded, surprise flickering in the velvet brown eyes. "Didn't you know?"

"I really don't know much of anything about your mother's family."

"He's retired now. But he's the one who got Dad his job in the beginning, okay?"

"Oh." Joy absorbed this, thinking back to the phone calls she'd overheard recently between Ray and Carolyn's father. His voice had been quiet, almost secretive. Joy realized Ray might be more comfortable sharing work issues with this man than with herself. She'd tried, goodness knew, to draw him out. But his replies were predictably monosyllabic.

"How's work?" brought "Fine."

"Is there something you want to talk about?" evoked "No—why?"

"How's band?" she asked Jenny now.

"Good. I moved up five chairs at the last tryout."

"As of when?" Joy was pleased, and more than a little chagrined she hadn't thought to ask before.

The waitress appeared, coffee pot in hand. "More?"

"Sure." Joy smiled her thanks, and the waitress dropped off two more creamers after she poured. "When did this happen?" Joy asked again.

"Just last week."

"That's awesome. I'm so proud of you."

A dimple appeared in Jenny's cheek at the compliment.

When they left the restaurant, Jenny leaned into Joy. Just for a second … but there was something so intimate in the brief gesture that Joy's heart fairly exploded with happiness.

"Let's go shopping, shall we?"

After the grandparents arrived—when the visit had begun to feel interminable, and Joy understood only too well what Jenny meant—she thought back to that moment when they were leaving the diner together. Over the years, she had developed a strategy of dredging up the pleasant memories. Through her unpopular years, through her parents' deaths, through the loneliness after, she'd recall moments of sweetness—something as simple as a particularly delectable bite of chocolate. Her mother's slightly off-key voice crooning to her when she was small: "Is it true what they say about Dixie? Does the sun really shine all the time? Do the sweet magnolias blossom at everybody's door?"

Joy could never remember the rest, no matter how many times she tried, though she could almost envision her mother whenever she passed a magnolia tree. If you looked hard enough, they were there, those moments. And wasn't that, after all, what made life bearable, and occasionally better than bearable, maybe even rich with promise?

"I *said*—"

The slight edge to Mrs. Whitworth's voice was present more often than not when she addressed Joy. "I said—where are the photographs of my daughter? What possessed you to eliminate all evidence from her house that she ever existed?"

The resemblance between her and Carolyn was striking. Lillian Whitworth was still a beautiful woman, with her dark hair and eyes. Her face was almost devoid of the usual signs of aging. There were no laugh lines at the corners of her eyes or mouth, and indeed Joy wasn't sure she'd ever seen her laugh. Perhaps that was why. The skin under her chin, however, was beginning to sag, just perceptibly.

Exactly. As if she *could* eliminate all evidence. Getting out the Christmas decorations, neatly stored and labeled in boxes in the attic, Joy had come across a set of napkin rings. Yellow-haired angels, snowy white except for their wings, which were shiny gold. She found one angel stuck in a corner of the box, buried under tissue and far from the others. Something was different about that angel, though at first, Joy couldn't identify the difference. Then she did. One wing was broken, the tip missing altogether. The surface was not rough or jagged, but smooth and glossy over the missing tip. The break must have occurred before the angels were finished. How upset Carolyn must have been when she came home with the purchase and discovered the blemish. Or had Carolyn made the napkin rings herself? If so, she would have been even more angry at the break.

Counting the napkin rings, Joy realized she didn't really need the one with the broken tip. That angel was an extra, and Joy wondered if she'd ever been out of her corner. Delicately, Joy had lifted the broken-winged angel and set her on the table, leaving one of the perfect angels in the box. She thought of her now, resplendent in her place at table.

"I really couldn't say exactly what happened to the photographs," she said. "I believe there's one on Marianne's dresser. Isn't there, Marianne?"

"She knows it's there," Marianne said. "Dad took down the rest."

"I see—I suppose they were too painful for him to have around." Lillian Whitworth had a way of lifting her head slightly to peer at Joy through the magnifying part of her bifocal glasses as though this close-up inspection revealed not only her physical flaws but those beneath the surface as well.

"You don't have a tree yet?" Lillian said, changing subjects abruptly. This woman managed with deceptively guileless ease to keep Joy constantly off balance, like a tennis player whose game was so varied you couldn't settle into a rhythm.

"How about this one?" Joy said. All the trees looked the same to her, but Lillian found flaws in each and every one.

Lillian turned the tree around slowly, lifting her eyebrows as she came to the back side where the tree had been leaning against another one.

"They are all going to be flat back there, aren't they?" Joy said. "It will fluff out after a bit."

"I don't think so." Lillian released the tree, brushing off her hands as she did, seeming momentarily as offended by the trees' imperfections as she was by those of everyone around her. For the first time, Joy felt a flash of genuine sympathy for Carolyn. What must it have been like—growing up with Lillian?

"I've found one!" called Marianne from another aisle, and they moved in the direction of her voice.

"I love the smell of a live tree, don't you?" Joy inhaled deeply, not sure whom she was addressing.

Lillian was the only one to answer. "But they are never quite right, are they? With an artificial tree, you have more control." She turned the tree, less slowly this time. It too was flat on the back. She sighed. "I suppose this one will have to do."

Marianne smiled, and Jenny punched her in the ribs. "Don't look so proud of yourself. That tree's no better than any of the others."

Later, Joy watched as the girls hung their ornaments and then as Lillian moved each one to a better location or a stronger limb. "You see how this branch is sagging under the weight of the ornament?" she asked Jenny, shaking her head. "You can't place them at the edge like that, or they'll fall off and break. We wouldn't want that, now would we?"

Jenny nodded her understanding, then backed away from the tree as if afraid of making another mistake.

"You've got to keep balance in mind." Lillian turned to Marianne. "See how close this blue ornament is to this other blue ornament? We can't have that, now can we?"

"Don't tell me about balance!" Marianne burst out. "I know about balance. Just decorate the tree yourself. That's what you're doing anyway."

Joy had been on the verge of screaming several times herself, and was almost relieved when Marianne beat her to it. Joy couldn't afford to add an ill temper to her long list of obvious shortcomings. She was disturbed, though, that this joyous occasion had turned so sour. "Marianne, why don't you set out the manger scene?"

Marianne stared sullenly at Joy. She had spent the first several hours of her grandmother's visit following Lillian around like a puppy. Apparently Marianne's tolerance had reached a limit. For a moment, Joy thought the girl was going to stalk out of the room.

Then, turning her back on her grandmother, Marianne moved to the sofa, where Joy held an exquisite little camel and a green-cloaked wise man bearing a gift that looked rather like a block of cheese. "Where do you want the scene to go?" she asked Joy.

"Where do you usually put it?"

Marianne shrugged.

"How about on that book shelf?" She held her breath, waiting for Lillian to point out why the book shelf was exactly the wrong place for a manger scene. But she was absorbed with the tree and made no comment on the manger.

"There now!" Lillian announced, standing back and surveying the tree. "That's just about perfect, isn't it?"

Indeed the decorated tree was beautiful, with its artful arrangement of expensive trimmings. Still something felt wrong. Joy stood frozen, the baby Jesus cradled in the palm of her hand, while the memories roared into place. Tears pricked her eyes, and she blinked them back until the pinpoints of light on the tree blurred into haphazard streaks of color.

"This is the one you made in kindergarten, Joy," Mama would say. Mama was so lovely, with her auburn hair tied back with red and green ribbons in a loose ponytail. A few tendrils escaped, framing her oval face. She wore love in that face as plain as if the word were written in letters on her forehead. "You see, that's me and that's your dad and that's you."

Joy would stare at the hand-painted block of wood and laugh. "Why is your hair so big?" she would say. Or, "Why are you so much taller than Daddy?" But she loved the eclectic collection of glitzy ornaments, some that were way too big to belong on a tree, others that hung precariously as if they might topple forward at any moment.

What she loved most were the stories behind the ornaments. Mama could tell her where and when each one originated, relating most of them to Joy's history but some before her birth. Joy loved to hear the stories about her parents' lives before she was born. Mama would tell the same stories over and over.

Then, during her teenage years, she'd become self-absorbed, had spoken harshly to Mama. "I know, I know, I've heard it a thousand times." These were the words she tried not to remember later but couldn't forget … when she'd have given anything to hear the stories just once more.

Drawn back to the present, Joy gazed at Marianne. "Don't you have any homemade ornaments?"

Marianne looked blankly at her.

"You know, the kind you made in school when you were little—"

Marianne scoffed at the idea. "I don't think we kept anything like that. They weren't good enough to put on the tree anyway." She placed Mary and Joseph on the bookshelf and looked at Joy as if waiting for criticism.

Joy smiled appreciatively and handed her the baby Jesus while Marianne's words replayed in her head. *They weren't good enough …*

"May I be excused?" Jenny asked. "I need to practice, okay?"

"Practice what?" Lillian removed an ornament and replaced it in what seemed to be the exact same spot.

"Her clarinet," Marianne said.

"Are you still wasting your time in band?" Her face a study of disapproval, Lillian whirled away from the tree to face Jenny.

"I don't see it that way," Jenny mumbled, looking at her feet. She wore red and green Converse shoes with bells on the back. The bells were silent now.

"We all know what the other kids think of band members—don't we, Marianne? But it's your choice," Lillian said.

Joy snapped around and faced Lillian. "That's right. It is." Joy had been in band herself. Jenny shot her stepmother a grateful look before ducking out of the room. Joy followed.

"Was your grandmother like this before?" Joy asked when they were out of earshot. Perhaps Lillian changed after losing her daughter, Joy thought, telling herself not to be so judgmental. Losing a child must be incredibly difficult, worse even than losing a parent.

"Before … when?" Jenny asked.

"Before your mom—"

"So, you mean before she died?" Jenny's shoulders hunched together. Her posture had grown increasingly slack since her grandparents arrived. She straightened slightly.

"Yes."

Jenny thought for a moment. "Pretty much."

Ray and Mr. Whitworth closeted themselves in the study for much of the afternoon. Joy lingered as she passed by the room, straining to catch a word or two. Beyond the mumble of masculine voices, she could discern little.

She lifted her hand to knock on the door. What would Carolyn do? She imagined the beautiful woman rapping lightly before she popped inside, the men's faces lifting in their delight to see her. She would smile, say something clever, her tone teasing. Joy imagined herself doing the same. "Are you two going to stay in here all day?" she'd say, and not, "Please, please rescue me from Lillian before I shoot myself."

She couldn't do it. She dropped her hand.

Later, when they emerged, their faces were somber. Something in their expression squelched Joy's other emotions—the relief at being rescued, her jealousy at being excluded, her curiosity about their relationship. In their place, a single emotion sprang to life. Fear. Her heart beat peculiarly, and for an instant she could see Carolyn's ghost walking toward her between the two men.

"Well, it's about time!" Lillian said. "We're almost ready for the gift exchange."

"I could use a piece of that fruitcake first," her husband said. A tall man, he carried himself with an easy grace. His hair, gray at the temples and still thick on top, was brushed straight back in a style reminiscent of an earlier time.

"Sure, I'll get it. Anyone else?" Joy said.

"I don't think he needs it. Do you, dear?" Lillian patted his stomach just above the belt. "We've been trying to avoid adding the usual Christmas five this year. Did you forget?"

He sighed. "You're right, of course. I don't need it."

Joy hesitated, uncertain whether to offer again or to keep out of it. To her eye, his belly looked remarkably flat for a man of his years, but perhaps there was a slight rounding. She sucked in her own stomach, trying not to imagine what Lillian thought of hers.

"I didn't think so," Lillian said, her tone firmer than her words. "Now … let's all keep in mind that there are going to be photos. And the photos will be around for years to come." She muttered something else under her breath, something Joy couldn't quite catch. What was her point anyway?

"I can't bear to see a room all cluttered with paper and ribbon. Can you?" She addressed Marianne, so Joy was spared from answering.

She couldn't avoid the memories though. Of another house. Strewn with crumpled paper and discarded bows—Mama wore one on the top of her head, her face alight with Christmas cheer. Had Joy nearly managed to forget how much Mama loved the holiday? How childlike she was in her enthusiasm, in her delight, both in her own gifts and, even more, in watching Joy's face as she opened hers.

"It's so much easier if you clean up as you go," Lillian continued, and Joy thought of something similar Marianne said to her when Joy was baking that abysmal pecan pie. *Mother always says …*

"What we need is an attractive receptacle, something that will look nice in a photo," Lillian said.

"I know just the thing," Marianne said, and the two of them vanished from the room, chatting companionably.

When they returned, Marianne was hauling a brightly painted Christmas trashcan—who knew there was such a thing? The tone of their chatter had altered noticeably. Lillian's voice had grown critical, Marianne's quiet.

"You *quit* cheerleading? That can't have been wise. Maybe if you called someone right away, you could still change your mind? Carolyn was a cheerleader every year of high school."

Of course she was.

"It's done now," Marianne said in a low voice but with a ring of finality.

Lillian turned her gaze on Jenny. "Don't you have something a bit more—"

All faces turned toward Lillian, waiting, while Joy glanced around the room. Where was the Christmas spirit? The beautiful tree with its blinking lights, the carefully wrapped packages with gilt-edged ribbons that Joy had tied and retied, unable to get them quite right, the exquisite little manger scene. The day should have been so warm, so joyful, but it was not. Again the image of her own family of long ago intruded. As always she pushed the memories away.

"I've tried and tried to keep my mouth shut—I thought surely your stepmother would intervene—but I simply can't believe you're wearing a tank top in December."

"It's hot, if you haven't noticed," Jenny said.

Good for her, Joy thought.

"A lady dresses for the season, not the weather." Lillian plucked at the perfect crease in her green wool trousers.

"I'm not a lady," Jenny mumbled.

"And at this rate you never will be." Lillian's tone was surprisingly sweet, but with a lethal sort of sweetness that made Joy want to gag.

Joy dripped with sweat, wished she'd worn a tank top herself instead of this ridiculous sweatshirt with its grinning reindeer. "Lay off her, will you?"

The room fell deadly silent. Her face white, Lillian stared at Joy for a long moment. When she spoke at last, her voice was cold as steel. "*Lay off her*—is that your approach to parenting? It's no wonder she hasn't a decent outfit in her closet. I suppose you let the girls dictate their wardrobe decisions"—Lillian looked Joy up and down—"although I can't be sure your choices would be any better."

Then Lillian turned to her husband. "Hank, I believe we've outstayed our welcome."

CHAPTER NINETEEN

"Thank God!" Jenny burst out when they had gone, and no one chastised her. The comment felt more prayerful than profane to Joy.

Though both she and Ray had tried to dissuade Lillian and Hank from leaving, their hearts weren't in it. At least she was pretty sure he felt the same way she did, for once. They exchanged a look that rippled right through her. As if they were truly beginning to think as one. To be one. And yet, suddenly, unexpectedly, her heart went out to the older couple. *Don't go,* she almost cried.

Even Marianne looked more relaxed now. "Shall we open the gifts anyway?" she asked.

"Yes, let's!" Jenny said.

Joy nodded her assent. "Only the ones from your grandparents."

Lillian's last words had been, "Save the gifts for Christmas morning, why don't you, and open ours along with your others?" A certain sadness in Lillian's eyes, the first hint of vulnerability Joy had seen, had almost made her soften toward the older woman. Lillian's hand trembled just perceptibly as she gathered her belongings—a bag of gifts, purse, coat, and accessories. Joy wondered if Lillian knew the fault for the visit's failure lay with her, if she regretted being the way she was, as Joy sometimes did. *We are who we are, and sometimes we tire of that self we're stuck with for life.* Under Lillian's eyes, the skin was beginning to crinkle, like the tissue paper in the Christmas gift bags. Perhaps the woman cried more than she laughed. Just for that instant, she ached with pity for Lillian. Hard to change your stripes. No one knew that better than Joy. Had Lillian ever attempted a change?

Joy tried to picture a younger, more vibrant Lillian, before she lost her only daughter. How lovely she must have been then, almost as lovely as Carolyn. Joy determined that next time she would try harder to connect with Lillian, to show Christian compassion … to set a better example for the girls. For now she couldn't help being thankful for the reprieve.

One thing about the Whitworths—they were certainly not stingy with their gifts. The majority of them, of course, were for the girls. While Jenny and Marianne shouted with excitement and the paper and ribbon flew, Joy's mind drifted.

The essence of Christmas magic—the joy of the season of wonder, of giving and loving, that had eluded her for so many years was right here in her grasp, with this family. Yet, even as she strained forward, memories washed in. And with the memories, the gift of the moment was nearly lost. Had it been only because she was young and gullible that everything seemed so large, so dazzling? The shops with their rows of toys. The Christmas tunes piped in. The enchantment of golden-haired dolls, and smiling elves, and the lure of catching a glimpse of Santa himself in one of the shops.

But more than that, what she remembered was the look on her parents' faces, in their shining eyes. The way they waited for her to react, how thrilled they were by her delight. When she believed she would have them with her always—or at least for many years to come—she'd taken that loving, that caring, that cherishing for granted.

One Christmas in particular emerged from the rush of memories—a tricycle she had yearned for that year. She had pointed to it, standing out from the others, so grand in its shiny blue coat of paint, streamers of blue and yellow floating from the handlebars. Something in her parents' expressions told her how much they wanted her to have the trike. She realized now how blessed she was to have someone who cared so deeply about her feelings. Not all children have that. Ever. At the time, this too had been taken for granted.

The tricycle of choice was more expensive than the others—she knew this much even then—but this tricycle was the one that drew her eyes, the one she wanted. Besides, what difference did price make—her parents' money was limited, but Santa had plenty, didn't he? When the tricycle she longed for appeared under the tree on Christmas morning, she squealed in delight, clapped her hands together, and took possession. Nor did she question how Santa knew the exact tricycle to bring, how he kept track of all the boys and girls and their wishes. She hadn't been that good, not really. For a moment, she felt undeserving, as if Santa had made a mistake. The way she sometimes felt now—to have fallen into this beautiful ready-made family. The family Carolyn deserved. Not Joy.

"Joy?" Jenny was saying. "Aren't you going to open yours?"

She looked down at the stack of gifts near her feet, then up at the watchful faces around her. "Of course. I just like seeing you open yours first," she said, though she had barely registered the contents of any of the packages.

She snapped back to the present, sorry to have missed a breath of the occasion. She untied the ribbon slowly on the top box, then ripped the paper more quickly and tossed it aside. Glancing around the room, she saw that everyone had done the same. Wads and strips of brightly colored paper graced nearly every surface. Inside, pressed between sheets of delicate white tissue, lay a linen blouse in a soft shade of buttercup yellow. Automatically, she checked the size. Perfect, of course. How had they known?

"Are you with us, Dad?" Marianne asked.

Glancing toward him, Joy saw Ray was just as preoccupied as she. What was he thinking about?

The hand-painted trashcan that Marianne had fetched for Lillian caught Joy's eye, and she crossed to pick it up. "Lot of good this did," she said, turning the receptacle upside down. It was completely empty, while the room was strewn with paper and ribbon from one end to the other, though a sizable stack of unopened gifts remained under the twinkling tree.

Everyone laughed.

"I rather enjoy a wrapping paper mess myself," Joy said.

"Wouldn't Granny Whitworth croak if she could see this?" Jenny said.

Joy thought of the older woman's recriminations about band and cheerleading and the girls' choices in general. "I suspect she's a very unhappy woman. Let's talk about something else." She looked toward Ray, hoping to bring him into the moment. "Can you believe Jenny's concert and Marianne's recital are falling on the exact same day so soon after Christmas?" As soon as she'd spoken, she saw her mistake.

He shrugged noncommittally, and she wondered if he even remembered the conflict, or if this was news to him.

"It wouldn't have happened if they were both school functions," Jenny said. "They would have coordinated things better."

"Is that my fault?" Marianne said.

"Isn't it unusual to schedule a Christmas concert after Christmas?" Joy asked.

"It is." Jenny spoke up when Marianne stayed silent. "It was this coordination thing I'm talking about. There was a bunch of stuff the school had to fit in before Christmas, so our concert got pushed. I really, really hope you guys can come."

"Well, I can't come, can I?" said Marianne. "So I guess you're not talking to me. I guess you're saying you hope they both go to yours so nobody goes to mine."

Gone was the good humor, which permeated the room only a few minutes ago, stripped away with the wrapping paper. "You have a lot more stuff like that than I do," Jenny said to her sister. She ran her fingers through her hair so that her cowlick was uncovered, causing her hair to spring out in an awkward lopsided fashion. "And this one is really important to me, okay?"

Ray crossed to where his younger daughter sat, shoulders slumped but eyes pleading. He smoothed her hair with his fingers. "We'll work something out. Maybe I can go to yours, and Joy can go to Marianne's." He glanced at Marianne, who looked less than thrilled with this solution. "Then, next time this happens, we'll switch up."

"How do you know it's going to happen again?" Marianne asked, but she looked more or less mollified by the solution.

"So you promise?" Jenny said. "Promise you'll be there?"

"I promise," Ray said, and Joy's heart sang with renewed hope.

"I have an idea," Jenny said shyly, and the other three looked askance in her direction.

"Why don't we try to focus on—you know, baby Jesus—the real meaning of Christmas?"

From the mouth of babes, Joy thought, humbled by this unexpected suggestion from this least likely of quarters. She glanced in Marianne's direction, fearful she might be rolling her eyes, but she was not. When neither Marianne nor Ray spoke, Joy found her voice. "That's a wonderful idea, Jenny. Thank you for reminding us."

CHAPTER TWENTY

Jenny was so excited she could hardly contain herself. She'd had to fight the impulse to confide in her stepmother or her sister. Experience had taught her that secrets had a way of leaking out. And she wanted her dad to be surprised. This was her real Christmas present to him. She'd been promoted to first chair second clarinet, the result of an unexpected tryout the day before school let out for Christmas break. Nobody was expecting the auditions, so nobody had a chance to prepare. Or get nervous.

As it happened, Jenny had been practicing the Christmas songs only the night before, partly because the concert was coming up but mainly because she liked the music. Besides, she didn't have much else to do, not since she and Claudia quit hanging out.

Apparently this was not the case for most of the kids. "You sound like crap!" Mr. Sled exploded that morning. "How are we going to perform in front of an audience sounding like this?"

He was given to mood swings, and Jenny was a little afraid of him. When her turn came to audition, she startled herself as much as Mr. Sled by nailing her passage perfectly. Mr. Sled nodded his approval. "Can you do that again?" he asked, and she did.

So here she sat, in the very first chair of the second row of clarinets, right next to the audience. What this meant was that her dad would not have to strain to find her. Black pants, white tops—their standard concert attire made it difficult to tell the band members apart from a distance, especially if your hair was mousy brown and mid-length like Jenny's.

That seat also meant she had a perfect view of the auditorium. Where was he anyway? She'd scanned the audience enough times to be pretty sure he wasn't already seated. She settled into a steady vigil of the entrance so she would know the instant he arrived. But now she took her eye off the doorway long enough to scan the crowd once more. No sign of him. Back to the entrance. Nothing there.

Could he have slipped in while she was checking the crowd? Mr. Sled lifted his arm, and the concert began.

Jenny forced herself to concentrate on the music. "What Child Is This?" was one of her favorites. For a time she lost herself in the notes, in the melody that rose and fell around her. How beautiful the song was. After Mr. Sled lost his temper with them, the band members had really pulled together. When all the pieces fit the way they were supposed to, like now, the result seemed almost magical. Sometimes she thought these moments were the only time she was truly happy. She wondered if anyone else felt this way.

When the song ended, she scanned the room once more. She spotted him on the aisle of a row near the back. Her heart thumped in anticipation, and a smile lifted the corners of her mouth. Did he see her? He was glancing down at his program, but he lifted his head now and looked straight at her.

It wasn't Dad. Her heart sank, and she continued to scan the audience. If he didn't come, she would never forgive him. The door opened, and someone stepped inside—a girl in an emerald green sequined top and vintage hip-hugger jeans sauntered in, a strip of bare flesh just visible between the jeans and the green top. Something twinkled in the vicinity of her exposed belly button.

Claudia? What was she doing here?

Claudia waved gaily, right in Jenny's direction, and Jenny had to restrain herself from waving back. Mr. Sled would kill any of them he caught acknowledging the audience.

Besides, Claudia and Jenny weren't even friends anymore. For a while after Thanksgiving, Jenny had avoided Claudia. They had been so close to getting caught by Dad with a joint, and Claudia didn't even give a hoot. Claudia was wild and selfish and ... dangerous. But she was also fun and exciting, and Jenny really missed her. By the time she realized just how much, Claudia had turned the tables and had given Jenny the cold shoulder.

At least that's what she'd thought. Until now. Claudia was probably waving at someone else. How embarrassing if she had waved back—thank goodness she hadn't.

The next song was already underway, and Jenny struggled a moment to find her place. Beethoven's "Ode to Joy." The title always made Jenny think of her stepmother, who was probably sitting at Marianne's stupid thing right now. Joy would have been so proud of Jenny, if only she were here.

To get through the concert, Jenny decided to pretend both Joy and Dad were out there in the third row, listening and beaming. She would not look again so she could manage to finish the concert before giving in to the urge to cry. A tiny hope persisted in the back of her mind, as she pretended and played, and played and pretended, that when the end was reached, Dad would be there.

But he was not.

Claudia, however, was. She was still hanging around after Jenny had swabbed out her clarinet, taken it apart, and debated what to do about a ride home. She thought about asking Sandra Duguid, who sat next to her, but Sandra was deep in conversation with her best friend, Darlene Walker.

"Where are your dad and stepmother?" Claudia asked.

Jenny considered lying. What could she say—they've both gone to the bathroom? She shrugged. "I dunno."

She didn't feel like explaining the pact, how Joy was at Marianne's thing and Jenny had been stood up by Dad. She chewed her lip as she asked Claudia, "How'd you get here?"

"My brother. How did you get here?"

"Joy dropped me off. Dad was working, but we thought—I thought—he was coming later."

Claudia drew in a deep breath, as if to say something important. Instead she just asked, "How was your Christmas?"

"Fine. How was yours?"

"Crappy. I thought about you and your family. I wished I hadn't screwed everything up so bad last time—"

"Really?"

"Sure."

Happiness welled up in Jenny, and if there was also a hint of danger lurking at the bottom of the well, it served to heighten the pleasure. "Okay." Claudia moved toward the exit, and Jenny followed her, a bit uncertainly.

"You want a ride?"

"Sure."

Jenny saw him then. The most gorgeous boy she'd ever seen, leaning against a tree with a cigarette hanging from his mouth, his thumbs hooked through the belt loops on his faded jeans. Several years older than her, he had that bad-boy sort of sullen expression you saw in movies sometimes. He was wearing a leather jacket, and his dark hair was slicked back—like

James Dean in a poster in the 50s-style diner. Claudia began to head in the direction of the gorgeous boy, and Jenny grabbed her elbow.

She gasped. "So, is that your brother?"

He looked at them, taking Jenny in from head to toe so that she blushed furiously. He must think she was a dork, with her clarinet case and dark skirt. Still her heart skipped a beat just to have those dark blue eyes on her for an instant.

"Yep." Claudia ping-ponged her gaze from Jenny to her brother. "Alex, this is Jenny."

The way she'd been watching the door and scanning the audience, Jenny was pretty sure she would have noticed if Alex had been inside the building. She gulped as she threw out the question, "What'd you think of the concert?"

"It was all right," Claudia said.

"No, I meant Alex."

Alex stared at her for a moment, and then the glimmer of a smile passed through his eyes, though it did not reach his lips, which were full and surprisingly red for a boy. "What do you think I thought?"

"I think you loved it." Jenny didn't know where her courage came from, as hard as her heart was beating … but after all, he would most likely never look at her again anyway. So what did she have to lose?

Something soft brushed her cheek, and she looked up. "Hey!" she said, seeing a mist against the parking lot lights of something like rain, only whiter and slower. "I think it's snowing!"

CHAPTER TWENTY-ONE

Joy was awed, watching Marianne on the stage. For a time, Joy was lifted outside herself, into the music and the dance, the symmetry and beauty of the young bodies. Not that they were all perfect, not like Marianne. Still there was a grace, even in the occasional mistake. In the recovery, in the intent faces. How young they were, and yet how serious about their art.

Among so many talented and beautiful dancers, Marianne stood out. Joy wondered if the other parents saw this too, or if they were fixated on their own child as she was on Marianne. But no. She was not that biased. Marianne had tormented Joy often enough. If she were vindictive, perhaps she would have longed to see Marianne stumble. But she could not. Nor did it seem possible.

The girl pirouetted and swayed, a flower caught in the wind. She lifted her leg, toes pointed, to impossible angles, and yet she made every motion look so effortless, so easy, as if her body were made for these positions rather than being strained to the breaking point through hours and hours of practice. Having been in band herself, Joy had secretly wished she'd be the one attending Jenny's concert tonight, where at least she'd understand something of what was going on. Now she realized you didn't need to understand. Only to feel.

Still, after a time, her mind drifted back to Jenny. She'd been practicing too, practicing a lot on her clarinet. Joy hoped with all her heart that Jenny's concert was going well. There had been a flush about the younger girl's face when Joy dropped her off at the school, an excitement that pleased, even as it frightened Joy. Was she setting herself up for some sort of disappointment, and if so, what?

Joy did not fool herself into believing either of the girls confided everything to her. Not their innermost wants and fears. Could Jenny have a crush on a boy in the band? Was it possible he reciprocated? That would be lovely. Such a boost for Jenny's ego, provided the boy was nice and not into any of the scary things you heard about with kids their age.

A shudder passed through Joy at the possibilities, at how quickly a girl like Jenny could have her innocence corrupted by the wrong boy.

Joy's mind wandered to Ray, to the conviction that he too was hiding something from her. How reluctant he'd been to take on the role of Bible study group leader. After overhearing his conversation with Marianne, Joy had probed, "It's an honor to be asked. Right?"

"I suppose," Ray had said with a distinct lack of conviction.

They had been on the balcony at the time. The day had been warm for the time of year, but the water churned angry white, spewing up a spray of fume. Beneath the white, the waves rolled in, a harsh greenish brown, about as unappealing as the gulf got. She could smell the salt in the air, stronger than usual, almost briny.

"Do you want to talk about what's troubling you?"

Ray looked at her mutely, then over her head as though something in the distance caught his eye. Joy followed his gaze. A pair of adolescent boys in black wet suits leapt in the waves, jumping high to avoid the onslaught but embracing it too. The water had to be cold. There was that Polar Bear dip in the Gulf each year on New Year's Day. Maybe these guys were toughening up for the plunge. As much as she loved the water, Joy could never bring herself to brave the cold, cold water. Maybe one day, if Ray or one of the girls would join her.

When the silence had dragged out, she'd suggested, "You haven't agreed yet, so you can still say no if you want to."

She had been baffled then, as she was now. Was his reticence because he was ashamed of her? Or of himself? The thought struck her again, the one she'd been avoiding. At the meeting when Alfred read about Pharisees and hypocrites—about cups that were clean on the outside but filled with excess—Ray's reaction had struck her as ominous. Still she'd dismissed the idea as unworthy.

Now the unthinkable seemed all too likely, as staggering as it was obvious. "Oh," she gasped out loud, and several of the parents turned to look or frown at her. All this time she'd been so worried about being compared to the gorgeous but dead Carolyn. What if she had a living competitor?

She knew how attractive Ray was, how likely women were to tease him, to flirt, to test his loyalty. She remembered how red he'd turned in their small group meeting when Alfred talked about the prevalence of illicit affairs when women worked instead of staying home where they belonged. She'd been stupid and naïve, acting as if he were immune to those kinds of temptations when of course he wasn't. No man was. An affair would explain so much—the reluctance to take on the position, his reticence at home, his distracted efforts at connecting with her and the girls, phone calls he took in private.

How she'd wanted to believe that she, Fatima Joy, could be enough for Ray! What a fool she'd been. There it was, one of those memories she had tried to suppress, longed to forget. Impossible to separate yourself from the memory long after the others involved in the incident had undoubtedly erased the entire episode …

Fatima was fourteen, a freshman in high school. Because her parents knew another girl's parents, one of the popular kids in her class invited her to a World Series party. The St. Louis Cardinals pitted against the Minnesota Twins. The girls, however, weren't actually interested in baseball. Nor were they really Fatima's friends, and they were off somewhere in another part of the house, giggling and chattering without Fatima.

She found herself in the room with the TV and most of the guys. Everyone was cheering for the Cardinals, of course. Some of the kids— either the most serious or luckiest of the fans—had actually scored tickets and were watching the game in person. Fatima, however, had a sort of crush on the Twins pitcher Joe Niekro, who was only twenty-three and had previously been one of the Chicago Cubs. Mama and Daddy, though born in Georgia, had lived for a few years in Chicago before moving to St. Louis and still rooted for the Cubs most of the time.

So she applauded whenever Joe struck out a Cardinal. All the boys whirled on her, and the sudden attention—in contrast to her usual invisibility—thrilled her. Craving more of it, she proceeded to cheer wildly when in fact the Twins defeated the Cardinals.

"Someone's going to have to teach her a lesson," said Carl Sawyers, a cute boy with longish blonde hair. "Who wants the honors? I'm lookin' at you, Greg."

"No, thank you!" Greg said vehemently. Fatima wasn't sure what any of them meant, but she knew she was being insulted, and in the worst possible way. Knew too that while she didn't want to be taught a lesson, she didn't want to be ignored or insulted either. What *had* she wanted?

Her excitement wilted away like morning glories in the afternoon sun, not unlike the way her exultation at marrying the gorgeous Ray Jenkins was wilting away in the cool face of post-honeymoon reality.

It was all she could do to sit quietly in her seat. The flooding memories made her want to cry, to scream, to confront Ray. Still she tried to immerse herself in the music, to ignore the nagging voice of doubt and warning. The recital ended and the girls took their bows—one boy in their midst, who got more than his share of attention and applause. Joy clapped until her hands hurt, wishing their tingle could obliterate the ache in her chest.

"She's yours, isn't she?" asked a big-haired woman beside Joy, pointing to the stage where Marianne was now stepping forward.

Mine, Joy thought, and she thrilled to the word. "Yes," she said, and for a second she succeeded in shaking off her doubts and suspicions.

"She's really good," the woman said.

"Thank you. Which one's yours?"

The woman pointed to a sweet-faced girl with long dark hair standing next to Marianne. At several points in the recital, Marianne had subtly nudged the girl into the right position, and Joy wondered if the dance instructor placed them together for this very reason.

"She's pretty," Joy said, searching for an honest but kind remark.

"Marianne helps her out a lot," the woman said. Joy smiled wordlessly, taking this in. The revelation put Marianne in a new light, less self-absorbed than she had believed.

"You were fabulous!" she told Marianne, debating whether to hug her. Around her girls and their parents were embracing easily, and Joy hated that such gestures did not come naturally for her.

She placed her arms awkwardly around Marianne, whose eyebrows were drawn together in a faint frown. She looked lovely, but less radiant than Joy would have expected. Her slight body was stiff, not yielding, but at least she didn't pull away. "You didn't see when I messed up?"

"No. I thought you were perfect." Had Marianne messed up when Joy's attention wandered?

"I was definitely not perfect," she said, and then added, "I hope Dad keeps his promise and comes to my next competition. It's a really important one."

Outside a soft blanket of snow had descended, coating the tops of the cars. Marianne lifted her face, the frown erased. "Ooooh," she breathed.

Joy followed suit, letting the large flakes caress her cheeks. "I had no idea!" she said.

"It's the closest to a white Christmas I've ever known," Marianne said, skipping around Joy in a circle of delight. With a running start, she managed to glide across the parking lot as if on skates. "Wouldn't this have been awesome on Christmas Day?" she asked as she skated back to Joy's side.

Around them, several of the girls, as well as some of the parents, scooped up handfuls of snow to toss at each other, laughing and squealing with mock anger.

"I hope there'll be enough for a snowman," Marianne said. "Wouldn't that be wonderful?"

"It would," Joy agreed, remembering another time, another snow, when she was younger than Marianne.

"I can't wait to get home," Marianne said. "Jenny will go crazy—she's always wanted to play in snow." But when they got home, the snow had stopped, and Jenny was not there. Neither was Ray.

Jenny showed up first, dropped off by some hippie-looking boy in a jacked-up Pontiac Firebird. Joy peered through the curtains, her heart thudding. Surely Jenny was too young for this kind of thing to be starting. Had she somehow wished this upon Jenny when she envisioned a crush on a shy boy her own age?

"Where's Dad? And who was *that*?" Marianne said when Jenny, all flushed and breathless, came inside. She indicated the car squealing out of the drive.

"That's Claudia's brother. Alex."

"And where is your father?" Joy could contain herself no longer. "Why didn't he drive you home?"

Jenny shook her head, the flush fading rapidly from her cheeks.

Understanding dawned. He didn't show.

"I was going to call, but I had to find someone to let me into the office. Then Claudia came and she offered …" Jenny shrugged. "You don't know where he is either?"

"No, I don't." She could not let the girls see how disappointed—and annoyed—she was.

"Do you think he's okay? Do you think he had a wreck?" Jenny looked alarmed.

Joy forced a smile to her lips, tried to sound reassuring and relaxed. "I'm sure he's fine. He probably got so tied up at work he simply couldn't get away. You know how it is."

"It never used to be like this," Marianne said, looking pointedly at Joy. Joy cringed at the implication and at her own fears.

All morning students streamed into Joy's office. Most of them wanted to know about her course, trying to decide—depending on whether or not they were currently enrolled—to stay in, add, or drop. But quite a few were from last semester, inquiring or, more commonly, complaining about their final grade. Finally she took a bathroom break.

A noisy queue waited at her door when she returned. Hoping the buzzing voices were more friendly than hostile, she plastered a bright smile on her face and called out, "Next! Come on in."

Shyly, hesitantly, the girl entered, twisting a strand of wispy blonde hair around her forefinger. She wore an oversized sweatshirt with faded flare-legged jeans. "I just wondered if you could tell me what I made on the final exam," the girl said. "I thought I had a solid B going into it, but—"

What *was* her name? Joy scanned the roster on the chance she might see and recognize it. She did not. She looked up, meeting the girl's round blue eyes. "What is your last name?" Joy asked, a lame trick intended to imply that she remembered her first name at least.

"Herrington."

Of course. Amy Herrington. She traced the line in her grade book from the girl's name to her score on the final exam. It too was a solid B. "What grade did you end up with?" she said. She would have to go to another page to see the final points.

"C." Amy's voice was quiet, as if being forced to utter something vile. "I've never made a C before."

Joy was on the other page now, and she suspected what had happened. For some reason, the names Herrington and Harris were not in alphabetical order on this page. They were reversed. On the page where she submitted her grades, they were no doubt correctly alphabetized. This meant not only that she'd given Amy someone else's C, but that Teresa Harris had received Amy's B.

Joy groaned.

"What is it?" Amy's smooth forehead puckered with concern, as though sorry she'd brought the matter up, fearful perhaps that her grade was to be lowered to something even worse.

Joy rushed to explain. "I'm pretty sure I see what happened. You made an 85 on the final, and you should have gotten a B in the course. I must have made a mistake. I'll send through a grade correction at once."

Relief engulfed the girl's round features. "Oh, thank you!"

"The error was my fault entirely, and I apologize. I hope I didn't create problems for you with a scholarship or your parents or anything."

"Oh, I'm not on scholarship." Amy sounded contrite, and Joy had a sudden impulse to scold the girl. "Stand up for yourself," she wanted to say. She should be angry with me, not apologetic for something she didn't do. The girl kept reminding her of someone else, but who?

"And my folks don't care. You see, they never went to college themselves, so they think anything passing is fine. It's just me. I'm always putting pressure on myself." Amy glanced over her shoulder at the queue, which was lengthening in the hallway. "I guess I better let someone else have a turn. Thanks again."

The girl tucked a strand of hair behind one ear. One part of Joy wanted to shake Amy for being so compliant, while another part wanted to thank her for not being irate. Ironic that the one person who actually deserved to be annoyed turned out to be the least critical.

"Next!" She cringed at the smug expression on the face of the student who entered. He'd been a pain since day one.

"I'm sure you made a mistake on my grade too," he said, and Joy regretted not having closed the door during Amy's visit. She remembered his name, though, remembered too how she'd even anticipated a complaint from him when she submitted the grades.

"I'm pretty sure I didn't," she said. "Why don't you close the door while I double-check?"

When the last student in the line had gone, Joy closed the door, sank into her chair, and dropped her head, which felt heavy as a tombstone, onto her desk.

CHAPTER TWENTY-TWO

"Does he have a girlfriend?" Jenny finally asked the question that had been nagging at her ever since she started visiting Claudia's home. The apartment was tiny, at least in comparison to her house. The kitchen and living room, for instance, were practically the same room so you could watch TV while you ate, which totally appealed to Jenny.

A shadow box containing a few trinkets hung by a chain over the table. At first Jenny thought she was looking through the box into another room until she realized the shadow box was mirrored. The television was pretty small, but she could see it just fine from the kitchen since the living room and kitchen combined were no bigger than her bedroom at home.

She and Claudia lounged in Claudia's room. The bedroom was actually one of the larger rooms, with black painted walls covered in posters of Madonna, Michael Jackson, and Joan Jett and the Black-Hearts. The door stood open wide enough for her to see the closed door to Alex's bedroom. She could also hear his music, a band she didn't recognize. She strained to catch the lyrics but couldn't make them out.

"Why do you care?" Claudia smirked. "Oh, I *see*." She contorted her features into such a parody of sudden comprehension Jenny was tempted to laugh, in spite of herself.

"I don't care. I was just asking."

"You've got a crush."

"I don't." Jenny flushed.

"You do."

"I don't."

"Do." Claudia examined Jenny's face so closely it seemed impossible to hide anything from her.

"Don't." Jenny felt heat rising to her face and knew she was blushing.

"Don't." Claudia reversed the pattern, and Jenny was confused.

"Do," she almost said, but caught herself in the nick of time. Still, she really wanted to know. "Well, does he?"

"He did. But you're in luck. They just had a big fight."

Jenny's heart hammered furiously, which was silly. She wasn't ready for a boyfriend, especially one Alex's age, even if he would look at her twice—which he wouldn't. "Really?"

"Yes, really." Wide-eyed, Claudia peered into Jenny's face once more, her eyes so close Jenny could see her own reflection in the pupils, which were slightly dilated.

As much as she wanted to hide her obsession from Claudia, every time she was here she'd find herself searching furtively for clues to his identity, his personality. Glimpses of his jeans in the laundry basket, the posters on the walls of his bedroom, even the food in the refrigerator—did he like mustard on his sandwiches, or did he prefer mayo like her?

She tried hard to look nonchalant, but every pore in her body yearned to learn more. "So—how long have they been going out?"

"Going out?" Claudia snorted. "Not long. They never do."

She stretched her long legs on top of the crumpled black bedspread and lifted one leg nearly perpendicular to the other, examining her green-painted toenails. They were beginning to chip rather badly. Smears of polish on the bedspread represented an assortment of the colors she'd worn since Jenny met her. Jenny scratched a tentative fingernail across one of the larger purple stains to see if it would flake off, having been well-trained by Mother never to polish her nails where she risked staining anything.

Eying Claudia's pointed toes, Jenny wondered—not for the first time—if, with training, Claudia might be as good as Marianne at ballet. Wouldn't that tick Marianne off? Right now, though, she was more interested in Alex, and she didn't want to lose the thread of conversation without learning a little more.

"So, is he really upset?" When Claudia looked at her blankly, she tried to clarify. "You know, about the breakup?" The music blared louder, and though she still couldn't make out the lyrics, she had the feeling the song was a protest of some sort. It sounded angry, maybe violent, and she wondered if Alex used music, as she sometimes did, to express his feelings.

"How would I know?" Claudia hopped off the bed to rummage through a cluttered drawer. She returned with a nearly empty bottle of green nail polish.

She shook the polish, which rattled as if a small metal ball were inside, then drew the brush out tentatively. "Crap. Why do they make the brushes so short you can't reach the bottom?" She tilted the bottle onto its side, and they both watched the green liquid slide slowly toward the opening.

Jenny tried not to think about how she didn't get a flower or a candy or a Valentine all day at school when others were cramming their lockers full of their Valentine's Day haul. Even Claudia had a few Valentines propped up on her dresser, and she was the sort to ridicule that kind of sloppy sentimental stuff.

Jenny scanned the room, familiar to her now, yet still a little shocking. Except for the large Michael Jackson picture scotch-taped to one end, Claudia's white, gold-trimmed dresser, slick on the top, seemed out of step with the rest of the room. Her thoughts returned to Alex. "Do you think it's over?"

"Do I think what's over?" Claudia had managed to get a decent amount of polish onto her brush now and was filling in the chips in her polish, creating a sort of uneven, layered effect, like the patched asphalt on the street outside.

"Alex and his girlfriend."

"Look, if you want my advice, you'll get over that crush in a hurry." Claudia sighed, swiping at a blob of green on the side of one toe. "I forgot the cotton balls."

"But you said I was in luck."

"Yeah, but I didn't say what kind of luck."

"What do you mean?"

"Do I have to spell it out? Trust me. He's just a heart breaker. If he does pay you the time of day, it won't be anything but bad luck."

Jenny figured Claudia was probably right, but still … she closed her eyes and imagined Alex emerging from his room to look for Jenny.

"I've been hoping you would come over today," he might say, handing her a small velvet box.

"But I didn't get you anything," she would apologize.

"What are you smiling about?" Claudia asked.

"Nothing—"

"Say, you want to watch a movie?"

"Which one?"

Jenny was amazed at the number of movies they had in the apartment, films her dad would never have let her and Marianne watch in a million years. She'd learned more about sex in the last few weeks from watching movies with Claudia than she'd ever gotten out of her dad's awkward explanations.

These movies gave her a warm, tingly feeling, and she felt guilty every time they watched one. When she mumbled something to Claudia about feeling wicked, her friend laughed in her face. "These aren't even the bad ones." she'd said. "These are our *family* movies, nothing worse than an R rating. You should see my mom's secret stash. Want to?"

Jenny had shaken her head, but she found herself wondering all the same. What could possibly be in the secret stash that was more shameful than what they'd seen already?

The familiar guilt rose in her throat at Claudia's suggestion but also a thrilling sense of excitement and curiosity she couldn't quite resist. What if Alex came in, she thought, when they were watching a sexy scene—which almost happened once before? She would die of embarrassment. Luckily, the scene ended just as he popped into the room. He even watched the next scene with them, quoting a couple lines of dialogue in unison with the actors, while Jenny sat there frozen, terrified that another sex scene might develop before he left.

"Who are your Valentines from?" she asked Claudia, who had finished her toenails and was dropping the empty polish jar back in the drawer for some reason.

"Nobody cool," Claudia said, flicking at one of the Valentines so that it toppled over.

Uncool like me. Alex, on the other hand, was totally cool. Way too cool for Jenny.

A few days later, she was back at Claudia's, sprawled on the tweedy sofa. Claudia lay on her stomach on the rug next to the sofa. The large beige rug with big flowers on it nearly filled the entire living room space. The episode of "The Fall Guy" they'd been watching was so boring they had turned the TV off and were debating what to do next.

Alex had been gone since Jenny got there, as usual. Then, suddenly, he was there, looking taller and more handsome than ever. His hair was messed up from the wind, and Jenny would have given anything to smooth it with her fingers, not that she would ever dare. He wore a blue jean jacket with the sleeves pushed up, open over a Ramones T-shirt. Jenny caught a whiff of something tantalizingly smoky—not cigarette smoke, more like a campfire roasting food with delicious spices. She had never actually been camping, which always sounded so enticing.

Maybe Joy would take her and Marianne camping sometime. The thought of Joy made Jenny feel unaccountably guilty. Why was she so haunted by guilt—was her conscience over-excitable or something? She wasn't even doing anything wrong. Not yet, at any rate.

"Why do you have that weird grin on your face?" Claudia asked her brother.

Jenny waited, trying to smile, trying not to stare, while she drank in his mouth and eyes, his hair and clothes. Had he made up with his girlfriend? Convinced this was the case, her heart sank, but mingling with the regret was relief. If he was off limits, she wouldn't feel so much pressure to make him like her, would she?

"Wouldn't you like to know?" Alex spoke to his sister but glanced in Jenny's direction.

"I do know," Claudia said. "I know everything."

"Oh, yeah? What time is it right now in Spain?"

"It's 8:07 tomorrow." Claudia glanced at her wrist as if making sure.

"Yeah, right."

"I know you. That's what I know."

"Meaning?"

"Meaning you've scored some good stuff. But you haven't partaken yet. And that means you're going to share." Claudia's grin was smug.

"You're crazy."

"Fine. But don't think I won't squeal. Don't think I won't suggest that Mom search every nook and cranny of your room, your clothes, your—"

"All right. I'll share. It's more fun together anyhow." Alex glanced at Jenny as he spoke, and she shivered a little, in dread or anticipation, or some other unknown emotion.

"Why aren't you sharing with Sarah Kay?"

"You know why. Remember, you know me."

"You really broke up for good?"

"Yep. Good riddance, I say." He glanced at Jenny again, and she could hardly keep her legs from trembling under his gaze. Being looked at in just that way was thrilling, as if she were a person, a girl, maybe even an attractive girl. She wished she'd worn her favorite jeans instead of these stretched-out ones, but her favorites were in the laundry.

"Your room?" Claudia suggested. "Or some place outside, under the stars?"

"Your choice. Yours and Jenny's."

Jenny's heart throbbed with the pleasure of hearing her name on his tongue. She looked at Claudia, and Claudia lifted a delicate reddish eyebrow. "Outside," Jenny said, thinking how romantic it sounded to be under the stars with Alex, doing … whatever they were going to be doing. Anything really.

"Why'd you come home, anyway?" Claudia asked her brother while they were assembling some supplies. A blanket to lie on, some pillows, a few snacks, and a thermos of some unidentified liquid.

"Maybe I was hoping you'd be here," Alex said, and he was looking at Jenny when he said it.

"Here, take these," Claudia said as they headed outside, and Jenny stared down at the brightly colored pills in her friend's hand.

"What are they?"

"You'll find out."

"But—"

Fear clutched at Jenny. Was she about to do something really, really awful?

"No buts." Claudia was firm. "We've been very good for a long time. We deserve this, and it's time you widened your horizons."

"My horizons?" Jenny's pulse raced. This was more than she bargained for.

"Remember the night of the concert when—"

"When my dad blew me off," Jenny finished.

"So what do you owe him?"

"Nothing." A corner of Jenny's brain registered that Claudia sometimes started her sentences with 'so' the same as Jenny. The habit—*her* habit—must not be so horrible as Marianne thought.

"You're darned tootin'," Claudia sang.

"We like Fig Newtons," her brother finished, whipping the blanket so that it ballooned upward, just like Jenny's hopes, before settling to the ground. Jenny swallowed the pills in a gulp so hard her esophagus ached.

"I liked your music," Alex told her a few minutes later when they were lying back against the pillows.

"My music?"

"The night of your concert."

"Oh, that." Jenny thought back to that night. The beautiful snow, how unexpected and wonderful. How cold she had been then, to be so warm now. Could it have been only a few weeks ago?

"But you didn't come in. Did you?"

He hummed one of the songs the band had played that night. Beethoven's "Ode to Joy."

"How did you know?" Jenny rolled over onto her side to stare at Alex in wonder. How handsome he was, with his dark blue eyes and dark, slicked back hair. One lock fell forward onto his forehead. She caught that smoky, musky scent once more, more intense this time. Was he wearing cologne—he didn't seem the type—or was that just his natural male scent? Surely nobody smelled this good without a little help.

"I could hear through the doors," he said.

"Why didn't you come in?" Jenny hoped she didn't have bad breath. She tried to remember if she'd eaten anything stinky today, like onions or garlic. She'd better avoid breathing on him just in case.

"I like to be alone sometimes. When I'm listening to music."

"Yeah," Jenny agreed. "Me too."

"What was your favorite part?"

"My favorite part?" she echoed, feeling foolish, hating herself for not being on his wavelength. What a ditz she was.

"Of the music that night?"

Surprised by the question, her mind went blank. Then, suddenly, she knew. She hummed a few bars for him.

He listened intently, brow furrowed, and then he laughed—a new sort of laughter. He wasn't making fun of her, he wasn't laughing because she was funny. He was laughing for sheer joy. She joined in, laughing as she'd never laughed before. This must be what people meant when they talked about getting high.

Dad always spoke of the horrors of drug addiction, showing her photos or news stories about people who were ill or homeless, people who overdosed or robbed stores for drug money. Those stories made Jenny think a person would be crazy to do drugs. Deep down, though, she must have known. There had to be an upside or no one would go there.

She felt as if she'd pressed the octave button on her clarinet, transferring the sounds to an entirely different level. A new range of emotions, where everything was heightened. Everything was wonderful. She loved Alex, and she loved Claudia. Better yet, they loved her too. She was engulfed by love, warmed by love.

As the night deepened and the air chilled, they huddled together, sharing their bodies' warmth, sharing their love.

After a time—and time was behaving peculiarly, so that she hadn't a clue how much had passed—through the warmth and the love, Jenny thought of Dad and Joy and Marianne, almost wishing they too could share this moment. But that was silly. They would never ... and at this realization, fear coursed back through her veins. What if she got caught? Would Dad know? Would Joy see?

"What time is it?"

Claudia told her. With her words, the warmth and the love thinned, evaporated, and Jenny climbed down from the cloud to her real life. "I've got to get home or I'll be grounded, okay?"

Later, safe in her own bed, she relived the experience, tried to recall the colors, the bliss. One time was—well, ecstatic—but one time was enough. As she drifted off to sleep, the word that played and replayed in her head was ecstasy ... ecstasy ... ecstasy.

CHAPTER TWENTY-THREE

Everything seemed to go wrong this morning. The way her hair stuck out on one side and refused to be flattened; the orange juice carton she knocked over when she rushed to grab the milk without removing everything in its way, creating a sticky patch on the kitchen floor (even after she scrubbed it three times); the irritability she sensed in Ray, Jenny, and Marianne. Or were they picking up on hers?

Her classes had gotten off to a poor start, and for some reason she always felt that the first week or so determined the tone for the rest of the term. And now this—the letter in her mailbox. Heart thumping, she walked rapidly to her office, ripped the envelope, and scanned.

Unfortunately we've decided to reject your submission. Because of the careless nature of the writing and obvious errors in the presentation of the tables (there is no Table 4, for instance), we must return the manuscript to you without sending it out for review. In the future, I must warn you against premature submissions, as they can only damage your future in academia …

Ignoring the students who lounged in the hallway just outside her office—were they looking for her or another professor?—Joy closed the door to her office and allowed her head to drop onto her desk. She would have to tell Natalie. What could she say? That this too was her fault?

She dialed Natalie's office number, then hung up before the ring. She should share the disappointing news face to face. But, first, a cup of coffee to steel herself.

She held her shoulders high and headed to the coffee room. Suddenly she was sweating profusely. Was it that warm in here? Coffee would make her even hotter, she realized, so instead she filled her Styrofoam cup with cold water.

She stared at a puddle of spilled coffee and then at the sign above the coffee pot, which she'd read dozens of times before. Today the words struck her differently. "If you make a mess, please clean it up." Today she wanted to lash out at the male professors, who often left dirty coffee cups or spills for someone else to attend to. Today, she felt annoyed at the way two of her male colleagues laughed and chatted as if nothing more serious pressed on them than the state of the stock market. She reached for a paper towel and sopped up the puddle. Then, abruptly, she stopped and deliberately abandoned the wadded paper towel in the middle of someone else's mess.

She returned to her office to read once more the unwelcomed letter. Yet, even as she scanned, her mind drifted. There was something troubling Ray he wasn't sharing. As hard as she tried, she couldn't quite seem to obliterate the image of another woman. She pictured the various candidates—women at the bank, women who'd been friends with Carolyn, the enemy could be anyone. Someone younger, more beautiful than Joy, someone more skilled at cooking and parenting and decorating. There was a small greasy stain on the sleeve of her gray jacket, and around the dark spot a faint ring, probably a watermark where she'd tried unsuccessfully to clean. How did some women manage to have their act so spotlessly together?

Still she couldn't quite believe him guilty of this particular betrayal. If he wasn't having an affair, what *was* troubling him? One way or another, she would have to get to the bottom of what was wrong. The notion of quitting her job came to her once more. Surely their lives would be smoother, less stressful altogether if she did.

In the meantime, she must deal with this rejection. On legs as heavy as if she'd strapped lead weights to them, she rose from her desk once more and headed down the hallway to Natalie's office. The door was closed ... not unusual for Natalie. She often worked with the door shut.

Joy rapped lightly. No answer.

She rapped again. Still nothing. Natalie wasn't in.

Relief swelled inside Joy, though she knew the reprieve was only a postponement. She'd have to face Natalie eventually. And then, suddenly, she saw the rejection in a new light. The letter wasn't good news, and she was truly sorry for Natalie's sake. Yet, for Joy, their failure could be just the signal she'd been waiting for. The signal to get off the fence and onto a new path. The path of full-time mother and homemaker. Even if Ray was having an affair, which she couldn't really believe, surely he wasn't in so deep that their marriage was beyond saving. They'd only been married six months, after all. Joy refused to think he'd have given up this soon. On the other hand, if she continued to spread herself too thin—doing everything halfway and nothing really well—he would eventually find someone else.

Her pulse thumped in a complicated thunderous rhythm of excitement and relief, fear and hope, as she felt herself on the brink of a decision. No, not on the brink. Over it.

She would tell him tonight.

If a cloud of doubt hung in some corner of her brain, the lightness of her legs as she headed back toward her office convinced her of the rightness of the decision. The weights had miraculously lifted, and she moved so easily she scarcely knew she was lifting one leg after the other. Thankfully, there was no line at her door.

Taking the coward's way out, she would write a gentle note and leave it in Natalie's mailbox with the letter. She scribbled a few lines, wadded up the paper, tried again, and repeated the process. Try as she might, she could not find an easy way to state her case. She strove for the right words to put an optimistic spin on the rejection. "We can tighten the paper up, and try another journal," she wrote. This last effort would have to do. She would help Natalie get this paper published if it was the last thing she did before leaving academia forever.

She was about to head back to the mailboxes when the phone rang.

"Where's Dad?" Marianne's voice had an odd note, excited, but not in a good way.

What now. "I don't know exactly. At work, I guess. Why?"

"I can't reach him. And I really need to."

"What's happened?" Joy glanced toward her doorway, where Gary Morgenstern hovered impatiently. He would have to wait.

After an endless moment, Marianne said, "It's Jenny."

CHAPTER TWENTY-FOUR

Joy gripped the steering wheel so hard her knuckles shone white. On the radio the Police sang "Every Breath You Take." Angry with herself for not watching Jenny more closely, for having ignored the warning signs, she had a sudden impulse to punch something—steering wheel, radio, her thigh. Her nature was not to punch things though, and she resisted the impulse. She'd probably sprain her wrist if she did. She settled for punching the radio off with unnecessary force. Jenny had been spending way too much time away from home lately, and Joy had let it, like everything else, slide.

"Mrs. Connors has agreed not to press charges," the police officer said with a look that spoke volumes of her assessment of Joy as a seriously deficient mother. The station smelled of cold metal and stale cigars, despite the 'no smoking' sign on the wall. Joy wondered what it was like for a woman to work in this place. With her regular features and short, curly auburn hair, the officer could be an attractive woman, if her expression were a bit more pleasant. The corners of her mouth twitched in an upward direction. A smile or a twinge of constipation?

"What's going on?" Joy addressed Jenny, who slumped in a chair. Jenny shrugged, her eyes focused on the floor.

Joy's jaw muscles tightened. "I repeat. *What's* going on here?"

"I don't see what's the big deal," Jenny said. "We—I didn't even get anything, okay?"

Joy had expected remorse, an apology, something to indicate a sense of responsibility for what had happened. She reached for the girl's arm and pulled her to her feet, none too gently. Should she leave her here, beg the officer to keep her overnight? Tough love. Did it ever work? Tough love, like punching things, wasn't in her nature. Then again, maybe her nature was deficient in some potentially fatal way. A person could learn to go against her nature … couldn't she?

"Where's Claudia?" she asked. "I know she had something to do with this."

Jenny shook her head, stubborn silence written across every feature. "I dunno," she mumbled.

Joy struggled to control an escalating anger that was new to her, an anger directed momentarily more at Jenny than at herself. Still holding Jenny's arm, she jerked it just perceptibly as she led her from the police station. In the car, she consciously eased her death grip on the steering wheel, relaxing the muscles in her jaw. "Was there something you needed—something you wanted to buy?"

Jenny's brown eyes met hers for an instant before darting away. A flash of something there intimated to Joy that she was on the right track, so she pressed on. "Clothes? Designer jeans?" She forced herself to sound calm. Like the good cop in a detective show. "I know how expensive those can be. *What?* Tell me please."

Jenny lifted one leg and examined the toe of her tennis shoe as if it were the most interesting thing she'd ever seen.

"Shoes?" Joy prompted.

Jenny propped both feet on the dashboard, and turned the radio on. The Eurythmics crooned "Sweet Dreams (Are Made of This)." Joy had always enjoyed this song, but it struck her now that she'd never really thought about the lyrics. Were we all—even without realizing it—looking to use or abuse someone, or be used or abused ourselves? Was there truth in this picture of human nature?

"Get your feet down, and talk to me," she snapped, slapping the radio off.

"The cop already told you," Jenny muttered. "I took the lady's purse. But the funny thing was … it was empty except for a bunch of junk. She had her billfold and all her money out on the counter, okay?" Jenny emitted an odd sort of laugh, and Joy's anger receded at the sound. A familiar laugh somehow, a chortle of failure.

How do I handle this? Joy needed help. *Ray!* "What's your dad going to say when he finds out?"

Jenny shrugged. "What does he care?"

Joy was stunned, made momentarily speechless. As shocked as she'd been throughout the day, this response appalled her as nothing else had done. She'd been expecting Jenny to beg her not to tell him. "How can you say that?"

"He doesn't care about me anymore. He wouldn't have missed my concert if he did. That was what started everything. It was all his fault."

"What? What's his fault?"

"It was just a lark. I don't know why they had to call the cops," Jenny said. "It wasn't like we got anything."

"We?" Anger surged through Joy once more, directed in part toward the other half of the "we" and partly toward Jenny.

"Me. It wasn't like I got anything. *Store policy.* They said they had to report it. " Jenny's voice took on a sassy edge Joy had never heard before, and once more Joy's level of fear and shock escalated. Jenny laughed again, a shrill, high-pitched wail this time.

"Are you going to tell me what's going on or not?"

There was a pause before Jenny answered. When she did, her voice was so low Joy could barely hear. "I can't." Then she was sobbing, the hysterical laughter replaced by a flood of tears.

Somehow the tears reassured Joy, and she softened in spite of herself. How deep was the problem, and what would she find at the root? She had no idea, knew only that she had to keep digging until she got to it.

With Ray. They had to do this together.

She was pleasantly surprised when she pulled into the garage to find his BMW already there. Seemed like a good omen. She would tell him everything, and they would sort the mess out together.

When she found Ray, though, he was on the phone. "It's all right, Darleen. You don't have to apologize."

Joy waited, not meaning to eavesdrop but caught by the expression on Ray's face. Intent and distinctly troubled. Who was Darleen? She tried to remember, and an image came to mind. A nondescript woman, unassuming and gentle-spoken. Joy had thought once when she stopped by the bank that Darleen might have a crush on Ray. At the time, she'd felt certain he didn't reciprocate.

Ray glanced up at Joy as he listened, but he didn't acknowledge her. She sensed that he was not so much listening as thinking how to reply.

"Don't worry," he said. "I'll take care of it."

As the conversation ended, Joy opened her mouth to speak. Before she could, Ray was taking another call.

"I'm sorry. Who did you say you were?" he demanded, and this time his voice was less kind. Joy couldn't tell whether the impatience was at being disturbed at home, or at something more ominous.

"Sure. Fire away, Sarah Kinsey." There was an edge to his voice, and Joy tried to think where she'd heard the name Sarah Kinsey before. She slipped away quietly. In the hallway, she hesitated. Now she was eavesdropping, but she couldn't seem to help herself.

"Good authority? What authority?" Ray said, his tone harsher still. Joy stood frozen. She remembered the name suddenly. Sarah Kinsey was a reporter for the *Financial Times*.

"Then, I'm afraid I'm not at liberty to comment." A note of despair had crept into his voice. "I repeat, I'm not at liberty to comment." Joy knew her talk with him about Jenny would have to wait.

CHAPTER TWENTY-FIVE

"Look. You know Dad will kill you when he finds out." Marianne stretched one leg over her head where she lay on Jenny's bed, nearly touching the pillow behind her.

Couldn't she be still for one second, Jenny thought. "Fat chance," she said.

"Are you really that stupid?" Marianne tucked both legs under her and sat upright, spine straight, staring at Jenny. "You really think he won't know?"

"I suppose you're going to tell him."

"He needs to know what's going on around here. How long can he keep his head buried in the sand? I'm convinced I am the only sane person in this family."

Jenny surveyed her ankle, where she and Claudia had tattooed a purple octopus. Marianne followed Jenny's gaze. "I hope that's a temporary tattoo," she said.

Jenny shrugged.

"So where was Claudia when all this was going on? Don't tell me she ran!" Marianne watched Jenny even more intently, so Jenny concentrated hard to give away nothing. She knew why Marianne was here. She wanted to know all the dirt. Why give her the satisfaction?

The phone rang. Jenny knew the caller would be Claudia, and she really didn't want to talk to her just now.

"Are you going to answer that?" Marianne asked.

"Nope."

"It's her, isn't it?" Marianne's tone was gentle. "I don't blame you. I wouldn't want to talk to her either." The ringing persisted, paused for a few seconds and began again. Marianne and Jenny stared at each other. "Do you want me to answer it?" Marianne offered. "I could give her a piece of my mind."

"No, thanks." Marianne's sympathy just made Jenny feel worse. Almost of its own volition, her hand reached in the direction of the phone, which had now ceased ringing. True, a part of her did want to talk to Claudia, to find out why she did what she did. Maybe there was a good reason. Like she already had a police record and one more goof would mean real jail time. This would actually be better from Jenny's viewpoint. She wondered if this was *irony*, a concept she could never quite get in English class.

"You want to play monopoly?" Marianne asked.

"No," Jenny said automatically. She always wanted to play monopoly, and Marianne was never in the mood. Still, she wanted to sulk now. She *needed* to sulk in front of Marianne and, besides, Marianne was probably after something. Why did everyone in Jenny's life have to betray her?

"Come on. It'll be fun, and take your mind off stuff."

"What stuff?"

"I'll get the game." Marianne hopped off the bed to locate the dilapidated monopoly box. Jenny watched her sister's narrow, boy-like hips in a pair of faded jeans she'd had for what seemed like years. She wondered if Marianne ever fretted about being so tiny, about not growing or developing breasts. Probably not. Breasts and hips would just get in the way for a ballerina.

"Should we ask Joy?" she suggested when Marianne came back and started setting up the board.

"No, I don't think so." She paused only a second, then went back to counting the game's fake five dollar bills, stacking them neatly.

Jenny shrugged, not caring enough one way or another to argue.

Jenny chose the steamship, as usual, and Marianne picked up the thimble. They played in silence for a time, except for the occasional "I'll buy it ... or your move."

Jenny loved this game. When she landed on Park Place on her third time round the board, having bought Boardwalk already, she couldn't help letting out a whoop of delight. "I'll take it!" This had never happened to her before, not so early in the game.

"Your choice," Marianne said. "But it'll take most of your funds, and I'll probably never land on it. I'm always shopping for luxury items and getting nailed with that silly tax."

"You will too land on it. By then, I'll probably have three houses."

"In your dreams," Marianne said. She drew a card from the community chest. "Oh, I do believe I've won a beauty pageant." She preened exaggeratedly, and Jenny giggled in spite of herself.

"Figures," she said, not really annoyed. She was too pleased about the property she'd just acquired.

"Tell me about that brother of Claudia's," Marianne said. "He's kind of cute in a hood sort of way."

Jenny bristled. "He's not a hood."

"I didn't say he was. He just has that look—you know, the bad boy look. Like James Dean in those old movies."

"Exactly!" Jenny said. And, though she knew she was yielding once more to Marianne's ulterior motives, she told her about him. She loved to talk about him—the way his eyes crinkled when he laughed, the way he sometimes treated her like an equal, the way they both loved classical music.

"Wow," Marianne said, her brow furrowed. "You've really got it bad, haven't you?"

Jenny shrugged, grasping for her armor of self-defense. "Not really. I just told you because you asked. He's way too old for me."

"You've got that part right anyway."

Jenny bristled.

"It's only four years. Lots of couples are more than four years apart. Even ten years," Jenny couldn't help arguing.

"Four years when you're forty is way different from four years when you're fourteen."

"I guess." Jenny rolled the dice and counted the spaces in her head. She loved drawing the cards from Community Chest, even though they were never anything great and sometimes painful. Like now. "Go directly to jail. Do not pass GO. Do not collect $200." She groaned, and moved her steamship to the jail.

"If you want my advice," Marianne said, "you'll stay away from him. And his sister too. If you don't, you may find yourself going to jail for real."

Jenny stared at her picture-perfect sister for a long moment. "At least I *have* friends!" she said at last.

Marianne's eyes flashed bright with anger, and then suddenly, before Jenny's eyes, the anger dissolved into waterfalls. Marianne, who never cried, was crying. Not sobbing, not weeping … more like her eyes were melting.

"You don't know what it's like to be me. Did you even know I had a ballet dance competition yesterday?" She made no effort to brush away the cascade of tears sliding down her cheeks. Jenny wanted to do it for her but resisted the impulse.

"No." Marianne answered her own question. "You didn't, and nobody else did either. I try so hard, and I practice and practice. And nobody even notices. It's just expected I'll win. And then you go and do something stupid like this, and you get all the attention."

"I don't *want* the attention. It's the last thing I want."

"I know, and that just makes it worse." Marianne drew her knees up, and buried her face.

"What do you mean?" Jenny was totally baffled.

"It must be so much easier to be you," Marianne said without lifting her head, her voice muffled so that Jenny couldn't be altogether certain she was hearing correctly. The words that seemed to be coming from her sister were so unexpected, and yet somehow believable too. "To have the guts to screw up and get in trouble, and not be the best."

"I'd give anything to be the best!" Jenny said, not to make Marianne feel better but because it was the simple truth.

"No, you wouldn't." Marianne lifted her head, her eyes sadder than Jenny remembered seeing them in a long time. Since Mother died, maybe.

"Yes, I would." Yet, even as she spoke, she began to doubt her words, to wonder if her insistence was, after all, for her sister's benefit. "I'm just not that good at anything."

Marianne went on as if she hadn't heard. "Because you don't try that hard. If you cared—if you cared like I do—you could."

Was this true, Jenny wondered. "Do you really think so?"

"I do. But don't change. It's no good being the best. It's awful." And now Marianne was actually crying—not just crying but sobbing in deep, gut-wrenching gasps.

Jenny reached out to take her tiny, perfect sister into her arms, not caring that she upset the monopoly board so that the stack of Community Chest cards toppled and the thimble and steamship left the board altogether.

Then, in the next moment, Jenny was crying too, and she didn't know whether she was crying for herself or for her sister. After a long time, she asked, "So, do you want me to tell you what happened with Claudia?"

"If you want to," Marianne said, her eyes brightening just a little.

So she told her. How Claudia pointed out the rich-looking woman and then distracted her while the sales clerk left the counter to check on a price. How Jenny was supposed to grab the woman's handbag but couldn't bring herself to do it. How Claudia kept talking to the woman, kept sending Jenny questioning looks that clearly said *What are you waiting for?* Finally, when the opportunity was almost lost, when the woman started to turn away from Claudia, how Jenny summoned all her courage and grabbed the bag. Then the woman saw her, and Claudia fled. Jenny froze, and all she could think of was how the wallet was lying on the counter, how she'd messed everything up.

"I'm so ashamed and so stupid," Jenny gasped, her breath turning to hiccups. Looking down, she saw the crumpled Community Chest card, still clutched in her left hand.

After Marianne left, Jenny assembled her clarinet while she replayed the things her sister said. Funny, how you could think you knew someone inside and out, and then they could take you totally by surprise. She was so absorbed in Marianne's issues that for a few minutes she forgot her own. She tentatively licked her reed. Was that a crack?

She hated asking for money for new reeds all the time. Especially now. And then the bad memories came crashing back. How could she have been so stupid? She'd been a fool to listen to Claudia, who ran at the first sign of trouble and left Jenny to face the music alone.

She pushed the images deep down in the place where she buried all the unpleasantness—the insults and hurts—the stuff she needed to forget. She blew into her clarinet, which sounded pretty good, despite the tiny crack.

As the music swelled, she filled in the rest of the instruments in her head until she heard a complete orchestra, way better than her school band. She thought of Alex, of the night they met and of the last time they were together in Claudia's backyard, under the stars. One of the things she loved about him was the way he shared her love of music. She shivered at the memories, at the way her mind just automatically filled in the word *love*. Things she loved about him. Did that mean she loved *him*? Could this really be it? She knew what Joy or Dad—even Marianne—would say. That she was way too young to know anything about love.

Only, she didn't feel too young. Her feelings were so sharp, so all-consuming, she had to wonder if emotions dulled with age—dulled so gradually you didn't realize what was happening. Could Dad or Joy possibly feel anything as intense as this? She didn't want to think about them. Thoughts of Joy and Dad brought back the stuff she wanted buried. She only wanted to think of Alex.

Did his lips really brush her hair in a quick kiss, or did she only imagine he had? No, she was pretty sure it happened. She strained to get the memory exactly right, to relive the rush of blood and joy and hope.

She'd been so surprised she froze. Another girl might have tilted her head up, met his eyes, and then he'd have bent and kissed her lips. She saw the other girl … prettier, sexier, slimmer than Jenny. Then she banished that other girl and saw herself melting into the kiss.

The phone rang again, and this time she answered without thinking.

"Did you tell? Please—tell me you didn't."

"I didn't," Jenny said, annoyed. No *"How are you"* … *"what did they do to you"* … *"how much trouble are you in?"*

"Thank God," Claudia said. "Promise me you won't. Not to your dad, or your stepmom. Or anyone."

Jenny said nothing.

"Promise me!" Claudia insisted. "Do you promise?"

"I don't know."

"I already have two strikes," Claudia said, exactly as Jenny had imagined she might. "That's why I ran—I simply can't get a third."

What did "two strikes" mean? Knowing Claudia, they could have been almost anything. Or nothing. They could be a lie. "I'm not a snitch."

"Alex has been asking about you."

"He has?"

"Sure has. He really likes you."

Hope swelled in Jenny's breast. She wanted to believe Claudia. How much she wanted to believe her … but she couldn't be that gullible. Not this time. Claudia was trying to bribe her, and she was probably lying. Almost surely she was. Jenny couldn't quite imagine Alex asking Claudia about her. Still. "So … what did he say?"

"He just wanted to know when you'd be coming over. He said he hadn't seen much of you lately."

A sort of wheedling edged into Claudia's voice. Hearing and recognizing this did not keep Jenny's heart from picking up its pace. "Really?"

"Yes, really. Now will you promise me?"

A gentle rap at her door made Jenny's heart lurch. It had to be Joy. "Look, I've got to go, okay?"

"Promise me—please."

Almost Jenny yielded. She wanted to promise to make Claudia feel better, to improve her chances with Alex. But she would not be bribed. Another rap, less gentle this time. "You're not the only one in trouble here," she said.

She could still hear Claudia's voice as she hung up the phone. "*Please …*"

"Come on in," Jenny called, laying down her clarinet and then picking it back up, trying to look normal, as if her world hadn't been turned upside down.

She blew a long slow note, knowing she could not ward off Joy's questions but trying anyway. When Joy didn't speak, Jenny played on. She could almost forget Joy's presence and succumb to the joy and anguish of Mozart's Clarinet Concerto.

"You're getting good," Joy said when Jenny stopped playing. "Really good."

Jenny caught a whiff of something sweet, like vanilla. Was Joy wearing perfume? Mother had always worn perfume—a musky, sexy scent. Heat rushed to Jenny's head at the thought, another reminder of Alex and her daydream. "No, I'm not," she said. "You should hear some of the first clarinets. They're way better than me."

"Maybe. But you've improved a lot. Don't sell yourself short."

"Thanks," Jenny said. Had she improved that much? She wasn't sure.

Joy sighed, a long, sad sigh. Jenny couldn't help feeling bad about how she'd let her down. She met Joy's gaze for a second before looking away.

She began to take her horn apart while she waited for Joy to speak. Then she put the clarinet back together and drew the swab through the instrument. How disgusting, the amount of spit that collected in these things.

"Why?" Joy said finally. "Why would you do something like that?"

Knowing this question was coming, Jenny had tested and discarded lots of possible responses. None of them seemed very good. She picked one at random. "It was just an impulse, okay?" she said. "You know, like you think about jumping off a cliff—or sticking your hand down a garbage disposal. But you know you won't really do it."

"But you did do it," Joy said, her light, sandy-colored brows drawn together.

"Well, I saw her handbag, and I thought about it. But then I knew I wouldn't, I'm such a coward. And I wanted to prove I wasn't—"

"Prove to whom?"

"Myself." She avoided Joy's glare.

"I don't believe you."

A sudden rage flared inside Jenny, one she didn't understand, didn't want to understand. Why shouldn't Joy believe her? It wasn't as if she went around lying all the time. "I don't care if you believe me or not"—she shook as she screamed—"You're not my mother!"

She didn't have to meet Joy's eyes to know the words stung … making Jenny cringe inside, making her want to tell the truth even if it meant ratting out Claudia. But she couldn't.

"I might have expected that from Marianne," Joy said quietly. "But not from you."

"Why not?"

"It's just—I suppose I always got the impression Marianne was more her mother's girl, and you're more your dad's."

"You might be surprised," Jenny said.

"How so?"

"Marianne may not be exactly who you think she is." Why did she say that? Jenny wondered if she was on the verge of giving up her sister to save Claudia. And if so, was Alex the reason?

She jerked her clarinet apart, angry with herself for being a sneaky, lying fool. But what choice did she have? There was nothing more she could say, and so she would keep her stupid mouth shut and take whatever punishment Joy decided to dish out.

CHAPTER TWENTY-SIX

Marianne had warmed up until she was sweating. Literally. She could no longer find an excuse for avoiding the challenge. Thirty-two fouettés, she knew she could do them. She would be perfect this time. She clicked her tongue inside her mouth to signal the end of any and all screw-ups of any sort, the beginning of a perfect series. Of course being perfect wasn't enough. Once she was perfect, she'd have to work on the wow factor. She sucked in a deep breath, started her music, and plastered a wide, fake smile on her face. You had to smile.

Standing momentarily flat footed, she bent her right knee while the left leg whipped around to the side, creating the impetus to spin. As she rose on pointe on her right foot, she pulled in the left leg until it touched her right knee. For the first ten turns, she was flawless, and the voice in her head was silent. Then it began. *What were you thinking—spilling your guts like that?* Marianne concentrated harder, ignoring the voice. Her smile stiffened until the edges of her mouth quivered. She would be perfect, she had to be perfect, she had to show Mother she could do it. After the accident, Marianne welcomed Mother's presence inside her head. Then, more and more often, the presence taunted more than comforted … in death as she'd been in life. If Marianne could just reach and complete thirty-two fouettés once perfectly, maybe that would be enough. Maybe this was the time.

As she stumbled, ruining the perfection, spoiling everything, the voice came again, more insistently this time. *What were you thinking? You know we never give ourselves away.*

Marianne sank to the floor, curled her legs in like a spider balling up to hide from a massive threatening boot. "I'm sorry, Mother," she whispered.

Haven't I taught you anything?

Marianne silently answered the voice in her head. She wasn't crazy, was she? Not crazy enough to talk to a ghost. Except in her head. *You have. I promise you have. And I'm trying so hard. You have no idea.*

Then why did you quit cheerleading? I still can't make any sense of that particular decision.

I hated it! And they hated me! Marianne fought back sobs, tempted to scream out loud. Mother had always hated tears, and so did Marianne. Only weaklings resorted to that device, and she would never garner sympathy from Mother—or her ghost—with tears in a million years.

You can't fool me. I saw you break down with your sister. I saw what you're capable of.

It's not a sin to be vulnerable, Mother.

The voice was chilly now. *I didn't say it was a sin. But it's a mistake. There's a difference you know.* The next words came in a hiss. *Soft people never get what they want. Don't be soft, Marianne.*

What are you talking about?

You know what I'm talking about.

No, I don't! You're not even here. You're just a figment of my imagination, and I'm not listening to you anymore. Yet, even with these words, Marianne thought of the character Figment at Epcot—how she and Mother loved that ride—and she felt guilty.

She pushed the guilt down deep. She rose and began her dance again. She was into her fifth turn before she remembered to click her tongue against the roof of her mouth. Never mind, she was doing well.

Even famous ballerinas couldn't always do thirty-two. When Emma Bessome performed fourteen in *The Haarlem Tulip*, fourteen had been considered a feat. So would it be such a crime if Marianne couldn't make it to thirty-two?

That's loser thinking.

She had to show Mother. Eighteen, nineteen, twenty. *Take that, Mother.* Ballet was a mind game, and Marianne was a pro at mind games. Wasn't she? Twenty-seven, twenty-eight. Only four fouettes left.

As she approached the thirtieth, having nearly completed her goal, the voice came again. *The time is perfect. Jenny is furious with Joy and with good reason. Use her, Marianne. Use her now.*

No. She wouldn't.

Marianne's body weakened. She stumbled and fell on the last turn. She lay there, trembling on her floor.

Don't you want Joy out of your life?

You know I do. Of course I do.

But did she? Joy could be pretty decent at times.

What do you have, Marianne? Tell me that. You gave up your shot at popularity when you quit cheerleading. Your dad's got Joy. Even Jenny's got a friend now. What have you got?

The sweat had dried on her skin, and she was suddenly cold. She lifted herself to a cross-legged position, brought her knees to her chin, and wrapped her arms around her legs. She thought the unspeakable: Joy's not so bad sometimes.

Aha! I knew you were thinking that way. Fool! You want to replace me too. Don't you? You're forgetting everything we meant to each other. Once. But now I'm dead and forgotten. The voice inside her head rose and fell in fury and self-pity.

No, I'll never, ever forget you. But it's not real anymore. Even if Joy goes, you can't come back.

I'm here now, aren't I? She's no good for your dad. Look how unhappy he's been lately—since she came. Do you think that's a coincidence? The voice was different this time. It came from the room, and not from the interior of her brain. Marianne looked up, toward the doorway. Of course there was nothing.

And, yet, she could see her. So perfect in her cashmere sweater, not a trace of sweat no matter how warm the day, her pencil skirt smooth over her slim hips, her legs muscled but not thick, slender and shapely in very high heels. The skirt and shoes were red, the sweater cream, Mother's hair, a dark cloud around her pale face. Then the image blurred, turned sour, hostile, the red mouth twisted and ugly.

Don't desert me, Marianne. You're all I have left.

And then she was gone, and the rapping on her door was real.

"Come in," Marianne called out, her voice strange in her own ears.

Jenny appeared in the doorway, her eyes puffy and red, her hair a bigger mess than usual. Still it was she who looked at Marianne with concern. "What's wrong?"

"Nothing." Marianne rose to her feet and positioned herself once more for the series of turns. "I just can't seem to get my routine right."

"You will," Jenny said. "Just keep at it. Never give up."

Marianne was startled. This seemed an odd thing for Jenny to say, as if she was mouthing Mother's thoughts. Did Mother haunt her as well?

"I came to ask a favor," Jenny said.

"Oh? What is it?"

"Call Claudia for me. Tell her I'm not so mad at her anymore."

"Why don't you call her yourself?"

"They took my phone away." Jenny sounded hurt and more than a little bitter.

"I see."

Do it, Mother's voice buzzed in her head. *It's what she wants. She's playing right into your hands.*

What would be the harm? Marianne met Jenny's anxious gaze. "Why don't you pop into my bedroom in a few minutes? I might just happen to step out for a bit, you know, just about long enough to make a phone call. A long phone call," Marianne said.

"Thank you!" Jenny rewarded Marianne with a wide smile.

"In a few minutes," Marianne had said. To make the time go faster, Jenny assembled her clarinet and blew a long, low note. Not that she was going to call Claudia. Not necessarily. She blew hard, making a harsh ugly squeak. She rummaged through a messy stack of music, looking for something to match her mood. Sad and blue, angry and confused. Calling Claudia would be a mistake; she would not take Marianne up on her offer.

She licked her reed, repositioned it, blew a few notes of several favorites, wanting to lose herself as she sometimes could. Not today. Today nothing suited. Deliberately she created another ear-tingling shriek. As discordant as her emotions. She was so angry at Claudia, at Joy, mostly at herself.

And so, after a few minutes, she headed to Marianne's room, clarinet in hand, as Marianne must have known she would. "Take all the time you need," Marianne said on her way out the door. "I have a lot of stuff to do."

Alone in the room, Jenny stared at the phone from the edge of Marianne's bed. Why was Marianne being so helpful? The whole thing was sort of worrisome, but she had enough worries without adding Marianne's motives to the list. Jenny dropped back onto her sister's bed, legs dangling, staring at the ceiling, and cradling the clarinet beside her.

How long had she been like this? Minutes or only seconds? She slowly rose. As if in a trance, she left the clarinet on the bed. Picking up the receiver, she dialed the first part of Claudia's number, then hesitated. After all, there was really no point, except to relieve the boredom for a minute or two. She replaced the receiver.

Now, at least, she had the option. She could call Claudia, or not. It was her decision. Of course she'd have to decide pretty soon, or Marianne would be back. She shifted her weight from one leg to the other, stared at the photo of Marianne and Mother on the dresser. Where had Jenny been when that photo was taken, she wondered. She picked the frame up to look more closely before setting it back down. With the corner of her shirt, she rubbed at the fingerprints she'd left on the smooth silver frame.

Finally she gave in. Picking up the phone, she dialed the entire number. When Claudia answered, Jenny discovered that she had no voice. Only a faint squeak.

"Who's this?" Claudia sounded bored.

Almost Jenny hung up.

"Is anyone there?"

If she didn't say something fast, Claudia would hang up. "It's me," Jenny breathed quickly.

"Jenny?"

"Yeah."

"I'm so glad you called." Claudia's voice was unusually enthusiastic. "Are you—not mad at me anymore?"

Jenny shrugged. Then, since Claudia couldn't see the shrug, she said, "I don't know—I guess not."

"Can you come over?" Claudia asked.

"I'm grounded." Jenny sank to the floor, as if to prove her point, another gesture Claudia couldn't see.

"Oh. Sorry."

"Yeah. Being grounded stinks."

"You're telling me!" Claudia said.

"Have you been grounded?"

"Not this time. But about a hundred times before. Like you said, it sucks."

"What do you do?" Jenny asked. "How do you get through it?" How odd life was, Jenny thought. There had been plenty of times when she didn't leave the house except for school and band. Exactly like now. Except that staying in had been her choice then, and now it wasn't.

"I sneak out," Claudia said.

151

Of course—of course Claudia would sneak out. But Jenny could never do that. Not in a million years. "How's Alex?" she asked, to change the subject—or maybe she just wanted to say his name.

"Not so great."

"Why not?" Jenny felt even worse to think Alex might be sad.

"He's not talking to me much. He knows."

"Knows what?"

"He knows what happened to you, and he blames me," Claudia said. "He really likes you, Jenny."

"He does?" She wanted to believe Claudia, but she was probably stupid to trust her ever again. Jenny plopped back onto the edge of the bed and picked up her clarinet, then laid it down while she waited for Claudia's answer.

"Dang it!" Claudia said.

"What's wrong?"

"I just smudged nail polish all over my toe." A few choice words followed. "Did you ever wonder why you always see those girls with cotton balls between their toes?" Claudia didn't wait for an answer. "Every time I use them, I wonder if it's really necessary. Then every time I don't use them, I get my answer. Hold on a minute while I find the polish remover."

Did she have the nerve to bring Alex up again? Could she stand not bringing him up again?

"All right, I'm back," Claudia said. "Now where were we?"

Jenny reached for her clarinet, pulled it into two halves, and opened her mouth to speak. Claudia went on before she could. Jenny had been holding the receiver to her ear with her shoulder and now dropped it, missing part of Claudia's words while she rushed to retrieve it. She dumped the clarinet halves back on the bed and pressed the receiver to her ear. "He does … honest," Claudia said.

"What?" Was Claudia talking about Alex? "I dropped the phone. What did you say?"

"I said Alex really does like you."

There was a satisfied smirk in Claudia's voice. Jenny's heart thudded an erratic rhythm against her ribcage. "So, did you get caught?" she asked abruptly.

"When?"

"When you snuck out. Did they catch you?"

"No way! They never knew a thing."

"How did you do it?" Jenny asked. Her heart continued to pound out a warning. *Don't do it, don't do it. You'll get caught.*

"Are they home?" Claudia asked.

"Only Marianne. Why?"

Claudia yawned loudly, but there was an underlying note of pent-up excitement, even in the yawn and definitely in her words. "Would she tell?"

"I don't know. Anyway, they'd figure something was up when they got home and I wasn't here." Still her mind raced at the possibility. She did have options.

"Not if you were back by then. How long will they be gone?"

Her spirits sank. "I don't know. They are hard to predict."

"What if you wait until they're asleep—do they ever check on you in the middle of the night?"

"I'm not a baby!"

"That's not what I meant. I thought they might because of the grounding."

"I don't think so." Jenny stood up and began to pace while she thought about Claudia's question. They sort of trusted her not to sneak out, and so maybe they wouldn't think to check up on her. Though the thought pleased her, she also felt guilty somehow.

"That's good! How about tonight?"

"I don't know. If they found out, I could be grounded for the rest of my life." She halted in front of her sister's dresser and stared at the face in the mirror, familiar and unfamiliar all at once. The eyes were red and the hair disheveled. She would have to do some work on herself if she did the unthinkable. What had at first seemed like a wild idea was starting to seem almost doable. Adrenaline surged through every pore in Jenny's body at the prospect.

"How long are you grounded for?"

"Forever, almost." At least that was how Jenny felt.

"All right then—what do you have to lose?"

"I'm too much of a coward," Jenny said. She couldn't do it.

"No, you're not." Claudia's tone was firm, insistent. She no longer hid her excitement, which struck an answering chord in Jenny, but also a warning note. "You've changed, Jenny Jenkins. Haven't you noticed?"

CHAPTER TWENTY-SEVEN

Joy leaned over the railing to stare down into the gulf. She had learned to appreciate this house, in spite of all the ways it reminded her of Carolyn. Or perhaps what she loved so much was the setting. No, it was both. The house with its pale yellow paint perching like a delicate bird on its stilts. The lofty, sun-filled rooms. Even the elaborate décor, though Joy would have opted for something less formal, more homey. The view took her breath away each and every time she allowed it to, and she vowed to let it more often in the future. She chided herself for getting caught up in the troubles of the moment too often, in forgetting to experience the wonder of sea and sky. There had been a brief rain this afternoon, and the air had that just-washed feeling she loved.

At moments like this, she had to wonder how anyone could not believe in a master plan, in a creator. Yet, when she thought of her parents—and the things God allowed to happen to them—it was just as impossible to believe fully. All her life, she had vacillated between the extremes—the impossibility of believing and the emptiness of not believing. Not all her life, she corrected herself, just all her adult life. Since she was sixteen and the unimaginable became her reality.

She and Ray had a dinner date tonight. Unlike most couples she knew, she was almost always dressed and ready to go before Ray. Not that he was overly vain. No, it was just that Joy was quick, had always been quick in selecting a garment and applying a minimal amount of makeup. Often just lipstick, or perhaps a quick brush with a loose powder, a touch of mascara for a special occasion. She'd been wearing a vanilla-scented perfume lately, wanting to smell nice for him … not that he noticed.

Perhaps she should strive to do more to bring out her better features—Acadia claimed Joy had plenty of those, though Joy herself was none too sure. With Acadia's help, Joy could probably look a bit more together. Her fashion sense, however, was not what weighed on her mind this evening.

JOY AFTER NOON

The sun hung low in the sky, a huge orange globe, the clouds over the gulf tinted a rosy peach. How wondrous, and how she loved this time of day. A funnel cloud took shape, silvery violet against a vivid blue sky. The water was green, almost emerald, and the path down the center of the ocean was gold, like a road to eternity. Were her parents there, waiting for her? Could they see her now, at this very minute, urging her to make the right choices in life, rejoicing or agonizing over her marriage to Ray? Could they see what lay ahead for her even though she could not?

She wished she had no more on her mind than the anticipation of a rare evening out with her husband. Her love. She thought back to their honeymoon and how the infinite possibilities had seemed to stretch out before her, like the golden trail, which was turning faintly rosy now, leading through the gulf, going where? He was so handsome, so perfect, it had seemed to her then. Incapable of infidelity, of forgetting his daughters' recitals or concerts. Without imperfections, with which she herself abounded. If he didn't chime in with appreciative laughter or rejoinders when she referred to characters from literature or movie classics, she'd assumed her references to be unworthy rather than that he'd failed to recognize them altogether. Now that she knew him better, as she began to see through the strong, silent exterior to the flawed but still wonderful man beneath, she loved him no less, maybe even more. Tonight she would tell him her decision to stop teaching. She had to, or she might never muster the courage.

Where the waves broke, the water melded into jade green, brilliant with white foam. Jade. Long ago, she'd once imagined naming a daughter Jade—a color she liked, liked the sound of the word too, which conjured up images of clarity and beauty. Mainly she liked the word because it reminded her of her father. Might she and Ray someday have a child together? Crazy, that she had been too timid, too unsure of herself to bring the matter up. Pathetic.

She thought back to her first experience with jade. Her dad had a letter opener that he used each day when the mail arrived. The letter opener, which looked like a fancy knife, had a beautiful green insert in the handle. He let Joy play with it, cautioning her to be very careful. "It's as sharp as a knife," he would say. "Don't tell your mother. This is our secret."

"Why is it so green, Daddy?"

"It's very special. I'll leave it to you when I die."

Joy had been alarmed. "You're not going to die, are you, Daddy?"

156

"Not for a long, long time. Not until you're an old woman."

She giggled at that, unable to envision herself as an old woman.

In high school band, she had worked hard selling personalized greeting cards as part of a fund raiser for new uniforms. Her prize, based on points accumulated, was to be a real jade bracelet. How excited she'd been! When the gifts arrived, her bracelet wasn't there. "It's on back order," the band director said.

Crestfallen, she sat quietly in her hard chair while, around her, the other students smiled over their winnings. After that, she asked him daily for a time. Then the calamity struck, wiping the bracelet from her mind. Eventually she remembered, asked about it one day much later. But so much had happened in the interim. The band director had been replaced with another. "Well, yes," the new director said. "That came in. That bracelet was lying around here for a long time. I don't know what became of it."

And that was that. The bracelet didn't really matter by then. Besides, she had the jade letter opener she could never bring herself to use. If she had gotten the bracelet, she might not have been brave enough to wear it, to face the pain.

Joy shivered. She would need a heavier sweater tonight. One lone navy umbrella remained on the beach at this hour, its spine broken so that it leaned precariously. Like the victim of a violent crime, the umbrella would not survive for long.

Gulls squawked as they headed into the waves in search of dinner. Joy's mind remained on her parents. Dad died instantly, but Mama had lingered on for a day and a half. Long enough for Joy's hope to be sparked. And then dashed. Broken. Oh, how she wished they were here with her now, so she could ask them for advice. If not here, somewhere in this world … somewhere reachable by phone. But they were not, and she would have to proceed alone.

Joy lifted her eyes to the heavens to send up a plea for help.

"Ready?" Ray came up behind her, and she swung around to face him. He looked handsome, as always, in his khakis and crisp white shirt, a yellow sweater thrown casually over one shoulder. Tired, though, and strained. Her parents would have loved Ray, would have been thrilled for Joy at finding him. Wouldn't they?

"Yes," she said, her heart thudding—the time had come. "I just need to grab a sweater."

"Are you sure you're okay with eating here?" Ray asked.

Her head spun with the news she was about to break, with the words she would use, so that she almost missed his tone, which was faintly apologetic. She hadn't eaten here before, but Reds 'n Ribs looked interesting enough. "Of course. Why wouldn't I be?"

"No reason."

Before dating Ray, Joy hadn't eaten out all that often. Even though she rarely cooked, she made do at her apartment with microwavable dinners, pot pies, and sandwiches. She didn't enjoy eating alone in a restaurant, and she didn't appreciate cooking enough to go to the effort for herself. Occasionally she baked a pan of cornbread, devouring it greedily with cold buttermilk, a dish her mother used to prepare. Joy had loved the combination of the warm bread and tangy milk.

Joy was sixteen the year everything changed. Before that, life stretched out in front of her like the Big Muddy, which took the traveler north toward Chicago or south all the way to New Orleans—the options seemed limitless. The river vanished into the horizon so that she could only imagine what lay ahead. And mostly she didn't do that. Most of the time she was too caught up in the present even to conceive of a world where everything she knew and trusted and counted on could be wiped out in one fell swoop. Until it was. Although the joy drained from her, eventually Joy would go north to school, and yet still wind up here, on the Gulf.

She closed in, shut people out, not really allowing herself to love or hope again. Not until Ray. How would she ever be able to go back to that solitary existence if things with Ray didn't work out? A sudden presentiment swept through Joy with such intensity that she was no longer sure she wanted to say what she had resolved to say. Yet, her premonitions had never proven to be justified in the past. When the worst did happen, she'd had no warning whatsoever. She believed in sacrifice, didn't she? If she could save her marriage, virtually any sacrifice would be merited.

Together they mounted a gangplank entrance into a nautical-themed restaurant of tantalizing, if fishy, smells and casual ambience. The host approached, a middle-aged, balding man with a tidy beard and a broad smile. "Inside or out?"

Several families with noisy kids populated the larger tables inside. Glancing toward the outside seating area, Joy spotted only one couple, who leaned together across the picnic table to clasp hands. Outside would be quieter, and she and Ray both had sweaters.

Almost simultaneously she and Ray said, "Outside."

They smiled at each other. "It will be quieter out there, and I have something to tell you," he said.

She was startled, as she'd been on the verge of saying the same thing. "You do?"

"Yes."

The host indicated a choice of tables, and Joy selected the one farthest from the courting couple. She and Ray slid into opposite sides of the red picnic table, and their host handed each of them a large plastic-coated menu.

What could his news be? Nothing good, judging from his face. "I have something to tell you too," she said.

"Oh?" He quirked an eyebrow. "Ladies first."

Now that he was staring at her, she stalled, changed the subject. "Why were you so—so concerned about whether I'd be okay with this restaurant?" She strove for a teasing tone. "Is there something I should know?"

A glimmer of a shadow passed behind his eyes, and his jaw tightened, just perceptibly. "Carolyn never wanted to eat here."

He mentioned his first wife by name so rarely that the word fell from his lips like fish scales. Joy was struck speechless for a moment. "Why not?" she asked at last.

"Not fancy enough, I guess."

"I like that about it," Joy said. "What's good here?"

"The royal reds, of course."

"Would you believe I've never tried them?"

Ray gawked in mock horror. "What? Then we definitely must have them today. They melt in your mouth, I promise."

"Okay."

"But—I have to warn you—you have to peel them yourself, and your fingers will smell like shrimp for hours, maybe days to come."

"You'll have to show me how," Joy said. "I'm pretty clumsy."

"No worries." Ray ordered for them both.

Still stalling, Joy launched into a story about the first time she ate shrimp cocktail, and Ray reciprocated with stories of boyhood fishing excursions and fish grilled over a campfire. The waiter showed up with platters of shrimp before Joy had gotten around to her announcement. "Wow, that was fast," she said.

"They must have known we were coming."

"All right. So how does this work?"

Ray demonstrated with a large red shrimp and a tiny fork. Joy tried to follow suit, and juice from the shrimp squirted directly into Ray's face.

He rubbed his eyes.

"Oh, no!" Joy said. "I told you I was clumsy—did I get you right in the eye?"

"No, I think you barely missed. What do you say I do the peeling, and you just enjoy yourself?"

"Should I be grateful or offended? I promise I'll be more careful with the next one."

Ray laughed. "Let me get my sunglasses first. They'll act as a shield." A strong breeze lifted Joy's napkin and carried it in the direction of the romancing couple, who had abandoned their hand holding in favor of rib consumption. She chased the red paper napkin down and managed to retrieve it just as it started to soar again.

Joy tackled a second shrimp and did a little better this time. "Do you eat this part?" She indicated the flesh clinging to the head.

"I don't," Ray said. He dipped a clean headless piece in the drawn butter and, leaning toward Joy, placed it directly in her mouth.

His fingers brushed her lips, and she shivered with the intimacy of the gesture. "Oh, my," she murmured when she'd swallowed the succulent morsel.

"Told you," Ray said. "I'm glad you like it. Now, what were you going to tell me?"

"Let's eat first," Joy said. "I can barely eat and carry on a conversation, much less peel shrimp, eat, and talk."

The jovial Ray had vanished, though, and they ate in silence for a time. Finally she blurted, "I've decided to quit working."

"What?" Ray set down the shrimp he was peeling and stared at Joy. "Why?"

She sucked in a sharp breath. She'd planned this speech—how to make it sound as if she was making the decision entirely for herself and not for him. Putting Ray on a guilt trip would defeat the whole purpose. More than anything in the world, she wanted to make him happy. Her planned arguments evaporated now that she'd taken the plunge, and she searched for one reasonable explanation. "I feel like I've been working for the wrong reasons."

"What do you mean?" Ray's face was ashen, so she hurried to explain, to reassure him, to make him see.

Some of her arguments were coming back to her. Yet, the reasons which seemed so logical when she rehearsed them in her head felt flat even before she voiced them. "I mean, you make plenty of money at the bank. So it's not like we need the money. Not like some of the couples we know who really have no choice."

Ray's face turned even whiter as she spoke. She was making a dreadful botch of this, but she was in too deep to stop treading water. She had to keep on.

"What I'm trying to say is I'm not all that happy at work anyway. It's not really satisfying lately, and my priorities are constantly getting all muddled. So I'm not doing anything very well. Getting a PhD and spending so much time doing research made me think I had to get tenure, or I'd be a failure. Really, though, they're sunk costs."

Ray's face had grown so still, so lacking in the relief and joy she'd hoped to see there, she faltered, felt herself sinking, the waters closing in over her. "You know what sunk costs are?" she stammered, and then felt more foolish than ever.

Of course, he knew what sunk costs were. He was a bank executive after all. The truth slammed into her. Their marriage was a sunk cost in his mind. A mistake he needed to move on past, so the last thing he needed was for her to quit her job and become totally dependent on him. He would never love her the way he'd loved Carolyn, and quitting her job wouldn't make one whit of difference. He had seen this even if she had not. Suddenly the smell of the delicious shrimp was faintly nauseating.

She would not beg. She straightened her shoulders and asked, "What were you going to tell me?"

His jaw tightened, and he started to speak, then closed his mouth again. The waiter approached. "Are you Mr. Jenkins?"

161

"Yes. Yes, I am."

"You have a phone call. You can take it inside."

Ray hesitated for a second until Joy said, "It's all right. Go ahead and take the call."

"Please take a message," Ray said to the waiter, and Joy's heart clenched in dread at what Ray was about to tell her that was so important he couldn't be distracted. His jaw tensed again, as if a steel ball was shifting positions inside his mouth. "You really want to quit your job?" he asked.

Joy nodded wordlessly, suddenly not sure that she did. What if she quit her job and their marriage fell apart anyway—where would she be then?

"Is there something else? Tell me, Joy."

The thing she needed to say the most was how insecure she'd been about his love for her. She couldn't tell him, not now. She shook her head. "I can't. I'm sorry, it's nothing."

Nothing and everything. "Is it the job? You don't really want to quit?" He asked this with an odd expression, almost hopeful. Was he hopeful that she did or that she didn't? She couldn't read him.

She picked up a shrimp and ripped the head off. Or was it the tail? She wasn't sure what she was doing. With her fingers she dug out the brownish gunk and tossed it into the bucket, vaguely aware that she was getting almost as much under her fingernails as in the bucket.

She answered honestly. "I don't even know how I feel about working, or not working anymore."

"Then what?"

They were alone out here. She wasn't sure when the rib-eating, hand-holding couple had left, but she was glad they were gone. It was never going to be easy to say what needed to be said, but she would not let their marriage dissolve without Ray's hearing the truth from her once. "I just—I just wanted you to love me. Like you loved her," she said, her voice little more than a whisper.

"Like I loved who?"

"Carolyn."

He stared at Joy as though the name was unfamiliar to him. At last he spoke. "I didn't love Carolyn." He hesitated and then corrected himself quickly. "I mean—I suppose I loved her once, in a way. She was the mother of my girls, but I never loved her like I love you." His face closed, and he picked up a shrimp and began to peel it.

Her heart leapt. She really, really wanted to believe him, but all she could see in her mind was that box and its contents—the transparent red garment, the letter. She picked up another shrimp though the last one lay uneaten and half peeled in her plate. "I found the box," she said, not meeting his eyes.

Ray stared at her for a moment. "What box?"

They both put down their shrimp and stared at each other.

"The box with the letter and—and the red teddy." Her words flew out in a rush, and she was glad the lighting was dim out here so he couldn't see the bright flush of her face and throat.

"What?" He rose from his seat and, leaning across the table, grasped her shoulders, none too gently. "What are you talking about?"

"I'm sorry. I know I shouldn't have opened it, but—I—"

Ray's face darkened and his jaw clenched. "I repeat—what are you talking about?"

"You really don't know?"

"I really don't."

"I'll show you," she said, brave now because she was facing the truth head on. "When we get home."

"Now," he said. "Let's go now."

As they passed by the waiter, Joy remembered the phone call. "Did you have a message for us—for Mr. Jenkins?" she asked.

"No. They hung up before I got back."

They drove in silence. The angles of Ray's face—of chin and brow—were harsh, his eyes grim, his mouth a straight line. Joy had no idea what he was thinking. Her heart raced. Was she making her worst mistake yet—bringing the past back to him so acutely when she'd only wanted to put it behind him?

She dropped her face into her hands as they pulled into the driveway. The scent of shrimp reminded her of the red teddy. It too had smelled faintly fishy, or had she imagined the odor of sex? How long could an odor live in a garment or in the mind? Would Ray smell it … and remember?

She led him briskly, her feet keeping time to her heartbeat, toward the pantry. His gaze followed her as she dragged a kitchen chair to reach a high shelf in the closet, as she pushed through old boxes, glassless photo frames, plastic containers with mismatched lids. At last she found what she was looking for. She pulled the cigar box down, silently handed it to him.

A chill passed through her limbs while he slowly opened the box, as though expecting a coiled serpent inside.

He lifted the blood-red, flimsy fabric, and Carolyn's musky scent rose. Suddenly nauseated, Joy wanted to flee, to see no more. Instead she stood frozen, eyes glued to Ray's face, steeling herself to observe what coils lay beneath, to reveal the serpent in its entirety. Now it was Ray who froze. Joy who pushed ahead.

"The letter," she whispered, and she lifted the envelope and handed it to him. *My dearest, my darling, my only love for all eternity, I can taste you as I write this, can sense your presence always with me, your smell, your touch …*

Ray's face flushed a deep red, and Joy knew she'd been wrong to show him. This reminder was more than he could bear. They stood in silence for seconds that dragged into years. Joy was lost in the sea of Ray's emotion, fighting to breathe, to reach the surface.

He spoke at last. "I never gave her this," he said.

Her relief morphed into happiness, followed by shame and sorrow.

"I'm sorry," she said. They spoke in hushed tones—either because they didn't want to alert the girls to their presence or simply because of the nature of the revelations, she wasn't sure which.

"It's okay. I knew."

"You knew? You've seen the letter before?"

"No. Not that. Not this. But I knew there was another man. A lover."

"What happened to him? To them?"

He still held the letter. Carefully he folded it and returned it to the box. He lay the red garment back on top, and replaced the box on the shelf.

Joy had unleashed all the demons, and they couldn't be shoved back into the box now, into their hiding place deep in the pantry of Ray's nightmares. Still they could try, she supposed.

He turned to Joy and pulled her to him. He kissed her lips, and his tasted of salt. Was he crying for Carolyn? "Never think I love you less," he said. "Whatever happens, never think that."

Was it possible he spoke truth? And if so, was she capable of hearing it, of comprehending it? Slowly she nodded, filled with wonder.

"What?" he said, drawing back to look at her.

"I can't help it. I'm just so happy, though I shouldn't be—"

He interrupted her words with another kiss, the salt of her tears mingling with his.

"There's more," he said. "I have to show you something else."

His face turned to stone again, the tenderness vanishing as if the moments of joy had been only a dream. "Get in the car," he said. "I'll take you there."

Joy hesitated, wondering if she should check on the girls first. Then again, they were teenagers, after all. And she was both troubled and curious to see what had effected this change in Ray.

CHAPTER TWENTY-EIGHT

They drove in silence out toward Point Mildred, a narrow peninsula of land to the west of Sugar Sands, less than a hundred yards wide in places and about a mile and a half long. They drove past the upscale condo associations and club houses, the golf course, the cottages and holiday homes, until the drive was dark and lonely, the only sound that of the hum of the car. Then they were out of the car, standing near the edge of the black water, listening to the waves crash into shore. In the distance, the faint glow of a light from an oil rig. Nothing else.

Carolyn had drowned. Everyone knew this. It had been a terrible accident, but there had been a hushed quality about the incident too. Had she killed herself? Joy had heard rumors, but she'd dismissed them as unworthy gossip. Someone like Carolyn would never take her own life.

"It happened in the middle of the night," he said, so softly she could barely hear. "You asked me what happened to Carolyn and her lover. He left her. He was the only man Carolyn really loved, or who loved her the way she wanted. She longed for a fairy tale romance—something I couldn't give her. I wasn't her prince." He fell silent, and they watched the waves crashing in, alternating between anger and passion in their foamy depths.

"And you think he was—her prince, I mean?"

"I suppose. Perhaps if we'd divorced and she'd married him, they could have been happy. Or maybe the scandal, the illicit nature of it all, was what made the affair so thrilling for her."

"Who was he? I never heard this part. Not even a rumor."

"Oh, there were rumors. A few. The elders kept everything pretty quiet. Carolyn's lover was married too. A youth minister actually, supposed to be setting an example for the youth, for our girls. That's why no one thought anything was wrong—myself included—when they spent time together. At least in the beginning, I thought their meetings were about the girls. And then they started spending time together without the girls …"

"How awful for you, and for Jenny and Marianne—did they know?"

"I don't think so."

Joy remembered a youth minister who moved away suddenly, and a quick flash of memory jarred her. Of glances exchanged between some of the church ladies when someone entered. Could that someone have been Ray? Joy tried to dredge up the memory more clearly. His name was Karl, she remembered suddenly. She hadn't probed at the time, had not known the minister well, having no children of her own, had not known Ray then at all. "Is that why we don't have a separate youth minister anymore?"

"That … and finances. He was asked to leave, and he did. First he tried to get Carolyn to come with him. To leave me. She almost did. She told me she was going to, but at the last minute she changed her mind, or he did. I'm not sure which." He fell silent, and again Joy waited. How difficult this confession must be for hm.

When he finally spoke, the immense sadness in his voice strained her heart. How she ached for him, even before his words registered. "This wasn't the first time she'd cheated. When she was in labor with Marianne, she told me something awful. Something I've never shared with another living soul." He grew quiet, and Joy could sense, almost see, the shudder travelling through the long, lean frame she loved so much. She knew what he was going to say before he spoke. "She said Marianne wasn't mine. She said she'd been looking for someone to appreciate her, to love her the way she deserved."

"Who's Marianne's father, then?"

"She said I didn't know him. His name was James, and he had red hair. I told myself she was lying, that she made up the whole thing to hurt me. When Marianne was born and her hair was—you know—I asked her about James again, and she laughed in my face. The affair hadn't meant anything, she said. She had only been searching. I believed her. But there were others after that, and I don't think she loved any of them. Not until Karl."

An owl hooted in the distance, and still the waves pounded. "This is where *it* happened," he said. "You see, don't you? Carolyn needed so much adulation, and I was never enough for her. Could never praise her enough, appreciate her enough, love her enough. I tried. Not often, but occasionally. The trouble, I think, was that when I did, I felt like I was *acting*, and that she could see right through the performance. So I didn't try enough … hard enough … or often enough. I let her down."

"Then why did you marry her in the first place? I mean—you must have loved her once."

"I did, in the beginning. At least I thought I did, convinced myself I did. Looking back, I'm not so sure. I was infatuated. But I think my infatuation was as much with Hank and Lillian and their lifestyle as it was with Carolyn." He paused, bent over to pick up an empty shell, then tossed it long and hard into the waves. "I remember the first Christmas I spent with Lillian and Hank in their home. How grand their house seemed to a boy from the other side of the tracks. How polished and perfect, like Lillian herself. Like Carolyn.

"Funny, I would have said I only had eyes for Carolyn that day. And yet I cannot remember for the life of me what she was wearing. But I can see her mother so vividly, right down to the earrings that caught the light when she turned her head. Baubles, they were, like the lights on the enormous Christmas tree. She had on this soft cashmere sweater, blood red with a matching scarf draped elegantly over one shoulder. Her slacks were a shade of soft gold that glimmered when she moved … and she moved like a queen. She asked me what I was planning to do with my life.

"I told her I didn't know. I felt so young and foolish. Hank was the one who suggested banking. I was flattered that he talked to me like an equal and not like the irresponsible college student I was. All I wanted was to be worthy of this man who showed me respect for what I might become someday." Ray frowned, a faraway look in the eyes Joy loved so well. "No, that isn't entirely true. I also wanted what Hank had. I guess it was greed, pure and simple, that made me long for a house like theirs, a poised wife like Lillian, even the tree with its gifts wrapped and stacked so artistically they could have been empty inside—like a staged set for a *House Beautiful* shoot or a movie."

"You're being too hard on yourself," Joy said. "It's normal to be lured by beauty. By perfection, and by the promise of the kind of life most people can only dream of."

"There was that. To be honest, I think I was a little in love with the idea of being in love. That night, after her parents went to bed, Carolyn and I went outside and walked under the blanket of stars. Their lawn, if you could call it that, felt like a formal garden to me, with rows of manicured shrubs and plants, with stone benches and replicas of Greek statues. We sat next to one of the goddess Athena. I knew Carolyn wanted me to kiss her, so I did. I think we kissed more in those early days of our courtship than we did in all our years of married life."

The thought of him kissing Carolyn still hurt, and Ray must have sensed her pain for he slipped an arm around her shoulders, squeezed gently. She couldn't be jealous, not of the real Carolyn, only of his youthful image of her. Joy could read Ray now, could see through the stony face to the pain beneath and she ached for him. What a fool she'd been, reading him so wrong, so completely wrong on every front. "I'm sorry," she said.

"The thing is ... she never got over Karl. She blamed me for not being him, for not loving her the way ..." He broke off. "It was all my fault."

"No, it wasn't," Joy said. "I felt that way too—after my parents died. I blamed myself for so many things. And, worse, I blamed God."

He reached for her hand, and his was dry and warm, despite the chill of the night. "Why did you blame yourself?"

As she sought the words to answer, she realized her experience and his weren't the same at all. She blamed herself—this much was the same—for being mean to them at times, for not telling them how much she loved them. But she did love them. She loved them so much ... she hadn't realized how much until they were gone. "I never told them how I felt," she said at last.

"They died in a car wreck?"

"No. I know I told you that—I'm sorry I lied." Joy sucked in a deep breath. "The story I told you is what I always tell people when they ask. Fewer questions that way. It's not what really happened. They were shot. I don't like to talk about it."

"I'm so sorry. I understand if you don't want to tell me."

"No, I do. I need to tell you, and I should have told you sooner. I should never have lied to you. They were out doing good—they were such ridiculous do-gooders—in a bad neighborhood—isn't that too funny?" Joy laughed. She stopped when Ray didn't join in her laughter. "There were a bunch of gangs in that neighborhood, and there had been some violence recently. But nothing like what happened that day. When the shooting started, everyone in the house went face down on the floor. There were others shot. My parents were the only ones who—who died. They weren't fast enough, they weren't prepared."

"Did they catch the shooters?"

"Nope. It was a drive-by. They tried. The cops were all over the place for a while. Eventually, they let the investigation go."

"Oh, Joy." Ray put his arm around her, and she shuddered into his embrace.

How did this turn into her story? Ray came here to tell her about Carolyn. She needed—they both needed—to put Carolyn behind them. She could come to terms with her parents' killers later. Somehow she now knew she could.

"Still, it's not as bad as drowning. At least in some ways—" What was she trying to say, or not to say?

"She didn't like to swim," he said. "Not even in the daytime."

What was he not saying? That Carolyn's death wasn't an accident? Her parents' death had been tragic, yes, devastating to her. But it *had* been an accident. Some small comfort in that.

Looking past Ray's shoulder out into the darkness, Joy could envision Carolyn's lovely pale skin, gleaming in the moonlight as she swam out deeper and deeper until she hadn't the strength to get back to shore, even if she tried. Did she try? Did she change her mind at the last minute, before the ocean claimed her? Perhaps she saw her life clearly then, the way they say you do when you face death. Perhaps she realized how much she was giving up, and for what? Carolyn wanted perfection, and perfection was not to be found. Not in this life. Not for Joy and not even for Carolyn. And yet she had so much. Surely she'd seen that. In her last breaths surely she'd asked for forgiveness.

Joy shivered, and he pulled her closer against him. "Do you suppose we could find something open at this hour?" she asked. "For a cup of hot chocolate?"

As they drove away, she looked back one last time. The vision of Carolyn, pale and ghostly in the black waters—the woman who had haunted Joy for so long— morphed from domestic splendor to dark despair as she faded from view … at last.

CHAPTER TWENTY-NINE

Jenny lay flat on her back in bed, staring at the ceiling and then at the bedroom walls that were so bare of posters. And personality. "I LOVE ROCK N ROLL!" she shouted, not caring who heard. When she squeezed her eyes shut, she could see the black and white poster of Joan Jett and her band so plainly, as if it were right there with her instead of a million miles away on Claudia's wall. She could feel the rhythm of the song

Marianne tapped on her door and popped her reddish gold head inside, followed by her whole leotard-clad self. "What did she say?"

"Nothing much."

"Come on, you can tell me. I'm your sister." Marianne pronounced the word like being sisters really meant something to her, and maybe it did. Jenny just didn't know who to trust anymore.

"She just wanted to be sure I hadn't ratted on her, okay?"

"And?"

Jenny looked into Marianne's eyes, trying to read them. They were unfathomable, like a cat's. Curiosity surely, maybe genuine interest, but something else too. Lurking deep behind the greenish yellow-flecked orbs. Was Marianne jealous? She remembered their earlier conversation.

"She wants me to sneak out tonight," she blurted.

"Are you going to?" Now the eyes shone almost gold, bright with pent-up excitement, as if she could live this adventure vicariously through Jenny.

"Of course not," Jenny said, and then, "Would you?"

Marianne shrugged her narrow shoulders. "You only live once."

"You won't tell if I do?"

Marianne crossed her heart, and Jenny noticed that Marianne's chest wasn't quite as flat as it used to be. Was Marianne changing also?

"You want to come with me?" Jenny asked on a sudden whim, not sure how Claudia would react to Marianne's presence, or Marianne to Claudia.

The possibility struck her that Alex might fall for Marianne, who was more beautiful, more talented, and closer to his age. She held her breath while she waited for Marianne's reply.

"No, I've got too much to do," Marianne said. "Besides, she's your friend, not mine."

Jenny flushed with guilt mingled with relief. She wondered if Marianne had sensed her second thoughts about the invitation. "Are you sure?"

"I'm sure. But you go and have fun. I'll cover for you if I need to."

"Thank you!" Jenny sprang from the bed to hug her sister. "You're the best."

Later, when Marianne had gone and Jenny had called Claudia, Jenny searched her wardrobe for the perfect thing to wear. She wondered what Claudia was wearing, thought about calling her back to ask. But Claudia had seemed kind of strange when Jenny phoned to tell her she was sneaking out.

"That's *mah-ve-lous*," Claudia had drawled, sounding more sarcastic than thrilled. "Be ready in five."

Claudia was so pretty, so curvy and—well, sort of sexy. Jenny flushed. Not that Claudia was drop-dead gorgeous like her brother. Still, Jenny could imagine guys reacting to her much the way she reacted to Alex. Jenny, on the other hand, was … well … just plain boring Jenny. There was no way Alex really liked her. His sister had used her. Again.

Jenny figured it was literally impossible for Alex to get there in five minutes, but still she kept peering out to see if he was pulling up.

"What's wrong?" Marianne asked when Jenny raced between the living room and her bedroom for the fourth time. "Oh, I don't know what to wear, and he could be here any minute."

"Let's see." Marianne hustled over to Jenny's closet and slapped quickly through the hanging clothes. She glanced at the stack of jeans, started to pick up a pair, then spun on her toes, ballerina style. "I've got it. Follow me."

"Okay, but hurry."

So like Marianne to organize her clothes to the umpteenth degree, with sections of tops grouped by color and style, skirts by length and color, dresses and pants in their own sections. As far back as Jenny could remember, Marianne had worn size zero. Marianne reached for one of these, a tiny but stretchy black number Jenny couldn't remember ever seeing Marianne wear.

"Try this on," Marianne ordered.

"Are you kidding? That thing wouldn't fit on my big toe," Jenny protested but she was pulling off her jeans and pulling on the little skirt even as she spoke.

Though a tight fit, the fabric stretched enough to slide over her not-so-skinny hips. She patted her belly. "I look ridiculous and fat, don't I?"

Without waiting for a reply, she began, hurriedly, to work the skirt back down over her thighs. Marianne put out a hand to stop her. "No, you look sensational. Now we just need to find you the right top." Marianne went to a section of pull-over tops and here too she located one of a clingy, stretchy material. The shirt was a soft mint green with a boat neckline

Jenny sighed in protest. "I know I'm going to look fat in that. Don't you think something loose of my own would be better to cover my gut?"

"You are not fat," Marianne said. "I don't know where you got that idea. Now just put this top on so I can see if it works with your coloring the way I think it will."

A faint honk caught her attention, and she ran to the window again. Still no sign of Alex's car. Hurrying back to Marianne, Jenny caught a glimpse of herself in a decorative mirror that hung in the hallway. Was that flushed teenager really her?

She slowed her pace and, with a trace of dignity, returned to her sister. "What do you *really* think?"

"Turn around," Marianne instructed.

Jenny spun around, nearly losing her balance and toppling breathlessly onto Marianne's tidy bed. "I don't think I have a career as a model, do you?"

"You never know … you look great."

"Really?" Jenny was almost afraid to look in Marianne's full-length mirror, but she did so now. The girl she saw wasn't petite like Marianne or sexy like Claudia—not bad, though—fresh-faced and bright-eyed and way too eager.

This time the honk was definitely nearby, so she hugged Marianne and fled, heart racing wildly, toward the driveway, toward Alex's car.

CHAPTER THIRTY

Joy inhaled the aroma of bacon and waffles. How nice to be the only customers in Waffle House at this hour. No cigarette smoke, which was usually the downside. Ray leaned across the table and clasped Joy's hands in his larger ones. Warmed by his touch and by the revelations of the evening—some sad, but others so reassuring—Joy knew this was a moment in life she would remember always.

The hot chocolate arrived, steaming and topped with a liberal swirl of whipped cream, and Ray released her hands. While she waited for the chocolate to cool, she scooped the cream off with her spoon and indulged. Ray lifted his cup to his lips and sipped.

"How can you do that?" Joy said. "Doesn't it burn your mouth?"

Ray shrugged. "A little."

"Now you'll have that sandpaper feeling for days. I know I would if I drank it that hot."

"Joy, I made a lot of mistakes with Carolyn. And I've been on the verge of making them all over again."

His words startled her. "What do you mean?" Joy blew on a spoonful of hot chocolate and took a tentative sip. Still too hot for her. She set the spoon down and waited. Strange, how she'd spent so much time wanting to be more like Carolyn, and now she cringed at the thought of being like her in any way.

"I never told her what she needed to hear, and I've been failing you in the same way. I knew what she wanted to hear; saying the words, however, would have rung false. In our case ... I love you so much, I didn't think words were necessary."

Joy picked up her cup, swirled the liquid while she thought, sloshing a bit over the top. She savored these words from his lips, words she had craved for so long. Still she knew there would come a time when she needed to hear them again. She couldn't let him off too easily.

"Women always need to hear the words," she said. "Doesn't everyone?"

"I know that now. I'm sorry—I've been a fool."

Joy shook her head. "Not just you. I've been afraid to ask you what's going on. It's my fault too."

Ray drained his cup and set it down.

"I can't believe you've finished yours before I took the first sip." She laughed, a little nervously. "There's something else, something you were going to tell me earlier. I almost forgot."

"There is."

She reached out to clasp his hands this time. Here in the bright warmth of the small diner, she could handle whatever was coming. She thought back to the dark chill of the beach, the ghost of Carolyn they'd left behind. All seemed possible to her at this moment in time. If Ray was fearful, she would be strong. Knowing he loved her, she *could* be strong. Strong enough for them both, if need be.

"I'm in trouble—we're all in trouble—at work. The bank is in dire straits, has been since the merger really. I never thought that merger was a good idea, but I had no idea just how bad the deal would turn out."

At his words, Joy remembered the phone call that came when they were at the restaurant, the caller who'd hung up before the waiter got back. "Is that what the phone call was about? What could be so urgent they would run us down at dinner?"

The door opened, and a group of laughing, chattering teenagers entered. The waitress Karla called to the newcomers, "Sit anywhere." She sauntered back to Ray and Joy's booth. "Can I get you something else—before I get swamped?"

Joy realized she had eaten very few of the shrimp at Reds 'n Ribs. She glanced at Ray. "You know what? I'm starving. How about you?"

He shook his head. "No, but you go ahead and order something."

Joy hesitated and glanced toward the group of teenagers, then turned to Ray. "Or would you rather go somewhere else to talk?"

"They're on spring break," Karla said, shaking her head. "Seems earlier every year."

Four girls and two guys squeezed into a booth for four at the other end of the diner.

"You haven't even finished your chocolate," Ray pointed out. "We can talk here as well as anywhere."

"They won't bother you," Karla said. "I'll keep them under control."

Hunger won. "Could I get a patty melt and fries?"

"It comes on rye. Is that okay?"

"Perfect." Her chocolate had cooled enough to drink, so she gulped it down while Ray talked. He spoke of shady accounting, pressure from higher up, and personal finances, of decisions and indecision and errors. Errors of accounting, of judgment, of choice. Of pushing the limits of the accounting rules until they strained and finally burst.

Joy swirled the chocolate syrup in the bottom of her cup, surprised to find it empty. She had barely tasted the beverage. "Have you tried talking to Brendan Glass? Does he know how you feel?"

"He knows. I've wanted to be more open with you than I ever could be with Carolyn. Then this whole mess came up, and I was ashamed to tell you. I didn't want you to think less of me."

"I wouldn't—I'd never—"

He held up his hand. "Don't be so sure. Not until you've heard everything. Good, bad, and ugly."

I've heard enough, she wanted to say. Ray's expression indicated he had not yet finished, so she clamped her mouth shut and waited.

"I wanted to spare you. I thought I could sort the mess out on my own. When Sarah Kinsey called, all I could think was what the scandal would mean for you and the girls if everything came out—the faulty accounting, the lies to the shareholders, the hidden reasons for the merger. Things I didn't even know about myself at the time, like how much money some of the execs pocketed in the process."

She had to ask. "But not you?"

"Not me." He sighed. "If I go public now, I'll have to quit. And we don't have much in savings to fall back on."

Joy stared at him, astonished. The beautiful house, the expensive furnishings, the BMW. She had assumed they were well off financially. How naïve she'd been, how clueless for someone with her knowledge of finance and business.

"Carolyn liked nice things," Ray said, as if reading her mind. "Not just nice. Luxurious." He paused, reddened. "I shouldn't blame her though. It's an easy habit to pick up—living in a certain way. New cars, golf, the works. All costly, and I haven't put enough aside to allow for unemployment."

Ray swallowed, and Joy thought she'd never seen him look quite so vulnerable. Strange, as serious as this business about banks and finances and mergers was, still career troubles fell into an altogether separate category for Joy … far from her concerns about their marriage and his feelings toward her. For him, though, she could see that this stress was every bit as serious as the other. Just as vital. Just as much a part of who he was.

A lot of things were clicking for Joy. The dance competitions and the band concert he'd missed, the way he'd been so distracted at home, all the signals she had misread. The problem was huge, and yet not insurmountable. It was only money after all. Or was there more to the dilemma she had not yet realized?

"Have you broken any laws yourself just by keeping silent until now— is there a chance you might go to—to prison?" She could barely get the words out.

"I don't think so. To be honest, I'm not sure. Depends, I guess, on lawyers and judges, and what kind of signals they want to send about accountability and cover-ups. The whole thing is so ugly, and I'm so ashamed."

She squeezed his hand, hard. "Are you ready to go to the press with what you know?"

With the prospect of prison time, their lives, as well as their livelihood, were at stake. Not to mention those of so many of Ray's employees and friends. Easy enough to tell herself she could be strong when she didn't understand how much hung in the balance. Could she, though, when so much was at stake?

"We have a principle we talk about in some of the classes I teach," she said slowly. "Full disclosure … usually in the context of telling the shareholders and the creditors everything that would make a difference in a decision."

Ray groaned. "I know, I know. I've made a lot of mistakes. My coming forward now may appear like I waited until everything was going to come out anyway."

"That's not what I meant." It was in the context of their marriage where she most wanted, *needed* full disclosure. She struggled to find the right words. She didn't want to rub things in, but she was sick and tired of being afraid to speak up. She would not let him, or herself, off too easily; she felt in her bones that this was a pivotal moment. "I don't want us to fall back into this pattern of misreading signals and failing to tell each other what's going on in our heads. Ever again."

"You're right. I'm sorry."

Karla set a sandwich in front of Joy, who eyed it with surprise. She'd completely forgotten ordering the patty melt. "Sorry it took so long," Karla said. "I got distracted and didn't place your order right away. My apologies."

"No problem." Joy laughed, astonished that she could feel levity in the face of so much bleakness. Karla hurried off, looking vaguely perplexed. "Seems like we're all apologizing today," Joy said to Ray, who nibbled one of the fries. Good—his appetite had returned. "I'm sorry too—I know it wasn't all your fault. I should have pressed you to tell me what was going on, and I should have told you what I was thinking. And fearing. Full disclosure."

"With the public too?" Ray reached for another fry.

"With the public too."

"So what do I do now?"

"Do what you know is right." Joy took a tiny bite of her sandwich and chewed slowly, mulling over what she needed to say next. "There is something else."

Ray waited.

"Here, you take half. I'm not as hungry as I thought." She pushed it toward him.

Ray's stomach rumbled noisily as he reached for the half sandwich, and Joy smiled in amusement. Amazing, she thought again, how lighthearted she felt at such a life-altering crossroad in their path. But it was one path, hers and Ray's. Not two separate paths. When they made the turn, they would take it together. "My job. I told you I was going to quit. You didn't look thrilled. Is this why?"

His expression was hard to read. "I figured that at least we'd have your income if I quit. But I'm ashamed of thinking that way. My troubles shouldn't affect your decision."

Joy pounced. "Not *your* troubles or *your* decision!" Hadn't he gotten the point yet? "It's *our* troubles and *our* decision. So shut up for a minute, you big oaf, and listen."

Ray threw back his head and laughed. "That's why I love you. Where have you been the past few months?"

Joy laughed too. "Too scared to come out of my shell, I guess. I'm out now, and I intend to stay out." She sobered, took another bite of her sandwich and noticed that Ray's half was already gone. How did he do that? She chewed, swallowed, nearly choked when the bite lodged in her dry throat. She reached for her mug—only a hint of chocolate syrup left in the bottom. She gulped, and the bite descended with a protest that made her esophagus ache. She looked for Karla, but the waitress was hustling with both hands full, and did not glance in Joy's direction.

Joy cleared her sore throat and continued. "Here's the thing ... I decided to quit my job mainly because I thought a stay-at-home wife and mother was what you wanted. I have been trying to be more like Carolyn."

His laugh came, a short, sharp bark. "That's the last thing I ever wanted."

"Well ... I didn't exactly succeed in the quest. Everything I've tried has resulted in disaster—in the kitchen, at entertaining, failing to sign the girls' papers. I thought maybe if I stayed home full-time, I might have a shot at getting things right."

"I don't care about any of that," Ray said.

"You don't care if the girls' papers get signed?"

"Well, I suppose I do. But I don't care about things being perfect. Carolyn drove us all crazy trying to be perfect." He signaled to Karla with the merest lift of a forefinger. She hurried to their table.

"Could we get some water here?"

"Of course."

Karla left, and Joy smiled at Ray. "That's a relief because I can tell you right now—perfect ain't in the books!"

At her inadvertent reference to books, Ray's expression darkened a trace. "I'm serious, Joy. I was drawn to you because you're strong and intelligent. You've got the confidence to stand up in front of a classroom of executives or future executives and tell them what you believe to be true. At the same time, there I was, succumbing to pressure to cut corners and hide the truth. Things too awful to confess."

"No. It wasn't."

"So tell me now. What do you really want? To quit your job—or not?"

Joy sighed. "I may not have a choice. If I don't get my act together pretty quickly, I might not survive the tenure process."

"Do you want to try?"

Karla set down two glasses of ice water, and Joy nodded her thanks. She thought for a moment while she finished the patty melt, washing the last bite down with water. "I do. I don't know that I'll make it, but I want to try. That will give us a couple more years of income, whether I get tenured or not, while you're …"

"Finding my way," Ray finished for her. "I just don't want you to make the decision for the wrong reasons."

"Which would be?"

"I don't want you to feel like you have to stay in a job you hate because I'm losing mine."

"I'm not, I promise," Joy said, and suddenly she was sure. To choose otherwise, she had been deluding herself. She thought of the girl with the fish-shaped birthmark. The student had been concerned about Joy, when Joy should have been the one looking after the students' welfare. Maybe it wasn't too late for Joy to become a mentor and a role model for students like her.

The times when she'd struggled this year to stay on topic, when she'd veered off onto tangential discussions—about sunk costs, about marriage and divorce, about relationships—had stirred something in Joy, something she hadn't fully realized at the time. These young people were at such a vulnerable point in their lives, and there was enormous opportunity here. Opportunity to make a difference, not just in shaping their knowledge, but their character too, and possibly even their souls. A little voice in her head scoffed at these lofty thoughts—at the notion that she, Fatima Joy, was remotely capable of undertaking such a momentous challenge.

"I want to teach and do research," she said aloud, not quite able to voice the other higher ambition, "so long as my doing these things doesn't interfere with *us*, with our marriage and our family."

Ray grinned. "Of course it *will* interfere … at times." He took her hands in his. "We'd be deluding ourselves to pretend otherwise. I believe those times will also serve to make us stronger in the long run. And better. Any job worth its salt is bound to interfere sometimes. So could the lack of a job—just in a different way. Don't you think?"

"I'm still new at all this."

"At what?"

"Marriage, parenting, the whole thing. But I see what you mean." Joy was seeing a lot of things more clearly. Still, would the eureka moment persist in the face of day-to-day living? As the sun came up and the lighting in the diner shifted, Ray's face was illuminated, revealing the creases around his eyes and the corners of his mouth. He'd aged over the months since they wed, though not in an unattractive way.

She leaned toward him, traced the lines with her fingertip. "I love you, Ray Jenkins."

"I love you too."

"Can I get you lovebirds something else?" Karla picked up Joy's empty plate.

"Don't you ever get to go home?" Joy asked.

"I've got a couple more hours," Karla said. "I actually like this shift."

"I wouldn't mind a cup of coffee," Ray said. "Smells like you're brewing a fresh pot."

"Sure enough. You too?"

Joy nodded. "Why not?"

Ray reached for Joy's hand and stroked the palm with his long fingers, sending a shiver of pleasure through her. Karla seemed to return with clean mugs and an urn almost before Joy realized she'd left. They sipped their coffee in companionable silence for a time.

Ray set his mug down. "I've got to make that call. I want to get it over with."

"Do you think you can get hold of anyone at this hour?"

The door opened, and a group of men in brown duck overalls, mud-splattered work boots, and assorted baseball caps elbowed their way in. "Hey, fellows. I'll be right with you," Karla called. "Let's see. Four coffees with cream and one black, right?"

"Do you want a practice round first?" Joy looked from the newcomers back to Ray. "I can be the reporter." She pulled a pen from her handbag, unfolded a napkin, and pretended to take notes.

"Let's see that!" Ray grabbed the napkin and studied the pattern of doodles. "Is that me in glasses or a raccoon?"

"Neither. It's a highly secret code, which I'll never divulge. You'll have to wait until you see it in print," Joy said.

"There's someone I need to talk to before I go public," Ray said.

"The girls?"

"Them too. I was thinking more about Hank Whitworth."

"Is that what the two of you were discussing at Christmas?"

"Yes and no. I told him a lot of it. But not everything," Ray said. "I just don't want him to learn about the scandal for the first time when it's in print—or on the air."

"Don't you think you should get some sleep first?" Joy was too keyed up to sleep herself. Were either of them thinking clearly?

"I'm pretty wide awake for the moment. Besides, Hank is an early riser." He paid the bill, and Joy thanked Karla, who chatted with the construction workers as if she hadn't a care in the world.

Marianne rushed at them the second they entered the house. Her usually perfect hair was a tangle, and her eyes were wild and red, the skin beneath them blotched and puffy. "Where have you been?" Without waiting for an answer, she went on, "I couldn't remember which restaurant, so I called just about everywhere in town. Then when I thought I'd found you, I was on hold so long I couldn't wait any longer." Marianne paused for breath. "So I got one of the neighbors to drive me. Then, when I got home, I called back, but they said you'd left already."

"Drive you where? Just tell us," Ray said. His tone was measured and calm, but the fear underlying it was palpable.

"Something terrible has happened—it's Jenny."

CHAPTER THIRTY-ONE

Joy moistened her dry lips with her tongue. How long had they been in this critical care waiting room? *Too long*. They tried to send Marianne home more than once. "You need sleep," Joy said.

"There's nothing you can do," Ray told his daughter.

The look Marianne shot silenced them both. They let her stay. And so she was there when the doctor finally stopped by. "Mr. Jenkins? Mrs. Jenkins?"

Joy nodded, leaping to her feet.

"I'm Dr. Young." The tall, slightly stooped young man took in Marianne at a glance. "Can I see you two—in private?" he said.

Ray nodded, and moved toward the doorway even as Joy objected, her heart pounding. "This is her sister, Marianne. She can hear whatever it is."

"She's going to be okay. However, we had to pump her stomach. She ingested some pretty vile substances."

"Substances?" Ray echoed, his face grim.

"Drugs? You mean drugs?" Joy was tired of evading the truth. She had to know the worst.

"But she's going to be okay?" Marianne said, and Joy saw that she alone wasn't shocked, wasn't even surprised.

"LSD, most likely. We don't have the reports back yet. But, yes, I think she's going to be fine. She was wearing a seat belt, fortunately, so she sustained very few injuries in the crash, as far as we can tell."

"Thank God!" Joy breathed.

"Amen to that," Ray said, his face still, only the rivulets of tears beneath the eyes reflecting his relief, like a trickling brook in a bank of stones.

"What about Alex and Claudia?" Marianne chewed on a fingernail while all three waited for the doctor to answer.

"Alex is still in critical condition. We won't know until morning."

"What about Clau—Claudia? Claudia was in the car too, wasn't she?" Marianne's usual perfect posture and precise articulation had given way to a jittery swaying from one foot to the other and an almost feverish jumble of words.

Dr. Young looked from Joy to Ray before answering. Ray nodded, giving him permission to speak.

"I'm sorry. She didn't make it."

"My God!" Ray breathed audibly.

"Oh, my God," echoed Joy, and then, "Where are her parents?"

Marianne had sunk into a chair, her face white as paper. Ray draped an arm around her while they all stared at the doctor.

"We haven't been able to reach them. You don't know where they are, by any chance?"

"No, I'm sorry," Joy said, thinking how little she knew about Claudia or her family. Why hadn't she reached out to that poor, troubled girl? The image flashed in her head of Claudia, sass-mouthed but sparkling, so alive, challenging Alfred at the Bible study meetings. Perhaps the very fact that she attended those meetings at all had been a cry for help. A cry Joy hadn't bothered to hear, too absorbed in her own troubles. Troubles that now seemed trivial by comparison. And what about Jenny, and *her* cries for help? Where had Joy been—and where had Ray been—while all this developed?

"Have you asked Jenny?" Marianne whispered.

"Your sister isn't conscious," Dr. Young said gently, "but she is going to be okay. Unless something unforeseen happens."

"What do you mean?" Joy's heart thudded heavily in her chest, like an internal hammer slamming against her ribcage. "Like what?"

"I mean there are always possible complications in a case like this. We don't have the labs back yet. We can be more certain in the morning, but I'm ninety percent confident." He smiled for the first time.

Joy did not correct his statement, did not point out that he had no basis for a statistic like that. She wanted to believe him, wanted him to increase the probability to 99.9 percent.

"You might as well go home and get some rest," Dr. Young said. "She'll need you more in the morning."

"I don't want to leave," Joy said, "not until she's conscious."

"Okay," the doctor said. "I can't promise when that will be."

"Possibly tonight though?"

He glanced at his watch. "Actually, it's already morning. And I'll have to be back here in less than five hours. I'm going home myself, and I suggest you do the same." He laid a hand on Marianne's shoulder before he turned to go. "I'm sorry about your friend."

"She's not my friend," Marianne mumbled as he left, slumping against the side of the chair, her head dropping onto a hard end-table.

"I'm taking you home," Ray said in a tone that left no room for argument. "I'll be right back," he said over his shoulder to Joy as he escorted a reluctant Marianne from the room.

Joy sank onto a sofa, her head spinning. She picked up a magazine and flipped idly through the glossy pages, comprehending nothing. Time lost its meaning so that she couldn't have said whether minutes or hours had passed when a rosy cheeked nurse popped into the waiting room. "Mrs. Jenkins?"

In a flash, Joy was on her feet.

"She's awake. She's asking for you."

"Thank you," Joy breathed. "Thank you, Lord."

She followed the nurse through the doors, then pushed through the curtain to where Jenny lay. She was connected by a maze of wires and tubes to a host of machines ticking their life signs, though Joy could make little sense of the erratic, squiggly lines. A blood pressure cuff squeezed one arm, while an IV pumped fluids through the other. An EKG monitored her heart rate. Wires protruded from under her gown, and a sensor was clamped onto her index finger.

Jenny lay on her back in a printed hospital gown, her hair tousled, her face a little flushed. She looked beautiful to Joy. She bent over to kiss the smooth cheek. How young she looked, her flesh as tender and unblemished as a baby's. In stark contrast, an oxygen tube ran into the edge of her nose. A second tube of indeterminate purpose ran into her nose as well, and beside the bed, the container of fluids coming from Jenny's young body made Joy flinch.

She thought of Claudia again … a dead Claudia—the red hair, the freckles standing out on the pale lifeless face, the flesh cold. A shiver ran through Joy. She should have done more for Claudia. The girl had been right there in their home, in their small group sessions, speaking out courageously. Unshed tears pricked her eyes, tears she could not let Jenny see. How easily it could have been Jenny. "Oh, sweetheart." She smoothed Jenny's hair. "I'm so glad you're okay."

"I'm sorry," Jenny said.

Joy swallowed hard, willing herself not to break down.

"Alex? Claudia?" Jenny asked. "Nobody will tell me anything."

Joy didn't know what to say. Why hadn't someone prepared her for this question? Why hadn't she prepared herself? "Shh," she said, terrified that the truth could put Jenny's own life in greater peril. "Your dad just took Marianne home. She was so worried about you, but we made her get some sleep."

Jenny's eyes closed, and Joy thought she'd fallen asleep. She leaned over and kissed the smooth face once more, pressed the fingers, still plump with the remnants of baby fat. What if something had happened to this child, something even worse than what transpired? They could recover from this. They were being given a second chance.

Jenny's eyes fluttered open. "He was driving so fast," she said. "I knew something awful was going to happen. I told him to slow down—"

"Shh," Ray said. He had slipped into the room when Joy wasn't looking. "You can tell us everything later."

"I just wanted him to like me," Jenny whispered, and her words struck a chord—a violent, discordant note—within Joy. Not being able to bring herself for so long to confront Ray, what kind of role model had she been for Jenny?

"Sleep now. We'll talk in the morning," Ray said, and Jenny's eyes drooped shut again.

A torrent of tears streamed down Joy's cheeks as she stared at the sleeping child. Having held them back until now, she felt the floodgate open, and there was no stopping the flow.

Through the blur of tears, she glimpsed the pink-cheeked nurse in the doorway, her eyes still clear and surprisingly alert at this hour of the day. A cartoon-patterned Band-Aid above one eyebrow seemed misplaced, reminding Joy of a Band-Aid she'd positioned in her childhood Bible on a colored page picturing Christ on the cross.

"She's going to be fine," the nurse said. "She just needs to rest."

"You're sure?" Joy managed to say through tears, her voice like a sob.

"The doctor seems sure. He's moving her to a regular room when it's ready. She's going to be in J316."

"Thank God." Ray's hand found and gripped Joy's.

"It's probably a good time for you all to get some rest too," the nurse said. Joy noticed her nametag for the first time. Cherry, how appropriate. Like Cherry Ames, RN, the protagonist in a series of books Joy had loved as a girl. Back then she'd been drawn to a lifetime of helping people. An ambition she'd abandoned when her parents died. *Why*, at a time like this, was her brain dredging up these irrelevant memories? Must be lack of sleep.

"Let's go home," Ray said. "For a while. Okay?"

Joy nodded, choked up with emotion and unable to speak.

Still gripping her hand, Ray tried to read her mind as they moved toward the elevators. "What is it?"

"I'm so relieved." Still, she couldn't stop crying.

"Is there something else? Tell me, Joy."

A wild-eyed, red-haired woman darted from the elevator, and Ray and Joy looked at each other. This woman had to be Claudia's mother. The resemblance was too strong to be a coincidence. "Should we go to her?" Joy asked.

They turned to follow the woman. When they caught up with her, she was already deep in conversation with a nurse at the desk, then was being ushered into another room.

"Tomorrow," Ray said, his brow furrowed, his eyes dark with empathy. "I don't think there's anything we could do for her right now. If you want, we can stick around a bit, just in case."

Joy shuddered. She imagined herself in the place of Claudia's mother and feared there would never be anything they could say or do that would help. Her hurt was almost beyond imagining, beyond human help. How easily Jenny might have been the one.

CHAPTER THIRTY-TWO

Joy curled into Ray's arms, feeling connected in a way that was new and wondrous, united even in their anxiety about what lay ahead. When Ray's breathing finally fell into the even pattern of sleep, she slipped out of his arms and made her way into the kitchen. She was startled to find Marianne there. "Trouble sleeping?" Joy asked.

Marianne nodded. She looked lovely as ever in a pair of mauve silk pajamas, though her face was still splotchy and her eyes red and swollen.

"We should have told you," Joy said. "But I didn't want to wake you. The doctor says Jenny's going to be fine."

Marianne hiccupped. A cup of hot chocolate sat untouched in front of her.

"Aren't you going to drink that?" Joy asked.

"Why? Do you want it?" She pushed the cup toward Joy.

"No, thanks. You drink it. Might make you feel better."

"Okay," Marianne said. She made no move to touch the drink. "Is she really going to be okay?"

"That's what the doctor said. He seemed pretty confident." Joy eyed Marianne's untouched hot chocolate. "Maybe I'll make myself a cup after all."

"It's easy—it's a mix," Marianne said.

Joy laughed.

"I didn't mean it that way," Marianne said.

"It's all right. I deserved that."

"You do realize chocolate is full of caffeine." The hint of a smile played at the edges of Marianne's mouth, the first Joy had seen there in days.

"I know it is. Somehow hot chocolate always seems like a nice, soothing, help-you-to-sleep sort of drink to me. I could warm a glass of milk for you if you'd prefer that."

Marianne burst into tears.

"What? What did I say?" Joy was baffled.

Marianne tried to speak, but only cried harder.

Joy located a napkin. "Here." She handed it to Marianne. "My mother used to say I never had a tissue at any moment in my life when I needed one. Some things never change, I guess."

Marianne blew her nose into the napkin, and the tears ceased abruptly. "You never talk about her."

"No, I don't."

"Do you miss her something fierce?"

Joy hesitated just an instant before answering candidly. "Yes. She's been gone a long time now. And I don't think about her all the time like I used to. It does get easier."

"Sometimes I talk to Mother," Marianne said, averting her eyes. Then, after a few seconds, she snuck a glance at Joy as if to assess her reaction before saying anything more, like dipping your feet into a swimming pool to assess the water's temperature.

"I used to do that. After my parents died. I wanted to tell them things I should have said when they were alive. So I conjured them up. Never worked. I could never get them to say what I wanted."

"What was that?" Marianne took a sip of her hot chocolate, and Joy rose to make herself a cup while she thought how to answer.

"That they *knew*." Joy sat back down and faced her stepdaughter. "That I didn't need to tell them because they already knew." She didn't want to cry, not now when she had been trying to put a positive spin on things for Marianne's sake. Joy could feel the sobs in her throat … in her nose … on her tongue. Only her eyes were dry.

"They probably did," Marianne said, and Joy was at once ashamed and comforted that it was Marianne who was soothing her instead of the reverse.

Joy removed the cup from the microwave and stirred the chocolate powder so hard it swirled over the top. "Their ghosts always seemed to be scolding me, or screaming at me. I don't know if the ghosts we conjure up are ever fair representations of who the people really were."

"You didn't know my mother—she was pretty horrible."

"Really?" Joy took a small sip of her hot chocolate.

Marianne gulped … said nothing.

"I doubt if she meant to be," Joy said.

Marianne's face was clearly skeptical. "She wanted me to be perfect, and I never could be."

"No, of course not. No one is."

"You don't know how bad I am." Marianne's small nose reddened, and the beautiful gold-flecked eyes—which had cleared over the past few minutes as only the very young can do—were suddenly pink again. "I feel so—so guilty."

"About what?"

"Everything."

Joy was so tired. Too much had happened in the past twenty-four hours. She stared at this lovely girl obviously riddled with pain. How poorly Joy had read her ... how needy she was, like Joy herself. She reached out a hand to squeeze Marianne's, not worrying that she might pull away. And she did not.

"I'm sorry," Marianne said, so softly Joy could barely hear. "I think the accident was my fault. I'm just glad she's going to be all right."

"How could what happened be your fault?"

"I can't tell you. Not yet. I'm too ashamed."

"Tell me." Joy held Marianne's eyes, sensing that Marianne really wanted to confide, needed to get something off her chest—whatever the girl believed she'd contributed to this nightmare.

"I don't think she'd have gone out if I hadn't—I encouraged her to go. I practically pushed her out the door."

"Why? Why would you do that?" Joy tried not to sound horrified, but she *was* horrified—in spite of herself.

"It seems so stupid now—I guess I thought—I was trying to get back at you for—I don't know, really. For not being Mother, I guess."

"At me? What did I have to do with—"

Still exhausted and rattled from everything that had happened, Joy wondered if she heard Marianne correctly. And then an inkling of understanding dawned. "You mean, by making it look like I—"

"Like you were failing to control Jenny." Marianne nodded, finishing the thought. "By getting her in trouble, when she was supposed to be grounded, I thought Dad would blame you. It was stupid. *I* was stupid. I see that now. Honestly, I never thought about her getting hurt. Or—or—" Marianne broke off, her face scarlet.

"You hate me so much?"

Marianne shook her head, swallowed hard. "That's just it. I don't. I really don't. I felt like I was doing something for Mother—something I didn't want to. Even when I was doing those things. I know you won't believe me, but I felt like Mother was using me, working through me to keep you and Dad from being happy together. I know it sounds crazy."

Joy thought back to all the things she'd learned about Carolyn, and shook her head. She was wide awake again. "Not as crazy as you may think."

"Can you ever forgive me? I'm really, really sorry."

Joy rose and pulled the slim girl against her breast, awkwardly but with tenderness. "Of course I can. We all make mistakes." Joy stroked Marianne's hair, still silky after all they had been through. Joy imagined her own was a mass of tangles. "Do you think you can sleep now?" Joy glanced toward the window, where the brilliant morning sun streamed through, as if today were an ordinary day like any other. "I guess it's not exactly bedtime."

"Not exactly." Marianne offered a thin smile.

The phone clamored for attention, and they both started. "I'll get it," Marianne rose.

When she handed the phone to Joy, her face was drained of color. "It's the hospital," she whispered, and Joy's heart leapt into her throat.

Joy found Ray in the bedroom on the second phone line. He got off hurriedly. "What is it?" he said.

"There's been a complication. We need to get to the hospital."

Already he was pulling on his trousers and buttoning his shirt. Some functioning part of Joy's brain noticed the buttons were misaligned with the buttonholes. She glanced down to see that she was still in her nightgown. "I'll only be a second," she said.

Joy collided with Marianne as she emerged from her bedroom. Marianne was fully but haphazardly dressed in a faded denim skirt and a flannel shirt with the buttons and buttonholes misaligned, too. Like father, like daughter. Funny, if any of them were in the mood to be amused. Within five minutes, the three were on their way. Joy realized that not one of them had buckled a seatbelt. The speedometer crept past seventy in a forty-mile speed zone. "Buckle up," she croaked.

The interior of the car smelled odd to Joy. Body odor seemed to be emanating from one of them. Twisting her head toward the backseat, Joy was pretty sure the smell was coming from Marianne, the most unlikely of sources. The smell of fear, perhaps? "Are you all right?"

No answer. Stupid question.

At the hospital, all the elements seemed to conspire to slow down their progress—from the crowded parking lot to the molasses-slow elevator. Finally, they were in Jenny's wing. They charged toward the door to her room, where an empty bed stared back at them.

"Oh, my God!" Joy gasped, her heart exploding in her chest. For a second, the room spun and she thought she might black out.

Marianne clutched her hand so hard Joy managed to regain control of her senses. "Where's Jenny?" Marianne whispered, and Joy turned to catch sight of her lovely face draining to a ghostly white hue.

Ray was already dashing frantically toward the nurse's station. I have to be strong, Joy thought, for Marianne and for Ray, whatever has happened. I can't give in to what I'm feeling, not now.

A nurse stood, reading their faces, hastened to explain. She waved her hands as she spat out words in rapid succession. "I'm sorry if you thought— she's back in intensive care. She threw a blood clot, and—"

"She's alive," Marianne breathed.

"Yes, she's very much alive," the nurse said, laying a gentle hand on Marianne's shoulder.

"How bad is she?" Ray asked.

The nurse glanced at Marianne, whose color was returning, though she still held Joy's hand in a death grip.

Joy glanced at the nurse's name tag. "It's okay, Kelly. You can tell us in front of Marianne."

"You'll have to ask the doctor," Kelly said, then seemed to soften. "I don't really know. I mean, I'm sure she's going to be okay, though blood clots can be serious. I'm sorry, I'm rambling. The truth is that I don't really know." She squeezed Marianne's shoulder, and Joy felt rather than saw the girl flinch.

"Where is she? Can you take us to her?" Ray asked.

"Of course." Kelly hesitated. "This is my first week, and I'm not sure if I can leave the floor. Also, I was the one who—let me call someone."

"Someone called us!" Ray exploded. "Please find that someone—now."

Kelly, who looked barely old enough to be out of high school, hustled off as an older nurse with a faint mustache appeared. "You're the Jenkins family?" she asked.

"Yes!" they chorused.

"Please come with me." The older nurse shot a disapproving glance in Kelly's direction; and, in spite of her own heightened anxiety, Joy felt an instinctive flash of sympathy for the younger woman.

"I'm Rachel. I'm the one who called you," she said. "Dr. Young will fill you in."

They followed Rachel to the elevators. Joy stared as the elevator lights hovered, then crept slowly in their direction. The elevator car was empty except for an older gentleman in a wheelchair attended by a male orderly in a blue uniform.

In a few moments they were in the company of the tall, slightly stooped Dr. Young. He led the threesome into a small consultation room adjacent to the ICU waiting room, and Joy's entire body trembled so badly she leaned against the door facing for stability. Was this the room for delivering bad news?

"How is she, Doctor?" Ray's voice was so tight, his words sounded foreign. She knew he was as frightened as she, and his fear intensified her own.

"She's sedated but conscious. I just wanted to prepare you before you went in to see her."

"What happened?" asked Marianne, her face rigid.

"She threw a blood clot into her lung, and she was having difficulty breathing when we moved her here."

"Why? What caused it?" Marianne asked.

"Hard to say, but complications are not unusual after a trauma. One of the newer nurses told her about her friend—"

"Claudia," said Marianne.

"Yes, Claudia. I'm not saying that's what caused the clot. However, she needs to stay as calm as possible right now." Joy thought of the nurse, Kelly, who had been so awkward with them. *I'm the one who—*

"Do you understand what I'm saying?" The doctor peered at them through thick glasses.

Joy nodded, and Marianne pumped her head up and down furiously. "Yes," Ray said. "Is she going to be okay?"

"I think so," said Dr. Young, and he offered a small smile. "She's on oxygen, and you'll see several other tubes as well. We're trying to dissolve the clot slowly, which is why we have to keep her very still."

"Can we see her?" asked Marianne.

"One at a time," he said, "and only for a few minutes. Don't say anything to upset her. Do you have any questions?"

As they followed the doctor out of the consultation room and back into the ICU waiting room, Joy realized she hadn't said a word. She tried to collect the scramble of her thoughts enough to find her voice. She would probably have a dozen questions once the doctor left. Right now her mind was empty, except for the blanket of relief that Jenny was alive and seemed to be in capable hands. She squeezed her eyes shut and offered a silent prayer of thanks and a plea for Jenny's recovery.

"How long will she be here?" Ray called after the doctor just as he vanished through the doorway.

Dr. Young turned back, his brow faintly puckered. "It's hard to say at this point … we don't want to rush the process. Do we?"

"No. Of course not."

Ray went in first, while Joy and Marianne sank into chairs in the waiting room. They were the only ones in the room, though a worn red sweater, a paperback novel, and a half-eaten banana on the table next to the sofa suggested someone would be returning. Or perhaps not. What if you got bad news? You would forget your possessions in a heartbeat. Joy's legs, which had ceased to tremble, began to shake again at the thought.

Don't *think* that way, she told herself. Not while next to Marianne, who was about ready to jump out of her skin. If fear was contagious, so was hope.

Ray returned within a few minutes, looking slightly less grim than before. "You can go in now," he said to Joy.

Marianne had risen when her dad entered. Joy tilted her head in Marianne's direction. "Marianne first. Then I'll go."

Marianne didn't argue. She was out of the room in a flash.

"How is she?" Joy asked Ray, her voice quavering only a little.

"Somewhat groggy and apologetic. I told her to save her strength and I got out of there before she could upset herself. I was worried she was going to say something about Claudia—"

An elderly woman returned to reclaim the sweater and book. Her gray hair was frazzled, and purplish circles ringed the tired eyes behind glasses. Joy suspected she hadn't slept in a while. Tossing the remaining banana in a trashcan, the woman settled onto the sofa with a groan and turned to Joy. "Is that your daughter in there?"

"Yes."

The woman smiled, revealing surprisingly white teeth ... dentures most likely. "She's going to be all right. I have a good feeling about her."

"Thank you," Joy breathed, as if the woman's feeling about Jenny could make it so. "And you?" She seemed incapable of forming a complete sentence.

"It's my husband."

Joy nodded. "What's wrong with him?"

"They're trying to figure that out," the woman said. "Or I could say, what's not wrong with him? He's got kidney issues and heart trouble, and a bad liver, so it gets to be a balancing act to keep him alive."

"I'm sorry," Joy said. Her stomach churned. The smell of overripe banana suddenly nauseated her. Before she could think of a tactful way to dispose of it, Marianne returned and Joy scrambled to her feet.

As she reached the doorway, Joy turned back to address the older woman. "What's your name?"

"Estelle."

"I'm Joy. I hope your husband's going to be all right."

Every fiber of her body cringed when she saw Jenny's pale, motionless body hooked up to even more wires and tubes than before. Her frail young chest rose and fell as she breathed in the oxygen. A part of Joy wanted to shriek at the child: "How could you put yourself in harm's way like this? How could you put us all through this torture?"

Later. Later, she would yell at Jenny, and Joy smiled at the thought. There would be a later. Estelle had somehow given her confidence. Joy's body relaxed just enough for the shaking to subside, though her heart continued to tap out an odd rhythm, the way it behaves in the moment you wake up from a nightmare—relief mingling with remembered terror.

Jenny's eyes fluttered open, and she smiled up at Joy. A feeble smile but a smile nonetheless. Her lips moved, and Joy leaned in to make out her words. She couldn't hear Jenny's weak voice. Joy shook her head. "Just rest," she said. "You shouldn't strain yourself."

Jenny said very clearly then, "Alex?"

"Oh." Joy realized she had almost forgotten the boy in her shock over Claudia and her anxiety for Jenny. She thought of Claudia's mother, and shuddered inwardly at the mere possibility of losing both children. "I don't know, but I'll find out."

Joy squeezed Jenny's fingertips, afraid to hug her. "Don't move. You need to stay very, very still."

Jenny nodded. "Please find out," she said.

"I promise."

Her mind raced as she left the room. Why wasn't Alex in this unit? Was he well enough to be in a room, to be released? Or could he be in a different wing, or …

Ray gazed up at Joy as she returned to the waiting room. "I have to find out about Alex," she told him breathlessly. "Jenny is asking."

"I know. She asked me too."

"And me," Marianne said.

"If it's bad—" Joy's thighs were quivering again.

"It's not." Marianne's face radiated joy at having relatively good news for once.

"We already asked," Ray said. "The news is not great exactly, but it could be much worse. He's got a concussion, and they are keeping an eye on him for a couple of days."

"Thank God." Joy sank into a chair. "Where is he?"

"He's in a room," Marianne said. "He's probably worried about Jenny. We should go see him—we were just waiting until you got back."

"I wonder if he knows about his sister." Joy glanced at Estelle, who was obviously listening to this exchange even as she pretended to be engrossed in her book. "They really think he's going to be okay?"

"Physically, I guess so," Ray said. His jaw tightened visibly, and his tone was uncharacteristically bitter. "Though I expect he's immersed in guilt. At least he should be."

"Do you think it will excite her too much if we tell Jenny?" Joy asked. Her muscles relaxed, and only then did she realize how tightly they had been drawn up. "I think it will stress her out worse if we don't."

"Can I go tell her?" Marianne's eyes pleaded.

Joy looked at Ray and he nodded. "Okay, but don't use the word 'concussion.' Tell her he seems to be fine … that they are just watching him to make certain."

Marianne, already on her way, paused to assure them she'd be careful.

CHAPTER THIRTY-THREE

Marianne couldn't help glancing at the monitors hooked up to her sister as she delivered her news about Alex. She didn't understand half the lines or jags. At least nothing was beeping at the moment.

"I'm so glad. So very glad," Jenny said. She had strained to lift herself toward Marianne while she waited for the report. She leaned back now, exhausted but brighter eyed.

"You look better," Marianne said, swallowing the lump that had formed in her throat. The lump that materialized every time she thought of her role in the fatal accident. "How are you feeling?"

"Better now that I know about Alex. But …" Jenny's eyes filled, and Marianne knew she was thinking of Claudia. Maybe she should leave before Jenny got more upset.

A male nurse—how many nurses did they have on this shift—popped in. A handsome man, with dark skin and eyes and a lock of thick dark hair that flopped onto his forehead. He smiled at Marianne. "I need to check your sister's vitals."

He wrapped a squeezing band on Jenny's arm and pumped it up.

"What do you call that thing?" Marianne asked.

"It's a sphygmomanometer."

"Wow, that's a mouthful. A fig-mama-monster?" She laughed at herself.

"Close enough. Are you interested in being a nurse?" He jotted down some figures and slipped a thermometer in Jenny's mouth.

"I don't know. Maybe." A new idea … one she sort of liked. "What was the reading?"

"115 over 70."

"Is that normal?"

"Yep. She's a lucky young lady." A beep sounded, and he removed the thermometer. "98.6, right on the button."

Marianne read the nurse's badge. "Should I leave, Joe?"

Jenny stirred. "Marianne, don't go yet … please. There's something I want to tell you." She looked imploringly at Joe.

"Five minutes," he said.

"Fig-mama-monster?" Marianne said as he turned to go, and she and Jenny both giggled. Marianne was so relieved to hear her sister laugh her eyes spilled happy tears. "I–should—go," she said.

"Wait, please. I need to ask you something."

Marianne dropped into the chair beside the bed. "Okay. Shoot."

"Where do you think Claudia is?"

Marianne froze. Had Jenny forgotten that Claudia was dead? Was that why she was able to laugh? Was her brain affected by the accident? What should she say?

Suddenly one of the machines hooked up to Jenny began to beep loudly and steadily. She ran into the hallway and located a uniformed attendant. "Please, can you check on my sister? Something is wrong!"

The woman followed Marianne into the room, pushed a button on the machine, and the beeping stopped. "She's fine. They just do that sometimes."

"I better go," Marianne said again.

"No! I don't think you understood my question," Jenny said. "I know Claudia … is … is … dead."

Tears filled Marianne's eyes and streamed down her cheeks. "I'm so, so sorry." Marianne bent over to hug Jenny, not worrying about the cords and wires at this moment.

"The thing is," Jenny said, "Claudia kept talking about weird stuff that night. I know she was—well, sort of high and all. Still, when I think back on it, I feel like she knew or something—knew she was going to die. She wanted to know where I thought we went when we died, and I told her about heaven. You'd think she might have laughed at me. But she didn't." Jenny paused to suck in a deep breath and smiled through her tears. Her breath stuttered as she let it out, but she seemed determined to finish. "She asked me if I thought it might be boring there, just listening to angels play harps and crap like that. Her words, not mine."

"What did you say?"

"I told her I thought the harp stuff was only a metaphor, like in English class. For everything being so good and the people so happy, like … like being on ecstasy, only better." Jenny flushed. "I'm so ashamed of myself."

"No, I'm the one. I'm older, and I'm so very, very ashamed and sorry and ..." Marianne kept repeating herself—measly, inadequate words to ever express all she was feeling. "You would never have gone out that evening if I hadn't—"

Jenny waved a dismissive hand. She pointed to a water pitcher and glass on a tray near the bed. "Could you get me a drink?"

Marianne filled the glass too full and some water sloshed out. Her hand shook so that she could barely control it. This conversation was terrifyingly real. Until now, the whole nightmarish experience had seemed like just that: a bad dream, one she would wake from tomorrow, and everything would be back to normal.

But it wouldn't. Not for Claudia, not for Alex, or their mother. And not for her and Jenny.

Marianne positioned the straw so that Jenny could take a drink. She gulped several sips of water. "Thank you. Now, where was I?"

You were talking about Claudia and ecstasy. Marianne said nothing, not wanting to remind Jenny, wondering again if her presence was tiring her sister too much.

"You know," Jenny said, "all those times she went to Bible study group with us, I think she was listening more than we were—I mean, than I was. That last night she talked a lot about Jesus and about some of the things he did and said. Like how he was a friend to the prostitutes and beggars and people like that when the Pharisees were turning their noses up at them. She said she thought Alfred was a Pharisee himself, but Jesus was pretty cool."

"Really?" Marianne found this hard to believe. She wondered if Jenny was delusional, if she'd had some sort of out-of-body experience related to the accident and imagined the whole conversation with Claudia. Her sister's eyes were grave, though, and she could tell that either this conversation with Claudia really happened, or Jenny believed it had. Although she looked weak, Marianne had the distinct impression that Jenny felt less burdened than before.

"Yeah. She told me she'd been into this religious stuff once before when she was younger, had even been baptized in another town. She said she'd done so much crap ..." Jenny's voice trailed off and Marianne knew she was trying hard not to cry. Then she continued, "Oh, Marianne, I can't believe she's dead. She was so alive. I think she was the most alive person I ever knew."

Marianne hugged her, at a loss for words. "I better go," she whispered.

"No, let me finish." Jenny's brown eyes were drowsy but determined. "She'd done so much bad stuff—like lying to me about Alex—that she couldn't see Jesus forgiving her. But I think he can, don't you?"

"What do you mean—about Alex?"

"She kept telling me that he liked me, you know, *in that way*. But that night—was it only last night? I can't seem to get my days straight ... it feels like another ... another ..." Jenny's eyelids drooped shut.

The male nurse appeared in the doorway and gestured for Marianne to leave. She bent over and kissed her sister's wet cheek.

CHAPTER THIRTY-FOUR

When Marianne returned to the waiting room, her beaming face made Joy glow with answering hope. Estelle looked up from her novel to smile at the girl.

Joy contemplated the significance of all she observed. Strange how, in the face of tragedy, every piece of good news had the power to lift. Why couldn't people be as receptive to the joy and blessings of everyday life? What was it in the human makeup that required depths to truly attain heights? Joy thought of the age-old question of why God let bad things happen—perhaps this was part of the answer.

Joy met Marianne's glance. "How is Jenny? What did she say?"

"Not much—I didn't let her. I could tell how relieved she was, though. It's just nice to have something positive to share. You know?"

Joy jolted with sudden remembrance. "Don't you have ballet today?"

"I'm not going."

Joy frowned. "I don't want you to miss out on qualifying rounds or anything."

Ray put down the newspaper he'd been reading. "It's all right. I know you need total focus to compete, and we can explain—"

"No." Marianne shook her head. "I don't mean because of Jenny. I'm not doing ballet anymore."

"*What?*"

"You're overreacting!" Joy's words fell on top of Ray's.

"This is not the time to be making major decisions," Ray continued, not waiting for Marianne's reply. He glanced at Joy as he spoke, and she knew he was thinking the two of them had been doing just that.

"I've been thinking about dropping ballet for a long time," Marianne said. "Being a ballerina is all about perfection. And I'm sick of trying to be perfect."

"I know," Ray said. "No one is perfect, not even ballerinas."

"I've got a new goal now."

They waited.

"I'm going to be a good sister to Jenny." A mischievous smile lifted the corners of Marianne's mouth. "At least for a day or two. By then, I'll have come up with something else."

EPILOGUE

One week later

Joy's hand rested on the console of their new-smelling BMW. She smiled as Ray stroked her hand. How much had happened since the day they returned from their honeymoon—a lifetime ago, and at the same time, only the briefest flash. Joy wondered if life with Ray would always be a paradox of some sort. Of having gone on forever and of having only just begun, though perhaps the newness would wear off with time. The past seven days of waiting and praying had been horrendous ... kind of wonderful too, in the way the experience brought them all together. Life itself was full of contradictions, wondrous and awful, all at the same time.

"You're both buckled back there. Right?" Ray asked the girls in the backseat.

"Yes, Dad, we're buckled." Marianne sighed. "Are you going to ask three times whenever we get in the car from now on?"

"I can't believe Claudia is gone," Jenny said, and they remained silent for a long moment.

Jenny broke the silence at last. "I'm so glad Alex is going to be okay."

Joy turned in her seat to smile at Jenny. She scanned Jenny's outfit—the new pair of jeans and Cyndi Lauper T-shirt Marianne had purchased for her sister out of her own savings.

"You still have a crush on him!" Marianne's voice was teasing, almost singsong.

"No, I don't," Jenny answered, a bit too quickly perhaps. "There's this guy in band though—"

"Oh yeah? What's his name?" asked Marianne.

"I don't know if I should tell you. I'll say this much—he's got the bluest eyes you've ever seen. And they are so startling because he's kind of dark, like he's always got a really good tan, and his hair is dark and curly."

"I bet I know who you're talking about!" Marianne said. "Does he play clarinet?"

"I'm not telling."

"Does he sit beside you in band?"

"I'm *not* saying."

"Is his name Steve?"

Jenny sighed. "How did you know? I didn't want to tell you yet—I mean, he doesn't even know I'm alive."

"How can he not know you're alive when he sits right beside you?" Marianne rolled her eyes in mock confusion, and Ray chuckled.

"You know what I mean! Now the whole family knows, and one of you is bound to embarrass me—"

"I promise, I won't say a word to him"—Marianne giggled—"about how you just *love* blue eyes, especially in a tanned face, or how—*ouch!*"

"Settle down back there," Ray said, his hand still caressing Joy's. "Jenny needs to take it easy for a while. Why don't you both try to think about whether there's anything we can do to help Alex's mom get through these next few weeks? Once the initial shock wears off, she's going to be in so much pain."

Joy's stomach turned a little at hearing Claudia and Alex's mother referred to merely as Alex's mom. *How quickly we adapt.* Still, their mother would always think of herself as Claudia's mom too. "That's a good idea. She's bound to be having a tough time," she said.

Joy couldn't even imagine how tough. Words were so inadequate, as would be anything they could do.

Ray added, "We need to believe you've learned a lesson from all this—"

"I *have.*" Jenny crossed her heart. "I promise I have. I'll never do drugs again."

"That's easy to say," Joy said. "I know you mean what you're saying right now—"

"I mean … forever," Jenny said. The childish heart crossing had been replaced by an expression so solemn and so mature on her young face Joy couldn't help but believe Jenny.

"I'll be keeping a better eye on her too." Marianne shut one eye and pulled the upper and lower lids apart on the other one to dramatize her words. "Ouch—she hit me again!"

"Let's talk about something else, can we?" Jenny's brown eyes pleaded with Joy.

"Like what? Like Ste-eve from band?" Marianne drawled.

"Like—when's your next ballet thing?" Jenny asked.

"Never."

"What do you mean?" Jenny asked.

"I quit."

"You … what?" Jenny sounded as incredulous as Joy felt.

Were they making a mistake by letting her quit ballet so abruptly? It hadn't been that long since she gave up cheerleading.

"Ballet was Mother's thing, really, more than mine."

"But you practice all the time!" Jenny protested. "How could you do that if you didn't like it?"

"I wanted to be perfect. Like her."

"She wasn't perfect." Ray's eyebrows were drawn together, but at least he no longer flinched at the mention of Carolyn.

"You don't have to be perfect to enjoy dancing. You're so talented, Marianne." Joy turned to look at Marianne, whose smooth brow puckered at this discussion. "I hate to see you give up. You could switch from ballet to jazz or tap. Promise me you'll think about your options at least. Okay?"

Marianne hesitated, her gold-flecked eyes so grave Joy felt certain the girl would refuse. But Marianne surprised her. "Okay, I'll think about it."

They were all quiet for a moment, and Joy thought how long she had been uncomfortable with the mention of Carolyn or with Ray's avoidance of the subject. Ray fiddled with the temperature controls. "Anyone too hot or too cold?"

When no one answered, he took Joy's hand again, squeezing her fingers suddenly so hard she nearly cried out. "I'm not perfect either," he said, talking to the girls more than to her.

Marianne snickered. "No kidding, Mr. Forgetful."

"I'm going to do better about that, I promise. But there's something else I've done. And something I need to do—"

The car quieted. Had the girls sensed he was about to reveal something which hung heavy on his conscience? He wheeled the car into their driveway. No one moved to open a car door. He talked and talked, more then he'd told the girls in a long time. Maybe ever. He talked to them as if they were his equals, or his superiors.

"I'm ashamed I've let it get this far," he said, and his face flushed a dark red. Wanting the girls to see him as a role model, instead he brought himself low. So low, so humble. Yet, in that humility, Joy saw great strength. She squeezed back on the fingers that still gripped hers.

"What are you going to do now?" Marianne asked.

"I'm going to do what I should have done a long time ago."

"Good," she said.

"Good," Jenny echoed.

"I need you both to understand what this means."

"What?" Jenny asked.

"This could become a court case. There's even a chance I might—" Ray swallowed hard, and his Adam's apple bobbed visibly—"might have to serve time."

The color drained from Marianne's face, while Jenny's flushed a deep pink.

"Probably not, though. Right?" Jenny asked.

Ray looked at Joy, and she nodded her agreement. "Probably not. We should be ready, though, just in case. You know the adage—expect the best … prepare for the worst?"

The girls nodded, and she wasn't sure whether the nods meant they knew the adage or that they would try to live its mantra.

"I think we're ready," Joy said.

Ray turned toward her. "You're sure?"

She nodded. "A little nervous of course, but we'll face whatever comes together."

"You know, I've probably prayed more this last week than I've prayed the whole last year. Maybe my whole life, now that I think about it," Marianne said. Joy twisted around in her seat to smile at her.

"Good idea," Ray said.

They prayed aloud together, each adding thoughts as they came to them, some more articulate than others, awkwardly at first, embarrassed sounding at times. And yet, they somehow formed a reasonably coherent whole. Joy knew she'd never understand, not in this lifetime, why her first family had been snatched from her so brutally. She was ready to get out her dad's jade letter opener, start using it, allow her mind to travel back to the good times she'd had as a child, cherish the memories, share them with Ray and the girls. When her final turn came, she said, "I only hope we can stay close like we are now. Please, God."

She opened her eyes. Now moist with tears, her vision blurred, yet filled with images—images of her loved ones … a sort of soft focus, like the glamorous movie stars in old films. She reached up to stroke Ray's scratchy jaw, then turned to soak in the girls. Her daughters.

Marianne had not changed much physically since the day Joy and Ray returned from their honeymoon to find her nursing a twisted ankle, her expression resentful. She was fit enough she could still be a fabulous dancer if she chose to continue. Her eyes, which had been hostile then, were filled with a new maturity. An inner light illuminated her, nearly taking Joy's breath away now as it had then.

Jenny stared at her sister, wide-eyed. The younger girl had changed more, at least on the outside. The image Joy recalled was of an insecure girl slumped over in the corner of the room, watching her sister with immense admiration. On that first day, there was another ingredient that was missing today. Longing … awe … envy? Now Jenny could hold her own. She sat straighter, her manner more that of an equal. Still pale from her hospital stay, she was blossoming nonetheless.

Ray cleared his throat, as he did when he changed a subject. "Another thing you need to know—we may not be able to afford the same standard of living for a while."

Joy thought of the apartment she'd vacated when she married Ray.

"What do you mean?" Marianne asked.

"Stuff. Clothes, shoes, maybe trading in this car for a cheaper one."

"What about the house?" Jenny asked.

"That too," Ray said. "Would you mind very much?"

The girls were silent for a moment, and then Marianne said, "Not really."

"What kind of car would you like?" Ray asked. "Assuming we can find a good buy on a used one."

"Could we get a Hummer?" Jenny asked.

"No way!" Marianne said. "That's a gas guzzler. How about a Volkswagen convertible?"

Ray laughed. "It needs to be comfortable for a family of four."

Joy's heart filled with an emotion that was new and yet not new, like an old friend you remember fondly but haven't seen in a long while. More than contentment. Pure and simple, the feeling was joy.

The End

ABOUT THE AUTHOR

DEBRA COLEMAN JETER has published both fiction and nonfiction in popular magazines. Her first novel, *The Ticket*, finaled for a Selah Award and Jerry Jenkins's Operation First Novel. Her nonfiction book, *Pshaw, It's Me Grandson: Tales of a Young Actor*, was a finalist in the USA Book News Awards. She holds a PhD from Vanderbilt University, and a BS and an MBA from Murray State University. She and her husband live in Tennessee.

www.ingramcontent.com/pod-product-compliance
Lightning Source LLC
Chambersburg PA
CBHW051341020726
47501CB00007B/2205